Lexus Sam

Lexus Sam

BP Gallucci

IGUANA

Copyright © 2014 BP Gallucci
Published by Iguana Books
720 Bathurst Street, Suite 303
Toronto, Ontario, Canada
M5V 2R4

Publisher: Greg Ioannou
Editor: Andrea Douglas
Front cover design: Paul Mellon
Book layout design: Meghan Behse

Library and Archives Canada Cataloguing in Publication

Gallucci, B. P., 1981-, author
        Lexus Sam / BP Gallucci.

Issued in print and electronic formats.

ISBN 978-1-77180-044-0 (pbk.).-- ISBN 978-1-77180-045-7 (epub).--
ISBN 978-1-77180-046-4 (Kindle).--ISBN 978-1-77180-047-1 (pdf)

        I. Title.

PS8613.A4598L49 2014   C813'.6   C2014-900865-1
                                               C2014-900866-X

This is an original print edition of *Lexus Sam*.

For Jillian Rose & Brode, with love

Book One

A doctor asked me once, "When did it start?"

Chapter 1

The blowing snow cut across his path in a downward slant, drawing stinging lines of white over the empty plain. A path of footprints, little craters in the sheet covering the hard ground, trailed away in a gently curving arc over the horizon — each print a signpost pointing the way to his girl with green eyes. But the drifting, falling snow filled them in bit by bit, and unless he caught up soon, it'd cover her tracks forever.

He pulled his scarf up over his mouth against the blowing snow and stepped off the road. He matched her stride step for step, walking in her footprints.

Something caught his eye, and —

— the scene burned away. The plain of blowing snow became tangled sheets of green snaked around his twisted, sprawled form in bed.

He raised his head off the pillow and sat up, propped on his elbows, and stared. Stared straight ahead, past his physical sight and through to the fading dream, those footprints in the snow.

He tried to hang on to it, tried to see those footprints in the snow for a little bit longer, but it was gone — replaced by the stranger's familiar room, by the strange reality of Adam Williams.

Recognition of the apartment in New York brought back little reminders, like pieces of string tied to the remnants of his memory.

He unwound the sheets, freed himself, and stepped onto the beige carpet of the bedroom. His eyes moved around the room, noting the details, testing and probing his memories — I picked out that carpet, the paint, hung those pictures — but the memories he found — of California and a small cottage a few blocks from the beach — did not match what he saw, lived.

He walked through the bedroom, familiar now from the routine of waking in it month after month, and rehearsed what he knew about Adam Williams, like a stage actor going over his lines — only he was an actor without a script, just a set full of props handed to him in one confused moment.

He switched on the lights in the bathroom and confronted the reflection in the mirror: light brown eyes, a crooked boxer's nose, long, wiry hair draped across the weathered face of a thirty-something man, a stranger staring back.

He gathered his hair, pulled it back, and tied it off in a short ponytail. He watched his eyes for a quiet moment, doubting but still hoping that this would be the morning when he'd have his moment of revelation — the bolt of knowledge that hit the people like him who recovered, who were blessed by the touch of God or fate or dumb luck and were returned their lives.

He waited and watched.

When he was convinced there'd be no lightning flash today, not even a flicker, he spoke to his reflection.

"I am Lexus Sam," he said. He turned on the taps and let the water run until it was warm. "Today you're going to check Rutherford's Williams. Then, see Dr. Renesque. Don't worry about what he says."

He bent and splashed his face with the water. He lathered some soap between his hands, scrubbed his cheeks and forehead, and rinsed it off.

He lifted a small hand towel off the countertop and patted his face dry. He folded it in half, then half again, and put it back.

4

He looked at himself in the mirror.
"I still love you, Sarah."
And switched off the light.

**

Lexus made breakfast — a kettle boiled on the stove, bacon sizzled on a frying pan, a couple of diced potatoes tumbled in a pot of salted water, and three eggs churned under his whisk in a plastic bowl — while his record player spun *Atom Heart Mother* by Pink Floyd. The needle skipped over the scratches, adding pops and hisses to the songs coming out of the speakers.

He kept half his mind on what he was doing and the other on the music, silently singing along, feeling its magic. The collection of old vinyl, stacked alphabetically in bright yellow milk crates, was one of the few things that felt right in the apartment. It fit with what he felt about himself.

The second morning after he came to on the street just outside Adam's apartment building, he went through each record, playing the songs he recognized, poring over the artwork and liner notes, trying to feel a connection to the person who'd bought it. He found that he loved nearly every album — except for the Eagles ones — and thought he could picture himself buying a few of them.

He lifted the bacon onto a plate lined with paper towels, drained the water off the potatoes, and dumped them into the sizzling bacon fat. Frying the potatoes in the fat was the key to good home fries — a little fact he retained from his past life, somehow.

He'd lost so much to … to what the doctor called "an event in the medial temporal lobes." And yet he remembered this.

5

Making home fries. And lasagna. And wine from scratch. And riding a bicycle and driving and so on and so on and so on — a list of skills — *memories* — haunted him — ghosts of his past whose whispers turned to howls whenever he gave them too much attention or thought. When his hands weren't busy, his mind not occupied on the simple, repetitive tasks he could get lost in, then these ghosts would stomp around like an angry mob of protestors, shouting slogans and thrusting placards high into the sky for him to read — each one a reminder of who he may have been, a small piece that was just enough for him to know he *was* someone, that he had a past, a life, but not enough to describe that someone in any meaningful way — in a way that would lead him, like footprints in the snow, back home.

Instead, he had two choices, two poor substitutes — hollow stand-ins for his past, his life, his memories — that were just store window mannequins draped with clothes — the fabric of his day-to-day reality — giving them the shape and form of a real body at a quick glance but utterly fake — stiff and unyielding, inorganic — under scrutiny. And anyone would scrutinize after being delivered one of these figures and told it was a living, breathing person.

Those mannequins, his choices, had names.

Lexus Sam or Adam Williams.

Take a black car and a vanity license plate or the props — a driver's license, a bank account — he discovered in his pockets, and form an identity out of them.

Make the mannequin a man.

He heated a slab of margarine in a pan, waited for it to sizzle, and poured in the scrambled eggs. They smothered the bubbling margarine with a hiss. He turned down the heat, picked up a fork, and whisked them. He flipped the potatoes and stirred them around in the bacon fat. Almost ready. He scooped four spoonfuls of coffee grinds into his French press, poured in the boiling water, stirred, pressed, and put it aside with the plate of bacon. He flipped the potatoes again, whisked the eggs, flipped them, and then turned all the elements off.

Ready.

The record reached its end and stopped playing with a loud click. Silence spread into the apartment like winter's cold and questions into his mind — questions he did not want to answer.

Focus.

You made breakfast. You are going to eat it, drink your coffee, read the paper — stay grounded, stay connected, if only through words on a page.

He turned around in his narrow kitchen. It was wedged in a closet next to his front door. The stove, small counter, and fridge shared one side, sinks and cupboards the other. He opened the cupboard on the far left, grabbed a navy blue plate and mug, and set them down beside the sink.

He divided the food into two portions and piled one on the plate, poured some coffee, and carried the plate and mug around the corner. He put them down on the table, flipped the record over and set it playing again, then opened his front door and picked up his copy of the *Times.*

He checked the date first — Thursday, November 20, 2008 — shut the door, and walked back to the table. He skimmed the headlines and repeated that date over and over and over: November 20, 2008.

He didn't expect the paper to say anything else — he remembered yesterday was the 19th — because, for the most part, the days marched on and on, one after the other, marking some linear progression most people knew and relied on. Together they made the movie of a life, progressing from scene to scene, logically, orderly.

7

Only his life had a huge gap. A reel was missing in the movie. Every morning he expected to pick up the paper and read some other date. He wasn't sure which, because he couldn't recall, precisely, the dates of the few memories he had left — but it wasn't November 20, 2008.

So he was stuck, lost, adrift in time and memory and identity — a forgotten explorer washed up on some alien shore with no charts, no maps to guide him back — or forward — as directionless as the drifting wood and debris, the shattered remnants of the vessel — a life — he sailed on the seas — remnants like the clothes he wore, a wallet, a key ring — all of it washed ashore with his unconscious form, dead in a way, but still breathing, feeling — the worst kind of corpse: alive and knowing.

**

Lexus sat at the kitchen table, cleared of dishes, with the telephone by his left hand and, to his right, a thick pad of yellow lined paper flipped open to the last line. It read, "F. Williams, 22 Elm Street, Rutherford, NJ."

He flipped through the phone book entries for Rutherford until he found F. Williams. He read the next line, which was for H. Williams, and dialed the number.

The phone rang and rang until an answering machine picked up. He let the recorded message run through and beep.

"Hi, I'm trying to reach Mr. H. Williams," Lexus said. "This is going to sound strange, but this is a sincere call. My name is Adam Williams. I am suffering from a severe case of amnesia and am trying to find my real family. I hope, maybe, you are part of it. I live in New York, and I'm thirty-two years old … if I sound like someone in your family who has gone missing, maybe even someone the police have told you is assumed dead, I might be him. I'd appreciate a call back, even if I have the wrong Williams family, so I can cross you off my list of potential family members."

He left his phone number, thanked the anonymous voice on the message, and hung up. He wrote the name and address on the next line in his ledger in neat, small print and wrote "left message 11/20/08" beside it.

He shut his eyes. Massaged the bridge of his nose. Waited, quietly, pausing in his unending chore like a climber thousands of feet from the mountain's summit — too high up to see the ground and too far away to see the top, stranded between two competing lines of thought — his two named mannequins: turn around and go back to safety, or continue, continue and hope there's something at the top.

Going back meant giving up — and giving up meant slipping into Adam Williams, his life, his past, his identity, his everything. It meant taking the props and knowing they were real. It meant saying good-bye to Sarah, his girl with green eyes. It meant admitting she was never real, he never loved her, never even *met* her. It meant a lot of things that were not as easy to accept as his doctor and his lover said.

And of course, going back held its own dangers. The climber turning around could slip and fall just as easily climbing up as down — but if going back worked, it held certainties — and those were pretty rare in this second life he awoke to under a flickering streetlight in New York City, like a drunk shaking off the night's liquor and stumbling home in the morning — confused, lost.

"I am Adam Williams," he could say, and have enough accessories to that life, that name, to convince an outsider — maybe even himself.

But I'm not Adam Williams.

I'm not.

So? Go on, keep climbing. That's what you want, what you need to do — but reaching the top of this mountain was only the start — a small comfort for his shaky sanity. It'd be proof of who he wasn't, not who he *was*; if the charade of Adam Williams was destroyed, then what?

Chapter 2

Lexus rode the elevator down to the ground floor, repeating the floor numbers in his head as they ticked off the digital display.

The elevator eased to a stop and opened its doors on the small lobby, carpeted in grays and black. He crossed the carpet and pushed open the door set into the lobby's far wall of frosted glass.

Greg waited on his right, perched on the bench underneath the intercom. Just like last week and the week before. Just like all the weeks stretching back to the night Lexus stumbled off the street — falling awake on his feet, aware in an instant of all the trivial facts you ignore when there isn't a break in consciousness — it's cold out; it rained recently; it's night. It was like coming out of a hypnotist's trance — he'd done that enough, now, to draw similarities — and taking stock of reality.

That night on the street, he found apartment keys in his right hand and saw a black car with "SAM81" on its license plate driving off. And Greg had been waiting in the lobby, too, as he was now. An extremely well-dressed panhandler. Shiny black leather shoes. Slender, tapered gloves. Cords. A tan scarf.

"I'm going, alright?"

He walked out the front door, into the cold, early winter air, hearing Greg scamper to his feet behind him — an overeager bloodhound on the fox's scent — and turned to walk up the street.

"Wait a sec, Adam," Greg said. His tone turned everything into a question. "Can I, can I at least …"

He paused, long enough for Greg to catch up.

"You keep calling me that."

Greg chirped a few notes of laughter. "Because that's your *name*, Adam."

"So I'm told."

They walked down a lane of three-storey row houses crammed against their neighbors. Wrought iron fences guarded front gardens of ivy and shrubs and miniature evergreens, each a precious, living treasure and a rare exhibit in a city of taxis and glass and stockbrokers and cops and little else, it seemed — a city so alien and imposing and packed and frightening, so unlike the beach paradise of that Californian bungalow he remembered, so uncomfortable that he couldn't believe he'd grown up in it.

Adam Williams had.

Adam Williams had been a New Yorker most of his life, according to the paperwork he'd found in a storage box in the main hall closet, tucked away beneath tailored suits he couldn't imagine buying. In the box he found bank account statements, bills in Adam's name, the forgettable paperwork of a life, buried like seashells half in the sand, lurking like cursed treasure that waited to be found. The high school diploma was from A.D. Secondary. Adam had graduated in 1994.

He remembered taking a cab out to the school the night he found Adam's diploma and spending the dark hours until sunrise walking the grounds, peering in the windows, touching the door handles.

Instead of reassuring him, of cementing him to New York City — and, by extension, Adam Williams — seeing that diploma pushed him further towards Lexus Sam and the conviction that something was going on, that something wasn't right. His time in California was so real, and yet here was an apartment in New York, school diplomas from New York, everything and everyone saying he — as Adam Williams — had always been in New York.

But they were wrong.

Somehow, they had him confused for Adam; somehow, they'd traded lives overnight.

Greg had been talking. His singsong voice twittered away in the background of Lexus's thoughts of the traffic, the sirens — the ambient noise of the Big Apple you wore around like earmuffs.

"I don't know what you want from me," Lexus said.

Greg's hand squeezed his forearm. "You know what I want —"

Lexus tugged his arm away. "Fuck off," he said, stopping in the middle of an intersection to turn and face his snuggling stalker.

"Adam, I —"

"No. Listen to *me*," he said, cutting Greg off and leaving him stunned. The same dramatic play. "I'm not who you think I am ..."

Greg looked at his polished shoes, nodding like a schoolboy, used to praise, who found himself in the principal's office, shamed, apologetic, hopelessly eager to make it up without understanding, truly, what he had done wrong.

"I just want you to get better," he said.

"And I can't be someone I'm not."

The lights changed, green to red, pinning them in the middle of the intersection like two oblivious tourists; horns blared from the cars and trucks that passed in both directions without stopping to let them cross.

"But I'm not asking you to." His voice caught on the last words.

Lexus just stared at him. He didn't know what to do, what to say, or how to convince this stranger of all the things he knew in his heart to be true and — more important — all the things he knew weren't.

13

He stopped, eyes shut, and ran through it again: I am Lexus Sam. I love Sarah. It was a rehearsed speech that did little to comfort or convince on a conscious level. But it's what he had.

He shook his head, turned, and plunged into the stream of honking cars. He timed his steps to cross in the gaps of traffic, while in his mind he ran through it again, everything he could remember — reliving the fragmentary glimpses of the girl with green eyes, her smile, the yellow rose tattoo on her shoulder. He thought about finding her engagement ring, seeing it in the shop window and *knowing* it was for her. And waiting in the hospital, nurses changing IV bags, making small talk. He couldn't pin down in his mind when he was there; he just remembered looking forward to her visit, any minute now.

He relished the details: the emerald eyes flecked with sunbursts of gold; the burst of yellow inked flower petals on her pale, freckled back; the way she clapped her hands over her mouth when she got laughing too hard.

But his little mental reel ran empty too soon for him to really remember. Always too soon. The last frame ended on the car accident, on that last look she gave him across the car before they hit.

**

Dr. Gilbert Renesque worked out of a tarnished jewel wedged between two renovated brownstones. A small, square bronze plate centered on the front gate spelled out the names of the seven doctors who worked inside in small, slanted script.

He pushed through the unlocked gate and climbed the three stone steps to the front doors. He pressed the intercom on his left and waited, his back to the door, watching the street.

"Yes?"

He turned back. "Lexus Sam, to see Dr. Renesque."

There was a pause.

"I'm sorry, Mr. Sam," the receptionist said, through the small intercom speaker. "I don't have an appointment for you."

"No?"

"No."

"You don't remember, then? From last week? And the week before?"

"Pardon?"

"Come on. Lexus Sam," he said, "just like last week."

There was a longer pause from the intercom.

"Oh, is it Mr. Williams? Sorry, right," she said. "Yes, *you* have an appointment. Come on in, third floor."

The front doors unlocked with a click.

He pulled on the long bronze handle and swung the heavy door outward. Late afternoon sunlight poured over his shoulder onto the front hall's scratched, varnished hardwood floor and the dust in the corners and edges, and etched his shadow in shifting black ink.

The office reminded Lexus of castle ruins left by royalty long dead.

He climbed the stairs, plodding, one at a time, with his left hand on the railing and his right buried in his jeans pocket.

I am Lexus Sam.

He climbed up to the third floor. The stairwell opened onto a wide, empty space furnished with only the receptionist's broad, uncluttered desk.

She smiled at him and pointed the eraser of her pencil at the door to her left.

"He's waiting for you," she said.

Lexus nodded and kept walking. His leather soles echoed at each step as he approached the door. Dr. Renesque opened it before he could knock — a wiry man with bony shoulders; he had a hungry look to his long face, half hidden by a trimmed black beard that grew high up his cheeks like spreading ivy. A few freckles showed on his high forehead, revealed by a receding hairline exaggerated by his hairstyle; a ponytail pulled taut.

"Good to see you, Adam."

"You too, Doctor," he said, the words coming out on their own as he followed Dr. Renesque into his office — a long rectangle with his desk at the back, facing the door. Behind the desk, an unwashed portrait window covered in a thick white film let in diffused sunlight.

Three couches in the middle of the room formed a square with the long wall to his left. They surrounded a wooden coffee table painted matte black and covered in gouges.

"Have a seat," Dr. Renesque said. "Can I offer you anything? Coffee, water?"

"No, thank you," Lexus said, crossing over the round rug at the front of the room. He sat on the couch to his right. He shrugged his coat off his shoulders, pulled it off, and tossed it to his left.

"So?" asked Dr. Renesque, from behind his desk.

"It's been a good week," he said, nodding. The wall opposite him was covered in black-and-white photos of other castles, different ruins. "I'm still keeping that dream journal ..."

Dr. Renesque opened a desk drawer and pulled out a leather-bound ledger. "And?"

And I am not Adam Williams.

I'm not.

"I saw Greg today," Lexus said, clearing his throat. "He was waiting downstairs."

"That's nice. He cares for you," Dr. Renesque said. "Actually, he called me a few nights ago to check up on our progress ..."

16

Lexus looked from one photo to the next, wondering where the places in them were, if he'd visited them, or if you still could — maybe they'd been destroyed, burned to the ground, lost to an earthquake, purposefully demolished to make room for the skyscrapers dominating Manhattan.

"I was a little surprised, of course, that he was asking me and not you ..."

He focused on one cathedral hung halfway up the wall and willed for the recognition, a memory, to come.

"... but then he told me about your last real conversation. Three weeks ago, was it?"

He nodded.

"You never mentioned to me that you two stopped talking."

He gave up on the cathedral and sat up, elbows on his thighs, hands at his temples.

"Well, that's not ... that's not how I see it."

"Oh?" Dr. Renesque asked, but it was barely a question.

"I mean, you say we stopped talking. But we never *were* talking," Lexus said. "As far as I'm concerned, he's this stranger who has me confused —"

"Adam ..."

"— for someone else. And sure, the guy's upset. I can see that. But so what? What can I do?"

Dr. Renesque scribbled on his notepad in quick, short strokes. "You know what you can do," he said. "You can focus on your treatment. You can help me. You can heal and get better and remember ..."

Remember.

Adam Williams?

Or Sarah?

"I haven't forgotten everything," Lexus said. "I remember Sarah; I remember a red pickup truck, an accident —"

17

"The first thing you can do to focus, to help me, is accept —"

"— and it's not just the accident that I remember —"

"— that you've never been in a car accident."

"— I also remember seeing her tattoo for the first time, this yellow rose —"

"Adam, this isn't —"

"— and I know all these little things about her —"

"— helping, to just talk over each other. Adam, are you listening? Adam?"

"— that I couldn't just make up."

Dr. Renesque pushed away from his desk and stood up.

"Okay, Lexus, okay," he said, walking around his desk. "Let's ... let's just leave that subject for now."

He stood with his back to the wall of black-and-white photos, facing Lexus, with the small, patient smile of a teacher or a father.

"I don't even know what my father looks like," Lexus said. "I try to think back and look for him. If I could just see him ... I know I'd lock eyes with his memory and *know*. Even if I've forgotten everything else ...

"But you know what? There's nothing here," he said, touching his temple. "Nothing. You'd think I'd remember *some* faces from my youth ... anyone, a teacher, my mother, brothers, sisters, friends ... the goddamned mailman. Fuck, *anyone* ... But there's just this girl. With green eyes ..."

"Lexus, wait," Dr. Renesque said, rushing back to his desk, "stay with your father."

Lexus shut his eyes.

My father.

He tried to think of something, some event — his sixth birthday, graduation, being taught how to drive — something he must have experienced, something he figured would have involved his dad. But there were no events, just a blank whiteness.

When he opened his eyes, they were full of tears that spilled down his cheeks — tears of grief that fell in mourning without focus. He didn't — couldn't — mourn anyone specific, so he mourned everyone — the family, friends, lovers, the people he'd left behind — maybe in California, maybe in another life, maybe only in dreams that felt more real with each night — those people who made up a world, a reality, a past, a present, a future — people who were gone with the finality of death.

So he mourned them, his anonymous everyone.

"Stay with what?" He cleared his throat. "There's nothing."

"That's not true," Dr. Renesque said. "It's just hidden from you. But why did you think of your father? Couldn't that tell us something?"

"Everyone has a father."

"True, but you thought of him first, before your mother," Dr. Renesque said. He stood up and shut the blinds. "I think that's important. In fact, I think that's what we'll focus on, under hypnosis…"

The doctor's voice faded to the background as Lexus tuned him out to go through the motions. He rummaged through the folds of his coat until he found his inside pocket and the little orange bottle of pills stashed there. He pulled it out — read the label for the hundredth time — and popped the cap off.

"…Today's dosage, let's see …," Dr. Renesque said, flipping back a few pages in his notebook, "four. Now, I know you have some doubts about this treatment, but …"

Lexus shook four pills onto his open palm. He dropped them onto his tongue and dry swallowed them one at a time while Dr. Renesque filled the silence with the same sermon he preached last week and the week before that: one about patience, faith, and the long, slow road to recovery.

Chapter 3

Lexus rested on his couch with his neck craned back and head nestled deep in the cushions. A cool, moist washcloth was folded over his forehead. Small twin streams of water ran from either end of the cloth and down his temples as the pair of ice cubes wrapped in the folds melted.

The self-titled album by the Doors spun on his turntable. The ghost voice of its dead singer crooned from the speakers. His voice was a deep, luring chant that filled Lexus with a righteous joy, a positive energy, and an excited, healed, hyped feeling that turned the cranks and gears in his mind and set him thinking while pumping the bellows in the furnace of his heart and stoking it ablaze.

Powerful magic.

Morrison's musical sermon was the perfect counter to the black art Dr. Renesque practiced on him week after week; the hypnosis left him wan, dried out, crumpled, exhausted.

But as the music flowed and Morrison chanted, the old magic worked. He lifted the washcloth off his forehead, sat up, and looked around the stranger's familiar apartment.

There wasn't much in it that was his. Some records. Some books.

But if I got up, right now, with the stranger's wallet and passport, I could leave. Just leave. Hit every bank machine on the way to the airport. Abandon it all. Fly to Costa Rica with fistfuls of cash and live like a king for a few hundred a month on a beach of the Pacific. Eat rice and black beans. Drink rum and cheap beer. Smoke. Fuck. Forget. Leave Greg and Dr. Renesque and the Williams families.

And Sarah?

Leaving meant leaving her, too. It meant abandoning the memory of the girl with green eyes; having to say good-bye to the girl who loved him — or had loved him, once upon a time — without ever meeting her, in his life, this realm of limited memories and ghost whispers.

He sat back, put the cool, moist cloth on his forehead, and listened to Morrison incant.

**

It was late Thursday evening. He sat, bent over his kitchen table, a mug of lukewarm coffee clenched in one hand, staring down a stack of a dozen pages of faded text from his computer's printer.

He slugged back a mouthful from the liquor-laced dregs in the mug and relished the pleasant warmth it spread down his throat. His mouth watered for more.

He turned the page on the printout — a transcript of the latest hypnotic regression session, e-mailed by Renesque's assistant.

His eyes danced across the words that read like all the other transcripts they had sent him — long, unbroken passages straight from his subconscious that retold useless accounts of trivial scenes in vague descriptions. They were answers to the wrong questions and had no focus on what Lexus really wanted to know — about Sarah or California, or more details about any of the memories he actually had.

Memories.

Dr. Renesque insisted on calling them dreams, hallucinations, inventions of a traumatized subconscious — anything but memories and evidence that the amnesia wasn't total.

So today's transcript, like the others, rehashed recollections of how he and Greg met, where he lived, and other mundane anecdotes that did not bring him any closer to knowing anything about the real person trapped somewhere in his head.

And whenever a question came up that seemed useful — asking about his childhood, his parents, his teenage years, where he grew up — his hypnotized self stonewalled it.

He took another sip and looked up from the page to stare into memories that weren't there. The alcohol worked behind his eyes, in his bones, and in his mind — soothing, numbing, and quieting the voices of doubt and fear and logic — the ones that told him he was wrong, he was wasting his time and this life. His doubts and fears screamed. Sarah's not real. There's no beach house in California and nothing but Adam Williams and his life in New York City — a life you could waste, miserable and confused and alone.

It was impossible to argue with the logical, rational sense of it, of Adam Williams, of that life, because it came with a lot of proof: props and possessions, credit cards, photo ID, diplomas, a birth certificate, and people — Greg, Dr. Renesque, neighbors — to back it up. But he didn't need logic or rational arguments to feel the truth of Sarah, their love, the beach, the accident, the memories too real to be ghosts or fantasies, too real not to believe.

He flipped back a few pages, skimmed, searched, waited, but felt nothing — no connection that felt like Sarah, like picturing her green eyes. The transcript read like a stranger's memories, dictated.

Dr. Renesque had an explanation for why he couldn't remember their sessions after he came out of the trance. It sounded pretty convincing. Lexus believed him at first, but as the weeks went by and Adam's life felt as foreign as ever, and Sarah and California felt as real as ever, he began to doubt; he began to read and reread and search for something in those transcripts that he couldn't name or describe but knew was out there, or rather, within.

He flipped to the last page and read the remainder of the transcript. It ended with Dr. Renesque coaxing him back, same as always.

He shut his eyes.

And saw Sarah's green eyes, glowing in the dim like a cat's, two emeralds in the realm without form behind his eyelids, burning bright.

The dim cleared. She came into view in a memory out of time, placeless, just Sarah looking up at him, her chin rested on his chest, not talking but not needing to, just looking and watching, smiling with her cat's eyes and speaking silently.

Sarah.

Her eyes vanished, leaving a thickness in his throat. Fog from dawn's passing.

He opened his eyes on the pages in front of him, aching with memory of a girl the stack of pages in front of him said wasn't real. He picked up the stack and flicked his wrist, scattering the pages across and off the table.

He stood up with a lurch, sauntered into his bedroom, and stepped through the clumps of dirty laundry that carpeted the floor. He sat down on his bed and switched on the nightstand's lamp. The yellow glow fell on a spiral notebook with a red, creased cover that waited within reach of his bed. He picked up his dream journal and flipped through the ink-filled pages until he found one about Sarah.

He cleared his throat and read out loud — diving back into each remembered dream. At first he had written them down in bare-boned sketches, formed in a few words, that weren't any better than what his subconscious rehashed week after week on Dr. Renesque's couch. But with practice, he began to recall more and more. His sketches became fleshed out into quick stories, small and sparkling and precious — emeralds smuggled across the border of dreaming and waking.

He read, chasing Sarah in every word.

Chapter 4

Morning came slow as sleep receded like the tide; morning's light seeped in under opening eyelids.

He rolled over in bed and grabbed his dream journal and pen off the nightstand, shifting and shimmying until he was in a sitting position. He flipped to the next empty page, and waited, mind blank.

Blank, no receding dreams, afterimages in his eyes; there was nothing for him to write and ponder. Again. If you added them up, there were four months of days starting like today. Four months.

He closed the journal and put it and the pen back on the nightstand. Okay. Okay. Get up, then.

He slipped out of bed and walked into the bathroom, looking at his reflection as he approached the sink. He saw a silent look from tired eyes that seemed faded and colorless.

"I am Lexus Sam," he said with his reflection, "and I still love you, Sarah."

He washed his face and patted it dry with a soft beige washcloth. He had found it months ago in a well-stocked closet full of linen and spare lightbulbs and a small red toolbox — all of it brand-new, too new and bright, like the fake plastic fruit used in department store displays. He brushed his teeth, spat, and rinsed his mouth out with a handful of water cupped from the running faucet.

He left the bathroom and turned the corner to the living room. He glanced at the clock. Quarter to eleven. Late. His stomach ached. Okay, okay. He thought about breakfast but was too hungry and tired to bother with the routine of making it. He found the cordless, dialed the number to Green Olives, and placed an order for six meat pizzas.

"Thanks," he said, and hung up.

That smothering panic, as nameless as he was, threatened to settle over him and the day — a suffocating fear of what he could be missing, the unknown life severed from this existence by the shadowed hand of fate.

He felt it, on him, over him, but he breathed, deep and slow, deep and slow. Okay. Breathing in. Okay. Breathing out.

Okay, focus.

Now what?

He looked around the clutter of his apartment for clues and saw the stack of textbooks by the door. Okay, right. Today you're going to the library to return those cognitive psych books and check out what they have on lucid dreaming. What else? He walked into the kitchen and opened the fridge door. Hit the grocery store on the way back. And go for a jog.

There, that's a day.

Or most of it.

He took a deep breath. Okay. Another day. And now? Right now, you're getting the newspaper, staying connected, if only through words printed on a page, right? Right.

He slid the chain out of the way, opened his front door, and stepped out into the hall. The paper waited a foot away, folded in half and secured with a fat blue elastic.

As he bent to pick it up, he caught the headline above the fold — "Governor MacTeague Pledges to 'Correct Our Mistakes'" — and thought of sun showers, sunlight refracting in

26

the rain and creating a rainbow, painting the world in its bright colors. Blinded, he stumbled —

— as his foot caught the lip of the next step. He steadied himself on the railing to the right. And slowed. A stream of people walked beside him, passing in either direction, hurrying, sauntering, hands on the railing, in pockets. A tall, lean man in a wool trench coat glanced down at him as he passed. Lexus blinked. Ahead of him, a kid in a puffy bomber jacket hopped up the steps two at a time. A lanky redhead walking in heels with loud strides put up her faux-fur lined hood. Her pale face disappeared within.

He stopped midway up the staircase. The crowd kept going. "Watch it, buddy," a voice barked in his ear. They streamed, pushed, sidled, side-stepped —

— What am I —

— like salmon swimming upstream. He noticed the man's reflection, a few bodies back, in the jeweler's glass storefront: an average looking guy, not too tall, square shoulders without being bulky, a narrow, dimpled chin. Only the hair stuck out — red and thin, his hairline like saplings planted to reforest a swath of clear-cutting. Just a face in the big city — someone out walking — but he was too familiar to be anonymous. He recognized this man —

— Wait, I do? How? It's just —

— with the thinning red hair. Not who he was or what he wanted, really, he just had an alias to go on —

— a stranger, familiar maybe, haunting, whispers from a dream, but nothing so concrete as *knowing* —

— Detective Rose.

It had to be.

He's following me.

Lexus looked away, hunched his shoulders —

— Why? Why does any of this —

— and ducked into the flow of people. The noise of the crowd drew him on more than anything. For a moment, he didn't know where he was heading. He stopped and looked around him, a lost tourist.

42nd Street.

The rally was outside the public library. They'd set up a podium on the steps between the two lion statues. The backdrop seemed suited for a caesar addressing his army.

He wouldn't be able to talk to him. Not with the crowds, all the fanfare, but he'd be able to see him in the flesh and up close and hopefully feel a moment of recognition.

He would. He knew it. The governor was another piece to his puzzle, another footprint in the drifting snow leading back to his forgotten, lost life.

The rally was close. He could hear the crowd's jabbering commotion — a rising and falling tide of individual conversations that flowed like sewage down the streets.

The police had shut down 5th Avenue between 40th and 42nd with dull gray barricades. The crowd was penned in between them like cattle, shifting and swaying like visitors to a faith healer, cautious but expectant.

Lexus turned up the collar on his coat and trudged through the wind.

The noise of the first gunshot was almost lost, not in the wild cheering — gunshots were loud, even in Manhattan — but in a moment of shock and disbelief — the mind's refusal to register and accept, at first, that what the eyes saw and the ears heard was real. That shock and disbelief was shattered as cleanly, as absolutely, as Governor MacTeague's skull by the second shot.

One moment the governor was falling down and to the left, his head and shoulders clear of the podium and in plain sight, his eyes shut tight, his mouth open in a round gape of surprise.

And in the next, his head burst.

Blood. Bright, ruby-red blood flowed down the freshly washed and swept steps.

Then Lexus —

— woke with a sharp pang of pain.

Blood.

Flowing down the steps.

"Easy, boss. Easy."

He thrashed, fists clenched, kicking. His body jerked in mindless spasms. But they passed. He exhaled. He opened his eyes on the white stuccoed ceiling of the hallway outside his apartment.

The pizza delivery boy, some kid wearing a mesh-backed hat with a faded picture of two green olives on the front, hovered nearby, holding a stack of pizza boxes.

"You okay?"

His heart throbbed behind his ribcage. It skipped a beat. And another. His breath caught with each murmur. It felt like he was drowning in open air.

Blood.

His cheeks and tongue ached. He'd bit them, hard. He swallowed blood, gagged, and sat up coughing. His vision swam. He wretched and gagged and cupped his hand over his mouth. It filled with bile and blood and whatever else was coming up from his stomach and throat. Some leaked through his fingers and flowed down his wrist.

And at the edges of his vision, he saw today's paper, crumpled, folded and held with a blue elastic, the headline above the fold.

**

After paying for the pizzas and stacking them on his table, Lexus checked himself out in the bathroom. Blood and vomit ran down from the corners of his mouth.

He washed himself off with cold water and wiped his face clean with a handful of toilet paper. He dropped the wad in the toilet, turned off the taps, and caught his eyes in the mirror as he reached for the light switch.

He frowned.

"I am … Billy MacTeague," he said, without thinking.

The name just fell out of his mouth and echoed in his mind. Billy MacTeague. Billy. The name plummeted down the dark gorge left in his mind by the amnesia. Careening, bouncing, its path zigzagged through the blackness. The sound of its fall marked its progress. MacTeague, it said, in one crash; Billy, in another. MacTeague. Billy. MacTeague.

Each little echoing bang of the crashing fall brought back facts, odd memories drowned in the dark well of his amnesiac mind, like a biography memorized for some history test: Billy MacTeague, governor of New York, elected in 2003 by a landslide majority. Called "Billy-Boy" by his friends. Irish descent. Father worked his way up to owning and running a vineyard. Mother was a librarian.

Each piece of information was like a headline that flashed up on a newscast streaming through his head. And then it stopped.

He shook his head.

Governor MacTeague is dead.

I saw it.

So I can't be him.

But.

I remember.

He grinned with the sensation of it: I remember.

"I am Lexus Sam," he said, laughing, "and … and I *remember* Billy MacTeague."

The scene of Governor MacTeague's murder lurked beneath his relieved joy — an awful, disturbing image — no, memory — but it *wasn't* a dream, wasn't some dark turn to his imagination — no, it was a memory — a real, true memory to hold on to, like Sarah, her green eyes, her resting chin, her smile — a memory he could confirm.

**

Lexus sat at the table, one pizza box open in front of him, half the pie gone, chewing slowly, afraid to make any sudden moves — like he was being stalked by the chance that this was just a dream, broken as easily as silence, and it'd take his epiphany — the moment of clarity he'd read about, begged and hoped for — with it upon leaving …

He kept still and silent and chewed each bite while his mouth watered and his stomach churned and heart and mind raced.

Easy.

But he'd finished half a pizza, and he still remembered. The dream held. Against common sense, common expectations, against fate, even, the dream held and held and held, and the seconds passed into minutes, and they'd pass into hours, still, if he sat like this, mouth full, watching the clock, he knew, he felt.

So the dream wasn't a dream.

It became truth, reality, integrating as fact among all the other facts you could accumulate through a life — even a life cut short and divided into a fraction by near-complete amnesia — integrating and becoming no more discernible, at the fact level, than any other little trivial, at times useless, piece of data in his head that survived.

I remember.

Governor MacTeague.

He finished the piece in his hand and shut the pizza box. He gathered the stack of boxes in his arms, lifted them off the table, and carried them into the kitchen.

Billy MacTeague.

When he came back to the table, he noticed it — the crumbled newspaper, still rolled up in an elastic. He must've brought it in. That hunted, unreal feeling swooped down on wings of dread that shadowed his thoughts.

The paper.

I picked up the paper, and —

— his foot caught the lip of the next step, and —

— he blinked. And he was back in his apartment, the paper in his hands. He looked at it, at the headline printed in black, uncompromising ink. It waited for his attention.

So he read.

"Governor MacTeague Pledges to 'Correct Our Mistakes.'"

He shut his eyes —

— turned up the collar on his coat, and trudged through the wind toward —

— the rally.

I remember.

Or.

Or you've just heard the name.

He skimmed the article. The governor was campaigning. There'd be an election soon. Of course. Governor MacTeague. He recognized the name, now, as Lexus Sam — he'd seen the ads plastered on every other lamppost and plywood fence he passed, heard pundits discuss him on newscasts and radio programs.

But that realer-than-real dream had pried something open. Something that felt beyond casual recognition, something surfacing from deep, deep within him: an original memory. It had to be. From before. Before whatever happened to put him on that road as a black Lexus drove off while he tried to recall where and who he was ...

So what do you remember?

A lot, he realized, as he thought about it.

William MacTeague went by "Billy." His father made a fortune in the banking industry and bought the vineyard he used to work at, in California. He won his first election in local politics on his sixtieth birthday by a landslide. The MacTeague family was big. Big business, politics. Lots of influence. William followed his father's steps into politics. Came out to the East Coast for an MBA. At Yale.

Billy had a sister, Leila. The black sheep. DUI charges. Cops even busted her buying coke, once, from an undercover. Dad tried to hush it up, keep it out of the papers.

If he concentrated, there'd be more; he sensed it as a roiling black cloud passing in front of the sun, pregnant, its rain bullets from a biography he had no reason for knowing.

**

The laptop's screen glowed in the dark apartment. The sun had set some time ago, but he hadn't bothered to switch on any lights. He cradled the laptop, stared into its glow, read, and learned, article by article.

Governor William MacTeague and his family were in the news a lot. Their life stories were public. Triumphs and failures, gossip and rumors, biographies and op-eds, the media hashed and rehashed it all. And a lot of it — hell, most of it — matched what he remembered.

Except the governor was alive.

**

"Billy!"

Governor MacTeague was up on the podium, no more than a dozen feet away, maybe less. He kept his eyes on his notes and a smile on his face.

Lexus inched forward through the crowd of hundreds, yelling, calling, and applauding, all around him.

Someone pressed against his back. Two women, one tall and slim, the other stout, held hands to his right. They wore identical boots, topped with fur. A thin Latino, looking like leather wrapped around a coat-hanger and chicken-wire frame, whistled around a cigar that smelled of vanilla, his eyes hidden beneath a brown leather fedora he wore tilted forward.

Lexus watched the crowd for several moments, shifting his gaze from right to left and back again.

He glanced at his watch. The governor's speech was scheduled to start. Now or never. He looked around. But what could he do?

Hey, Bee Mac!

Bee Mac? The governor's nickname — his handle back in his football glory days.

The governor shifted his gaze up from his notes and scanned the crowd. He smiled and then frowned slightly, puzzled, curious.

Remember the Pizarros!

**

The sound of a gunshot brought him back, gasping, like a diver who went too deep looking for some unseen glimpse hidden from all those who turned back early. His heart pounded. The gunshot echoed in his ears with each beat — bam, bam, bam, bam. He stood and walked to the kitchen. Easy. He caught his breath. Take it easy. He ran the tap. Shut his eyes.

Okay.

He filled a glass with water. His hands shook and spilled some down the side of the glass. He took a drink. Spilled more down his front. Shit. Calm down. It was just a dream. A nightmare.

A voice yelled in his memory.

Remember the Pizarros!

Echoing, it sounded like his.

**

The next morning Lexus finished one of the pizzas, cold, for breakfast. He put some coffee on, opened his laptop, and sat down with it. The pot brewed while he sat, hands on the keyboard, Google opened and ready. He just stared, vacant, listening to the echoes of gunshots and the voice in his dreams that sounded too familiar.

He shook himself free, typed "Pizarro," and hit Enter.

There were articles on the indictments brought against them, about who was in jail, on trial, and on the loose. The *Times* had a dozen articles on Alessandro Pizarro alone. He was their new don, imported from the Sicilian branch of their family and reported to be the youngest leader in the New York mob's brief and bloody history.

The NYPD already suspected Alessandro of giving the order for three different gangland slayings since taking the reins from Franco six months ago.

Remember the Pizarros!

He turned away, eyes wandering, aimless, around the apartment — Adam's apartment — and the things he'd collected — a nice couch, well-equipped kitchen, new, bright paint on the walls — while in his head a voice yelled over and over, punctuated by gunshots.

Chapter 5

Lexus walked with a stream of people down the yawning maw of the subway's entrance — a shallow cave in the sidewalk that people explored by the thousands.

He kept pace with the stream, thinking, glancing at faces as they passed. He tried to read something in their expressions when — if — they glanced back at him.

He adjusted the weight of the faded brown leather satchel he wore over his right shoulder. He'd slipped the diploma, a notebook, pens, a tape recorder, and an old digital camera into it before heading out to prove Adam Williams was a fake — or at least that his high school diploma was.

The crowd slowed to a shuffling pace outside the turnstiles — people searched their pockets for change, a short, round woman lifted her overstuffed shopping bags over the barriers and waddled through.

He stopped at the back of the line with his head down and watched the heels of the woman in front of him. He shuffled forward. Matched her steps. Waited. The line paid and pushed through the turnstiles. Subways came and went — stopping long enough to open their doors and dump a few dozen travelers out of each car.

He tried to picture Sarah as a teenager and place her in a high school — was it out in California? Manhattan? But he couldn't.

His memories of her formed an uncharted island in his memory — real and solid — but without context. He didn't have any coordinates to put it on the map of his life and times.

But A. D. Strong Secondary, where Adam Williams went, was a real school. And if the diploma is real? Check the yearbooks. Try to talk to teachers.

His thoughts fell over themselves and down deeper trails — the line pushed through the turnstiles — the subways came and went.

Lexus paid his fare, pushed through.

A few paces behind him, a man with thinning red hair followed.

**

A. D. Strong Secondary shared a driveway with several old apartment buildings that looked abandoned. Gray stains leaked down the brown and red bricks from each concrete balcony. Close to half of the windows were taped up with newsprint. Only a few browning shrubs clung to life in the little gardens out front.

The driveway was about a half-mile long, with the apartments facing it on either end. It ended in a fat roundabout with a couple of leafless trees, fenced off, in the middle.

The closest bus stop let him off across the street, at a community center. Lexus climbed the gentle slope to the back of the driveway, where the school hunkered down in the shadows of the apartments.

He walked up to the front doors, looking over the face of the building in the daylight; it didn't look any more familiar than when he first came and spent the night in a quiet trance.

He tugged the front door open and entered a lobby covered in waterlogged dark gray mats with two staircases climbing up to the second floor on his right and left. He walked through to a larger lobby; paintings of cubes and triangles hung on the walls, plastic potted plants and wooden benches, thick with scratched varnish. Wandering down short hallways covered in lockers and spotted with classroom doors, veneered in beige wood paneling, he found the head office — an inset in the hall with a glass half-wall topped with a plastic countertop. Behind this, a secretary sat, watching her computer screen.

He knocked on the countertop, twice, and cleared his throat.

"Hi, there," he said. "Sorry to bother—"

"Mr. McDougall?" she asked, without looking up.

"Pardon?"

Now she looked at him, tilting her head so the monitor was out of the way, and raised an eyebrow.

"You're early," she said, "but if you'd be kind enough to wait, Principal Easter will see you."

Principal Easter.

Recognition hit him hard, and he stumbled, mentally, mouth slack — thoughts tumbled: I know that name, I *remember*, but it can't be, won't be. This is another dream. And it'll end, now. Just like following those footprints in the snow, the dream always ended before he got anywhere, before he crested the horizon and saw.

But when the secretary kept watching, he cleared his throat and replied. "I'm sorry. I think you made a mistake," he said. "My name is Adam Williams, and I —"

"Oh, sorry," she said. "You're not interviewing ..." She turned her attention back to the computer monitor.

"I'm having some difficulty with my school transcripts. I'm trying to apply to —"

She began typing. "You went here?"

"Yes, I have my —"

"Name please."

"Adam Williams."

More typing. She peered out from behind the monitor again. "Sorry, but can you spell that?"

"A-d-a —"

"No, your last name," she said, ducking back behind the screen.

He spelled the last name.

"Huh." She stopped typing.

His breath caught. He waited.

"One minute please," she said.

"Something … wrong?"

"One minute."

She stood up from her chair, flicked a smile at him, and disappeared around the corner into the room behind her desk.

There are no transcripts. No records. No real evidence of this Adam Williams. Just props. Tear them down and get to the real business of finding out who you are, not just who you aren't.

The secretary returned, pulling her graying brown hair behind in a ponytail, with a small frown on her face — the displeased, annoyed look of a bureaucrat forced to work outside of the normal process.

"I don't understand it," she said. "We should have *some* records on file … Did you happen to bring your diploma?"

He nodded.

"May I see it?"

"Of course," he said, opening his satchel and pulling the stiff paper diploma out. "Here you go."

She scanned it quickly, nodding to herself. "Mind if I take a photocopy to send on?"

"No," he said. She walked to the photocopier in the back corner. "Is it possible my transcripts were just misplaced?"

"I don't think so," she said, her back to him, "but paper copies of older transcripts are kept in a warehouse. You probably graduated before the school kept electronic copies."

"Oh, I see ..."

A pretty young blonde walked out from the office's backroom — dressed conservatively in black and silver — a big change from the bright yellows and greens and reds of long dresses and silk scarves he remembered her in — a pretty young blonde with sparkling green eyes.

"Janet, if Mr. McDougall shows up, can you have him wait in my office?"

The secretary probably replied.

He couldn't hear her.

Sarah.

He'd found her. Sarah. His girl with green eyes. Here, now — memory and the present blending and validating each other.

She glanced at him, he smiled, and she smiled back — a quick flash that turned up the corners of her pale, pink-glossed lips. It was a reflexive smile that did not touch her eyes.

He felt a warning in that polite, quick smile; a prelude, like the shrill cry of a smoke alarm to the desperate panic of a real fire engulfing your home. It came just moments before the real harm rushed him and consumed the relief he felt, for an instant — the unexpected joy and pleasure and everything good he'd hoped to feel one day, that he knew he'd feel when they were reunited, despite whatever, whomever, kept them apart, kept him trapped in Adam Williams. But all of that burned up with the realization that she did not remember him.

Or never knew him.

She left the office, passing on his right without a word or another look. He struggled to say something that would get through to her — to the Sarah he remembered so clearly — but

he could only watch her walk down the quiet, empty hall —
struck mute by her lack of recognition, by all that meant.

**

The secretary took down his phone number — Lexus
regurgitated the digits in a numbed trance — and promised to
call as soon as the school board found his transcripts and mailed
them to the school.

"Is there anything else?" she asked, eyebrows raised, when he
stayed in the office — unable to think beyond the simple,
damning concept: *She does not remember me.*

Lexus managed, then, to shake his head, mumble his thanks,
and leave with the diploma crumpled in his clenched fist.

He walked halfway down the hall in the direction Sarah went,
just enough to be out of sight of the secretary — who looked to
be on the verge of calling the police — and then stopped, leaned
his back against the rough, exposed brick wall, and waited. And
thought. Or tried not to. But he couldn't help it.

She didn't remember me.

She never knew me.

Never.

And I never knew her.

My memories *are* dreams. Just like Dr. Renesque insisted.
And Greg. Shit, Greg. How could that be right? And his life with
Sarah wrong? Imagined? And the mannequin of Adam Williams
alive?

Bodies passed in front of his empty gaze. He caught trails of
color in his vision — their clothes, hair — and the smell of their
perfume, the odor of cigarette smoke in his nose; they might
have stared, or paid him no attention, or tried to talk to him, or

not — he only sensed them — sensed that for a brief moment he was not alone in the hall, not physically.

But he felt alone.

Completely.

He'd read that loneliness was an unnatural compulsion — an aberrant feeling, like the impulse that drove some whales to beach themselves.

Avoiding being alone was misguided, this article said. Everyone was alone, from birth to death. It was your natural state — the default way of life — the relationships you formed, the people you knew, were just interruptions.

But what if you didn't know the person you remembered? If your memories of someone were imagined, then that person, that relationship, was not only missing from your present but stolen from your past, too. It was beyond the simple absence of company that being alone was; it was something else, something worse — deprived.

The click-clack of high heels approaching drew him out of his spiraling thoughts. His drifting eyes focused on the wall opposite him, and the details sharpened. He noticed dust on the silver frame hung on the wall, framing a black-and-white photo of the original school — a narrow, rectangular building that shared the front door and little else with the school he stood in now. He also noticed the subtle difference in the colors of the exposed bricks — maroons, browns, grays — forming long diagonals running from left to right.

He turned his head and saw Sarah walking towards him in quick, short strides. She's mad. That's how she walked away from our first fight. The details blended back into obscurity. She drew his focus, the way her hair was different now, her long sweep of bangs cut on a diagonal, the left half of her face lost behind them; her small black-rimmed glasses were missing —

contacts, maybe, but didn't she hate contacts? — and she was wearing a dozen rings — silver triangles and engraved bands and crosses — when he remembered only bare, slender fingers. Her paler skin would seem out of place on California's beaches.

She doesn't know me.

And maybe I never knew her.

Is Sarah even this woman's name?

She slowed, eyes on him, one eyebrow raised.

"Hi, Sarah," he said. His voice sounded too tense. Dammit. But he forced himself on. One way or another, he was getting some answers. "This isn't the place for this, and this'll sound strange —"

"Hey, uh, you," she said, stopping. "We know each other?"

"Sure we do," he said. I think. Don't say that. "From … California."

A frown crossed her face, briefly, and he remembered her frown lines — two slight lines that ran up from the bridge of her nose, but when she relaxed, they disappeared — another detail that seemed to fit, at first, and then didn't.

"California? I've never been to California," she said, "so …"

Dammit.

One strike.

"My mistake," he said. "I guess … I got confused. But you have always wanted to go, right? Ever since you saw that surfing movie — I forget what it was called — on your fourteenth birthday. You decided then and there you'd grow up and live on the beach in California."

Sarah laughed — a surprised little yelp — that made her eyes sparkle like he remembered. Okay, that was real, too, and so was that raw, perfect beauty of her eyes. She shook her head slightly, smiling now, too, and watched him with obvious interest. "Now that is … surprising," she said. "I haven't thought about that

44

movie — in fact, I don't think I would've even remembered that, myself, if you …"

He smiled in return, nodding.

"But I'm sorry, I don't remember. We've met, obviously, but, well, can you remind me who you are?"

She was real. Sarah. As he remembered her. Well, almost. But her fourteenth birthday happened. He remembered her telling him. And she remembered.

"You really don't remember?"

She shook her head, eyes a little wider, now — playful, innocent, a look he remembered so well, that fit now so perfectly, he felt a lump seize his throat.

"No, I really don't," she said. "Were you there, maybe, and just have a great memory?"

He laughed.

Thoughts, emotions, surged and seethed in him, but he forced them out of his mind. For now. Sort out what this means, how you feel, all of it, later. For now, focus.

"The opposite."

"What's your name?" she asked. "I'm terrible at recognizing faces, but names stick with me —"

"You can call me Lexus Sam," he said, "but that's … not my name. That's the whole problem: I have amnesia. Near total amnesia. But I remember you told me about that movie and wanting to live in California …"

She stepped closer and touched his arm. "I'm sorry. That's awful." She looked up at him, the angle a near match for those memories of her resting her chin on his chest. "I can't even imagine."

They were on a beach, then. The surf lapped lightly against the shore. She held his hand. Good morning. The world turned, and the clouds drifted, and the waves rose and fell and rolled back. It was a living postcard from his memory that blended with the Sarah in front of him now.

"… give you something of your past back. Is that why you came here?"

"No, not really," he said, picking his words. "Sure, I've been looking for you, but I came here … No, meeting you was just a coincidence."

"You've been looking for me," she asked, with a smile and eyebrows raised, "because of one memory?"

No, not one memory: dozens of memories, hundreds maybe, memories of little else, in fact.

"I, I think I know more about you … It might seem strange, but you're all I remember. Parents, other friends, co-workers, family — nothing."

She frowned; it was slight and subtle, just a whisper of doubt across her open face. But her eyes still smiled; green, shining emeralds.

"Why me?"

Because we were in love.

Or I loved you.

He didn't answer.

"Listen, I have to get back," she said, and glanced at her watch.

"Right, of course."

"But I'd like to help, if I can. Maybe if we talked some more?"

Relief washed through him. Hope.

"Sure," he said. "That'd be great."

Chapter 6

Erik slumped in the back of the cab, waiting, while the meter ran and his mark talked to the slender, short blonde who sat across from him. He noted the details. Tight, knee-length, gray-and-black striped skirt, black blouse, ponytail, scarf around her neck. A low-key dresser, a bit conservative.

Erik couldn't read their body language, yet. Casual but distant. Old friends, maybe. Not a date, he guessed. Co-workers maybe, having coffee after work — except his mark didn't seem to work; he rarely left his apartment.

This was something new. A break from routine that so far had been pretty limited: make some phone calls, keep appointments in a three-storey walk-up, shop for groceries, go to one of three used record stores within walking distance of his apartment, and order pizzas. The only visitor the guy got was Greg Redfine, who Elle was tailing as part of the same contract. Greg never visited for long. Lately he'd just been waiting in the lobby.

Erik tried to work a kink out of his shoulders by rolling them and reaching back to massage them. He kneaded a handful of flesh and muscle and thought about what he was doing. A damn boring job. But it was the longest running, best paying job he'd had since that socialite's suspicious — and stubborn — husband kept him on retainer for a full year.

So. Do the job. Tail Adam. Report in once a week. Enjoy.

Tonight had started out the same as most. He'd set up outside Adam's apartment and waited. Around seven, he'd left his apartment and hailed a cab. So Erik grabbed another and followed him here, to the coffee shop. The guy had come here before; sometimes he would nurse a mug, read the paper, and leave. But tonight he had company. Tonight a chatty blonde showed up to talk and talk while the meter on Erik's cab climbed into the fifties and Adam nursed whatever drink was in that big beige mug he'd ordered an hour ago.

"I guess I'd better get out, after all." He shifted in his seat and pulled the wad of bills out of his front pocket.

He paid the cabbie, grabbed his duffel bag from the floor, and got out. It was a cold night, and the wind hit him as soon as he shut the taxi's door.

He picked the nearest open store — a furniture shop with a dining room set up in the display window — and went inside. A little bell chimed as he opened the door, and the lone clerk looked up from the magazine she was reading.

"Sorry, police business," he said, flashing a fake badge that read "Detective Rose." "I'll just be a sec."

He walked out of the way of the window — behind a dark-stained dresser — dropped his duffel bag, and knelt beside it. The clerk watched him unzip the bag, sort through its contents, and pull out a brown wig with slightly curly hair.

Good enough.

He fitted the wig over his short red hair and put a baseball cap on top. Shit. He hated fitting himself like this. If the coffee shop was dim enough and the mark was busy enough, preoccupied, Erik'd be okay.

He slipped off his jacket, unbuttoned his shirt, and took it off. He stuffed it in the duffel bag and pulled out a yellow and orange

Hawaiian shirt — bright and ugly enough to catch the eye, to draw it down from his face.

"What do you think," he said, pulling his coat back on, "do I look different enough from when I came in?"

The clerk smiled and nodded. "Sure you do," she said, "but what —"

"Great. Bad guys won't notice, then," he said, winked, and grabbed his duffel bag. He walked out of the store with her eyes on his back.

**

Lexus sat in an oversized wicker chair with tall legs like a bar stool's that made him feel off-balance.

The newspaper he brought along was spread open on the table in front of him. Color ads, grayscale photographs, and columns of text waited for his attention in the bottom of his vision.

But he watched the door and turned the unread page only when he thought of it. Everything felt fast and slow. Nervous, anxious, cautious, but excited, he waited. If she didn't show, he'd be relieved, upset, sad — but he wouldn't have to go through whatever this was, whatever he hoped tonight was. It'd mean not trying to explain and convince her; it'd mean he'd never have to see a look in her eyes that told him more than words ever could about how wrong and misled he was about her and him, about *them*.

It'd be easier if she drifted back to obscurity, beyond the horizon without leaving even the footsteps in the snow to follow. Then, maybe, he could rationalize her — and his memories of her — away. Then she wouldn't be the girl he remembered.

Never was. Then he could stop chasing her ghost. Start grieving. Move on, not as Adam Williams, not as whomever he'd been, with the Sarah of his dreams, but as Lexus Sam, fully and completely, without the illusion of finding home and his past in a girl with green eyes.

Then he'd hide from the world for a month or a year or ten — for however long it took to recover and get ready to face it again. And then, maybe, he could fall in love, again, but for the first time.

If she didn't show.

If she disappeared.

But she'd come. Disappearing was too easy, too clean. She'd come and maybe reveal the girl he remembered — except without their past, their chemistry, no loving looks and touches, no gentle embraces and hard kisses, no lust, no love, nothing beyond simple curiosity and a little generosity of feeling.

He shut his eyes, turned the page, and then opened them on Sarah's green, smiling eyes. She gave a little wave and pointed at the counter. He smiled and nodded back. He waited as she ordered a tall, thin mug topped with whipped cream.

She came.

**

Dr. Renesque sat in his darkened office with his shoes off, feet on the desk and fingers laced behind his head. He leaned far back in his chair and stared at the pattern of orange light on the ceiling. With the lights out, only the glow from the streetlights lit the room, casting bands of orange through the blinds and across the ceiling. Shadows of bare tree branches, crisscrossed and intertwined, and pencil-line telephone poles, ruler straight but angled, marked their territory in black.

Together, the whole thing looked like an elaborate inkblot. Shadow lines formed patterns and shapes. In them he saw images that led his mind to thought after thought — an empty swing and seesaw, then a Dali giraffe with legs too long and spindly to be real. Then he saw a map of a city grid, with roads like a river's tributaries.

Forget it.

All that.

Imagine Adam's situation; picture an empty childhood.

No memories of swinging on a swing, or going down a slide, or learning to skate or swim or ride a bike or throw a curveball or shoot hoops. Not that he had done any of those things as a child, but he at least *remembered* not doing them.

He remembered reading and drawing, haunting the finished, heated attic during his childhood. The weird giraffe in the shadows reminded him of the first time he saw Dali's works up close, in a sprawling exhibit in London's Tate Modern. With wonder in his eyes and mind he'd decided, then and there, to dedicate himself, to finish paintings instead of continuing the endless cycle of chasing ideas like butterflies through the wheat fields of his imagination. He'd always abandon his current work for that newer, fresher, better idea — an idea that would work this time, he'd tell himself, that would yield something he could sign and frame and call art.

But what if he didn't remember that? Like Adam — no recollections of any of his childhood, of the Tate, of Dali, of drawing, of all the ideas he'd once had of how his life would turn out — where he'd live, who he'd marry, his job — how would he judge his success or failure? How would he feel any sense of accomplishment or pride? Where would his motivation come from if he didn't have goals? And how could he have goals without memories of his desires?

Would you be an empty vessel, waiting to be filled? New memories must nurture new goals and hopes and motivation — even a personality.

Down the hall, the phone rang at his receptionist's desk. The sound penetrated his thoughts. But he ignored it, stayed with that — new memories, new personality. And if you could pick what new memories you had, what associations you formed? The phone now rang in his office. He let it ring. It'd be self-determination. Not in a political sense, but a personal one. The phone kept ringing.

He sighed and picked it up.

**

"Alright, mystery man," Sarah said, putting her mug on the table, "let's figure out who you are."

He glanced into his mug, silenced by nerves, by an awkward verbal clumsiness he didn't realize he had until now.

"So, I've got to say, you got my attention," she said, eyebrow raised, mock inquisitive, "enough to do a little digging — yearbooks, old photo albums, that sort of thing."

He nodded. "Any luck?"

"No sign of you," she said.

Even with all the time he'd had since she'd returned his call, the nights in between then and now, awake, and the quiet moments waiting in the coffee shop for her to show, he wasn't prepared. Not for this conversation. He could talk to *her,* his girl with green eyes, and slip back into that life with comfort and ease. But Sarah, this Sarah, not remembering, not knowing … Without the common bond of their fictitious past, he didn't know what to say, didn't see a path from here to there, to California and their little beach house and bliss, but he wanted it more than his life, his memories, his family — more than anything that made him, he wanted his girl back, wanted her to be as he knew she was.

"I remember, I think, you as an adult."

She raised her eyebrows. "You think?"

He nodded into his mug before taking a sip. "Well, you don't remember me," he said, into the mug, "so I distrust what I remember."

"What do you remember?"

He looked up. "Nothing, really," he said.

A lie.

But not if what he remembered wasn't real — if he and Sarah never happened, then everything he thought he knew was just fantasy — an elaborate delusion or some other psychobabble term Dr. Renesque used instead of calling it, simply, bullshit.

She shook her head. "No, come on," she said, "you didn't invite me out over nothing. And you remembered that story about my birthday, right?"

He took a long swallow of warm coffee, thinking, cringing inwardly, his cheeks warm as he blushed, considering telling her, this stranger, how he felt, that they were — or should be — in love, together.

Tell her.

"Okay, okay," he said, and put his mug down. "I don't know where to start, but I remember flying back to New York, renting a car, you driving ... we were going to see the baby, your nephew," he started telling her, before he could organize his thoughts and decide what he'd tell her and what he'd omit. "Your mother never liked me; I could tell right off ... You told me she thought of me as a stray cat you were nursing ..." And without pause, without time to gauge her reaction or let her interrupt and tell him he was crazy, that none of these things he remembered had happened, he kept going, kept churning his mouth and tongue, spewing words, the memories he had in his head — images, scenes like little movie clips only his mind's eye ever saw, conversations they'd had — the memory fireflies he'd swallowed and kept trapped in his lungs for as long as he'd been Lexus Sam but released now in a chaotic, glowing geyser to scatter and take flight.

Out of him, free, the fireflies hovering, flickering, burning globes of fairy light, forever beyond his control; free to fly, spread, like the Olympic torch passed hand to hand, or a disease mouth to mouth.

He siphoned off the flow of words, forced a deep breath into his emptied lungs, held up his hands — begging for a few more sentences, a few more seconds of attention, from Sarah.

"I know; it's crazy. I can't explain it. But I know these things. I've seen them. The birthmark on your left thigh. The red and white paint, like a candy cane, still on your old room's walls in your parent's place ... that yellow rose tattoo on your shoulder blade ..."

He finally stopped, looked her in the eye, and saw what he'd been dreading.

Chapter Seven

Sarah sat in her cramped office. Two heavy iron filing cabinets flanked her chairs, full of beige and gray binders labeled with faded white slips of paper. A rectangular desk cut the square room in half; the gap between its edge and the wall was just wide enough for her to squeeze by if she walked through sideways.

A fan looped idly above her. She read and re-read the contents of the filing folder in her hands, the file on Robert Derdock. He was one of the little shits at her school who had an even bigger shit of a father. His file was full of bad grades, worse comments from teachers, and a log of behavioral problems: detentions and suspensions racking up and up.

Janet peeked her head into the open doorway. "Ms. Easter? I'm heading home."

Sarah nodded and looked up from the file with a smile. "Okay, Janet. See you tomorrow."

"Good night."

She turned her eyes back to the file while her thoughts went back to the same old track they ran whenever she looked too closely at a problem student. This moron, Derdock, was a shit, plain and simple.

She sighed, closed the file, and turned to her computer instead. She scanned through her e-mails, procrastinating, while the hunger in her stomach grew and the sunset turned from orange to red.

She looked through her personal account first — one from mom, a couple of friends had written, some newsletters — but didn't read any.

Her work's e-mail account had a new message. She didn't recognize the address, someone from the school board. She opened it and read. It was a response to a transcript request Janet had sent. The board's clerk couldn't find any records or transcripts for an Adam Williams.

Weird.

Someone knocked on her door, hard.

"Principal Easter? It's the police."

"Just a second," she said.

She stood up, squeezed by her desk, and went to the door. A figure rocked back and forth, impatient, silhouetted behind frosted glass.

She unlocked the door and opened it on a middle-aged officer — a detective, judging by the beige suit and dress shirt he wore — with thinning red hair and a perfect round dimple on his chin.

"Is there a problem, officer?"

He smiled a bland, customary smile. "Nothing serious," he said. "Sorry for the interruption."

She moved back, giving the detective room to step inside, until the edge of her desk pressed against the back of her legs. "That's alright, Detective …?"

"Rose. I want to talk to you about Lexus Sam. I believe you know him?" He pulled a creased photograph of Lexus from his inner jacket and held it out for her to see. She nodded. "You had coffee with him, five days ago, correct?"

"Yes."

"Do you mind if I ask you a few questions?" He put the picture away and drew a small notepad and pen from the opposite pocket.

"Sure," she said, sitting, lightly, on the edge of her desk, "but can you tell me what this is about? How did you know I met with Lexus?"

The detective nodded and gave her another bland smile. "Of course, sure," he said, flipping the notepad's cover with a flick of the wrist. "This man has been under surveillance for some time now. I can't get into many details of an ongoing police investigation, but I can tell you that his name is *not* Lexus Sam. That's an alias he's been using for years. It's actually Adam Williams."

"What, really?" was all that came to her mind to ask.

Another nod. Another bland smile. "That's correct, yes."

"Why? What did he do?"

The detective shrugged. "Innocent until proven guilty," he said, "and I really can't discuss …"

She frowned. "Right, of course. But, anyway, I don't know him —"

"But you had coffee with him."

"Yes, I did —"

"His idea?"

"Yes, it was; well, no actually …," she said, and sighed. "Sorry, I'm just a little surprised. I'll tell you all I know: we met here, at school. He knew me — not just my name, but details about me, things he said I'd told him …"

The detective got his notepad out again and started writing. He gestured with his pen for her to go on.

"I didn't remember him. Like I said, I don't know him. But he was so sure we had met, and he has amnesia, so he can't tell me much about his past …"

"You don't remember then, how you met or how he knows you?"

She shook her head. "I even looked through old photo albums and stuff," she said. "I felt sorry for him."

The detective looked up from his notepad. "Then you two were never … together? Romantically, I mean."

She forced herself to laugh a bit, because it felt like the right reaction to a strange question. If I didn't remember him, I certainly didn't … But an uneasy feeling was fluttering around, telling her to end the conversation, now.

"I remember all my exes," she said, and shook her head. "No, we never dated. Like I said, as far as I know, we've never known each other — and that's what I told him over coffee. Now, if that's all?"

"Right, thank you," Detective Rose said, turning to the door. "We'll be in touch if anything comes up."

She nodded and followed him to the door. She returned his smile and then shut the door after watching him walk to the school lobby.

Adam Williams.

He'd said his real name was Adam Williams.

She checked her e-mail and re-read the message from the school board's clerk. Adam Williams had a diploma from her school, but with no transcript to back it up. Weird. Too weird.

**

Sarah sat in her grandmother's old rocking chair — the back made out of four thick pieces of leather stretched over a lacquered wood frame, the seat a mess of spilt stuffing, stains — and rocked forward, back, forward.

She tried to ease her thoughts into place, but she was too agitated. She was worried and curious and polluted by Lexus Sam, or Adam Williams, and his weird familiarity — his random insights into her past, into her — and his fake name and fake diploma, and that damn familiar way he looked at her when he finally got going — like an old lover, a husband who was supposed to be dead but instead shows up in the same aisle of a grocery store, total coincidence, just returns and gives a look, like, "I never thought I'd see you again," and if life were a movie the music would be playing, and Sarah would run into his arms and cry and laugh, and the lights would fade, and it would be happily ever after.

But she didn't know this fucking guy.

The lost husband can't just show up and claim the first girl he sees as his. It wasn't right. She got up. Still restless mad, mad at nothing but stuck in it like Dad would get. And some of her uncles. Tempers flared. Tears flowed, smiles spread. All-or-nothing emotions.

Some of my family's a bit ... she used to say, before anyone came over, but she had never found a way to end that sentence. They just were … a bit.

But then, no one was ever that surprised.

Someone buzzed up. She started. What time is it? Late. With a glance over the apartment — some clutter — she walked over to the intercom. It buzzed again before she could reach it.

She pressed the Talk button, a fat, stiff plastic square that reminded her of the buttons on a child's toy phone.

"Hello?"

"Hey" — it was her sister — "let me up!"

"Come on up," she said, smiling.

She buzzed her up, unlocked the door, and headed into the kitchen. Not bad in here, either. A few dirty pots were stacked on the stovetop, and a couple of bowls and plates waited in the sink.

She opened the cupboard underneath the sink and grabbed a bottle of Irish cream. Sugary cream had dried in the grooves of the twist cap, and it took a couple of tries to wrench it open. She filled a couple of glasses with ice, and the door opened. Julia, buried in a bright red coat, burst in grinning ear to ear.

"Hey, Julia," she said, "one sec."

Julia waved, peeling off her layers, petals off a flower. She dumped them in the big Papasan chair — an oversized wicker eggcup — by the front door.

"Is that Baileys?"

Sarah brought the glasses out and set them on the oval glass table that stood just outside her kitchen, in the main room. "I figured you'd want something," she said. "I've got to tell you my latest …"

With her jacket and sweater and scarf and boots and gloves off, Julia looked several sizes smaller — a little slender Mediterranean princess, right out of some visit-Italy tourism ad with her black hair and eyes, and dark maroon lipstick a few shades darker than that perfect beach-tan complexion she inherited from Dad.

Looking at her, it was hard to tell they were sisters — they even joked that they weren't, that Sarah was adopted to keep Julia company after mom refused to have a second. It was like all of the Italian genes — except the rampant emotions — went to Julia, and Sarah got everything German and Ukrainian, from her mother's side.

"I don't think I can handle another talk about Vlad the Impaler," Julia said.

Sarah rolled her eyes. "No, I haven't talked to *Yuri*," she said. "You bring him up more than I do."

"Well, Serafina, clearly I'm in love with him."

"Right." Sarah laughed and handed Julia her glass.

Julia took a small sip, pulled out a chair, and sat down. "Talk to Dad?"

"Not since his birthday."

Julia nodded. "Hire anybody yet?"

"I have a supply in there now," Sarah said, "but I think he'll stay on for the full term next year."

Another sip; another nod. "Come on, Fi," Julia said, her grin and eyes wide, "spill it. What's the big mystery with the new guy?"

Sarah laughed and shook her head. "Where'd you get that idea from?"

"From your boyfriend!" Julia said, laughter in her voice. "Come on, tell me. What's he do? Bartender? He has that ease with people, you know?"

"You're crazy. There's no mysterious bartender."

"Sure, sure, Fi," Julia said. "But you can't fool me. What's wrong with him? Something's wrong. That's why you don't want to talk about him. He's a drug dealer. Won't Uncle Rocco love that?"

Sarah laughed while Julia rambled on, forming her own little world a sentence at a time.

"Finished?"

"For now." She took another sip. "But listen, is this topic really off-limits? I'll drop it."

"First of all, you've never dropped a topic in your life," Sarah said. "But I swear on … on Irish cream and every drink that's tasty and sweet, that I do not — *do not* — have a new boyfriend, bartender or dealer or astronaut. I promise."

Julia pouted slightly, as close to serious and brooding as she ever seemed to get. "Sarah, seriously, I don't need to know details," she said, "but if you don't have a boyfriend —"

"I don't," Sarah said. "Fuck, Julia, I've got enough on my mind —"

"Then who did I see coming out of your apartment yesterday?"

Chapter 8

Lexus was returning home from an aimless walk through the night-veiled city when he heard the phone in his apartment ring from outside in the hall.

He got his keys out and unlocked the door just as the phone stopped ringing. He went to the kitchen, filled a tumbler with water, downed it, and filled it again. He walked over to his couch, half covered in empty pizza boxes, and sat at the far end. He put the glass on the coffee table, shrugged out of his coat, and fished the cordless from the junk piling up all around — the detritus of his cluttered, aimless days.

He checked the missed calls. "S EASTER" it read on the last entry. And there was a message. He dialed his own number, thumbed his password, and retrieved Sarah's message.

"Hi, Lexus? Or is it Adam? I need to talk to you. Do you know the board can't find anything on you? Level with me, okay? Because I believed you the other night. Or at least, I believed that you believed …"

There was a long pause.

"If you really do remember me, somehow, like you say you do, then do me this favor."

Lexus replayed the message, listened carefully, eyes shut, legs crossed underneath him on the couch, a nervous Buddhist in false meditation. He faked the outer calm, figuring if he was still and quiet enough he'd achieve some measure of concentration and clarity, but he didn't.

He fumbled with the phone, dialing Sarah's number while the digits were in memory, actions outrunning thoughts.

Maybe she won't answer.

He opened his eyes. Looked at the ceiling. Frowned. Thought. How are Governor MacTeague and Sarah Easter connected? Why would I remember both, if neither memories are real — or if both are true? There *is* a link. There has to—

"Hello?"

"Hi, Sarah," he said, his mouth dry, "I got your message ..."

"Lexus?"

"Yeah, listen I —"

"Not Adam? Adam Williams?"

"No, I don't think so," he said, standing up. "That's ... hard to explain."

"Were you lying to me, then?" Her voice rose.

He paced laps around the coffee table, listening, thinking.

"Because a cop came to see me, asking about you. And he's convinced —"

"What? What cop?"

"Detective Rose," she said, her voice even. She waited. He waited. "You don't know what that's about?"

He pinched the bridge of his nose. Detective Rose. He ran the name through the short list of names he remembered — the people he'd had contact with since his amnesia. He didn't think Detective Rose was one of them. But it did sound familiar.

"I have no idea."

"But?"

The gunshot blasted through his mind, again. He flinched. He pictured the look on Billy's face. Saw the blood run red.

"But maybe," he said, his voice low, "maybe he knows me from before …"

On the other end, Sarah sighed. "Great, just fucking great," she said "Why'd you have to be like a murderer, not just a regular guy?"

He smiled, despite it all, at that tone — that exasperated, fuck-this tone that'd jump into her voice, sometimes at the oddest times — like the time she was trying to find high heels that didn't make her taller than him — not that he minded having a girl taller than him — the same tone — the only tone — that'd get Papa Easter to back down when they argued, on the rare occasions he'd back off from a point he'd made.

"Lexus, you there?"

"Yes, sorry," he said, letting out a deep breath. "This is a lot for me to take, too. But I remember you. I know … things about you, things that are real. They are real, aren't they?"

She paused before answering, "Yes."

"Can you explain that? Because I can't," he said. "You want to know what's going on, well, so do I. I want answers. I want to know who I am … Fuck, I'll turn myself in if it helps. I'd rather that than drifting in this purgatory."

He collapsed back onto the couch, tossed the pizza boxes onto the floor, and stretched out. He cradled the phone against his ear, the other end silent, and looked for patterns in the stucco on his ceiling — seeing faces, frowns and smiles, imagining his ceilings as the surface of the moon, full of craters and mountains — while he waited for Sarah to say good-bye — because, really, what else was there to say?

"I'm coming over," she said.

**

The buzzer rarely worked in his building, so he rode the elevator down to let Sarah in. He faced the beveled metal doors and his distorted reflection. He didn't know what to think. He didn't know why she was here.

The elevator dropped below the third floor, the little readout counted off another floor in red digits, and slowed.

He looked at his socks. They needed to be washed. The white had changed to a dull gray color. The left one had a hole in the heel. He could feel it.

The elevator reached the ground floor with a chime. The doors opened, and he stepped off. His heart beat a little faster. And there she was. Bundled up in a white coat and pale green scarf, a winter princess in his eyes, waiting with her hands hidden in the coat's deep front pockets. She saw him and smiled.

He opened the door for her.

"Hey," he said.

"What's this 'Adam Williams' shit?" She stayed in the outer lobby, waiting.

He shrugged. "That's who they say I am."

"But you're not?"

He shook his head. "Nope."

She swayed on her feet, shifted her weight to one leg. "Why'd you come to my school with his diploma, then?"

"To prove it," he said. "There is no Adam Williams, so how can he have a real diploma?"

She frowned. She didn't look convinced. But she stepped through the door he held open and unbuttoned her coat. "You're pretty weird."

"Sorry."

She laughed and said, "Who doesn't like weird?"

She walked to the elevators. He stayed at the door, watched her move — her stride a dance, her clothes a costume — and thought back to one quiet, still morning a few weeks ago. A hangover had pounded the beat of a headache with hammers of pulsing temples, and an overcast sky had blocked the sun from his windows, his eyes, like the curtains drawn around a hospital bed by a merciful hand to shield a dying patient from the world. On that dazed, lost morning of hurt, he stumbled onto an esoteric path of digital breadcrumbs that led him to a website of scanned Polaroids.

The site said the concept was to capture a life and write an autobiography, without words. If you took the story of your life and condensed it to snapshots — little freeze-frames in the movie of your life — could you express yourself more accurately without words? And if you could, if that was true, and a life expressed in a few hundred still pictures better described that person than words, could that, eventually, invalidate words and replace language?

He didn't follow half of the philosophical trails the site's author ventured down, but the idea of your life as still pictures stuck with him — maybe because most of his pictures had burned up, destroyed in the onset of amnesia, so that each Polaroid he retained gained significance in scarcity — and this moment, this image, had to be one of those pictures and a turning point in his new life — either they'd go up, together, and stay together, or she'd satisfy her curiosity or relieve her anxiety or whatever motivation brought her to him, tonight, and leave as a familiar stranger.

**

Lexus let Sarah into his apartment and shut the door behind her.

"Sorry about the mess, but, well—"

"You're a bachelor," she said. "I get it. No worries."

He shut the door and latched the lock. "Want anything to drink?"

"Just some water," she said. She took her coat off and hung it up on the empty rack of hooks. "Have you lived here since … as long as you can remember?"

He walked into the kitchen and grabbed a couple of glasses from the cupboard. "Yeah," he said, plunking two handfuls of ice cubes in the tumblers. "I woke up on the street. I mean, I was awake and walking somewhere, I'm sure … but I just *knew* I was on my feet and on a street, suddenly, like waking up."

He filled up both glasses and left the kitchen.

"Have a seat," he said, gesturing to the table.

"Okay," she said, sitting down, "let me tell you what I know …"

Lexus sat across from her and listened. He sipped at his glass of water and tried, again, to remember the name Detective Rose. "What did he look like?"

She cleared her throat. "Late thirties, I guess … red hair, losing it … pretty average, I guess, in shape … honestly, he looked like a cop you'd see on TV."

He shut his eyes.

Average-looking, with thinning red hair.

He looked like a cop.

Lexus frowned.

"That's weird," he said, "I think I've seen him …"

Not that "seen" was the right word. No, not all. Remembered? Envisioned?

"Really?"

He nodded.

I wrote it down.

"Hang on a sec," he said, heading into his bedroom. "I might have …"

He'd hid all the clutter from around the apartment in his bedroom. The floor was carpeted in loose sheets of paper, notepads, and file folders. Stacks of overdue library books were fanned out across his bed, open to whatever page he'd read last. Dirty dishes he couldn't fit in the sink were stacked up on his dresser. He turned on the light and confronted the mess. Shit. He stooped and started sifting through the notepads. Most were yellow legal pads he'd swiped from Dr. Renesque's office one day as he'd left, when the secretary wasn't at her desk. He devoted each to a different subject — dream recall, self-hypnosis, causes of amnesia, dream interpretation, a host of psychology, neurophysiology subjects, and notes from a few medical textbooks — but he didn't need them now.

Where is it?

He climbed over the bed, knocking a couple of books to the floor, and checked his nightstand. He lifted the empty plate — and there it was, the worn red spiral-bound notebook.

He picked it up, crawled off the bed, and backed out of the room, retracing his steps through the debris. He switched off the light, shut the door, and started leafing through the book.

"I have a description here of the guy," he said, skimming through his recollections of the dream.

"You wrote it down?"

He glanced up and nodded. "Well, you tell me," he said, and cleared his throat. "I wrote, 'He's an inch or two shorter than me, well-built, and tough-looking. He's got a plain face and thinning red hair, cut short.' I also mention that he acts like a cop."

He looked at her, then back at the writing, and read a little further.

"I think his name is Detective Rose." He frowned at the page, at the truth of it, there, written in his hand. "But I don't know why. I've never heard that name before."

"What are you reading from?"

"Just a notebook."

She smiled. "I can see that."

He closed the notebook and held it behind his back.

"I have something else to show you," she said. She stood up and reached into her jeans pocket. "Here."

He put the notebook on the table and accepted the folded piece of paper she held out. It was a pencil-and-ink drawing of a yellow rose, with "$120" written beneath it. A yellow rose with a single thorn on a curling stem.

"You recognize that, don't you?"

"Of course," he said, looking up at her, "this is your tattoo — the one on your shoulder."

She laughed. "Fuck, do you know how creepy that is? That's the one you were talking about over coffee?" He nodded. "And you're so certain, aren't you?"

She looked scared now, pale and small — a patient confronting a doctor's fatal prognosis, a mourner approaching the open casket — forced face to face with some truth she wouldn't allow herself to know until now — some irrefutable moment.

What did she see, what truth did he bring to put that look in her eyes?

"I remember … you in a strapless black dress, at some party — maybe some family thing, actually — your mom freaked out, I think, seeing it for the first time …"

She stood, a dead gaze on him. Everything slowed. Gained significance. He watched, mesmerized by her, by the moment's stillness and magic — magic that came from the uncertain, the unpredictable.

His second life, lost between Lexus Sam and Adam Williams, was a train he rode backwards, watching out the window not at what was here, or what was coming, but what had passed — the scenery receding into the distance of memory, of useful recall.

"You're certain?"

He nodded.

But this. This was new. The train switched lines.

"I think, like being blind," he said, talking slowly, "your mind compensates. The memories I have, the few that are left, are so vivid …"

She turned, gathering up the loose fabric of her shirt, and lifted it up her back to expose the curve of her spine — as beautiful as a master-crafted instrument, the vertebrae like ivory keys on a piano that made music in the right hands.

She drew it up and around her neck, exposing bare shoulders broken only by the lavender straps of her bra. Bare and plain, the left missing the yellow rose tattoo he remembered so exactly.

She dropped her shirt, turned.

"Well?"

"But" — there's no protesting the truth of this — "you have a picture of it."

She stepped closer. "You're still sure it's my tattoo?"

He nodded.

"My sister brought it last night," she said, "my birthday present."

She took another step forward. And the stillness descended again, like the quiet, frozen moments after a gentle snowfall, layering, covering everything he saw, heard, felt — until he saw only her, heard her say, "I don't understand, but I feel …" — and could feel only her hair in between his fingers as he cupped the back of her head, drew her forward, felt the warm pressure of her lips resisting his, resisting, resisting, but submitting, gently opening.

Book Two

Last night I dreamt that I woke up. And then I did.

Chapter Nine

Lexus lounged on his couch, feet on the bare coffee table, head titled back, with a cold, damp cloth across his forehead.

A scratched copy of the *Closer* album by Joy Division played on the stereo. Ian Curtis mourned his lyrics aloud while a simple beat echoed over the drum skins.

Lexus sang along in a quiet, deep voice, relishing the textured lows of the album, feeling angry and down and emptied but defiant and comforted by Ian's words, voice.

"Something wrong?"

He looked up. Sarah was home from work. She stood in the doorway, overstuffed purse hung off one shoulder, scarf loosened and falling down her front like thick curls of ivy down a trellis, and a stack of magazines cradled against her chest.

Sarah, home from work.

It was their third week living together, the third week since she'd moved in, protesting, "I never do this, go this fast," but moving in and settling in anyway; the routines he remembered playing out before his eyes, now, only in Manhattan, not California, only as Lexus Sam, and not whoever he was in those dreamed glimpses of a life beyond the curtains of the waking world.

But still, he smiled.

"Yes. No," he said. "I don't know. Thinking about Ian Curtis."

Sarah walked into the apartment, dropping the stack of magazines on the table and hanging her purse over the back of a chair.

"Who?"

He watched her unravel her impossibly long green and yellow scarf from its twists and turns and knots around her neck — a magician's handkerchief that kept coming and coming and coming.

"This singer ... this kid, really," he said. "My mind's just wandering. I went to see Dr. Renesque today, so —"

"Again?" Sarah had her scarf off and was unbuttoning her coat when she stopped and looked up at him.

He nodded. "Again."

She sighed, leaning back and taking a long, slow stride, so that she sighed with her whole body, stretching it out in the exaggerated theatrics he found adorable. "*Why* do you keep going?"

She knew why.

But it was still a good question.

"Because he tells me to." He frowned at his own words, at how easily they came.

"That sounds like some of my dimmer students," she said, with a grin, "and you know what I have to ask, right?"

He shook his head.

"If he told you to jump off a cliff, would you?" she asked. Then she laughed. "Oh, come on, someone must've asked you that ..." She caught herself and stopped.

"As a kid? Probably."

She kicked and shrugged and tossed her boots and coat off, in a hurry now, and flitted across the room, too light on her feet, an angel in this waking dream — but her warmth next to his, her lips on his, were real enough.

"Right, right, sorry," she said in his ear, just a whisper, before laughing, "I forget you're a freak, sometimes."

He laughed. "Me, too."

She nestled in and put her feet up. "What did you talk about today? Me?"

"Yes, we did," he said.

"And? What about me?"

"He said this — us — is a coincidence."

"Oh, really?"

He nodded, not wanting to get into it, knowing part of him listened to Dr. Renesque — not because he thought Sarah *was* a coincidental match to his dreams or hallucinations, but because this, she, wasn't quite right as he remembered, because this wasn't what he remembered, them living here together, how they met. He had to doubt those memories, had to doubt the reasons they *were* together, because without those he wouldn't know how to win her over, get her here, make her fall for him — he, Lexus Sam, had no idea how to do that, but he had a blueprint, a plan drawn from those days in California, and he mouthed the words he'd said to her before, acted the way he used to act, and it worked, he drew her to him stronger, inevitably, than he could have without California. But then if that had never happened … should *they* be happening, now, in Manhattan?

He felt like he'd cheated life or Sarah, that he took a shortcut by following the path he took before, without earning it through the restless tension and nerves, the uncertainty of a fresh, new romance; he won without playing, without chancing losing.

Sarah believed his belief, trusted it this far.

But then she was on her feet, the spark in her eyes, peeling her top over her head, slow and smooth. The back of her shirt rose up her slender back like curtains raised at some grand theater before the show.

His eyes went to the bright yellow rose on her shoulder. Just as he remembered — or, rather, just as he saw in his false memories. Distinguishing what he actually remembered, after waking from his amnesia, from what he *thought* he saw was still hard, but key.

The tattoo matched what he saw. Whatever it was that he saw. It matched. The yellow rose of his false, and now real, memories. The same rose. That meant something. But she didn't have one when they met. And that bothered him, felt wrong.

It's funny, she had told him, *before, I don't think I ever would have agreed to a tattoo. I didn't think they suited me. But when my sister showed up with that drawing, saying she'd pay for it for my birthday ... it felt right.*

Sarah walked into the bedroom.

"Let's make the most of it, then," she said.

Lexus didn't get up, didn't move.

Dammit.

He waited, his eyes shut, frantically willing it but feeling nothing. Feeling nothing, again. Just like the week before, and the week before that.

Since Sarah had moved in and they'd fallen into a routine, he couldn't hide it anymore. After therapy, nothing aroused him.

She sauntered out of the bedroom, topless, beautiful, and silent. She knelt beside him on the couch, folding her long legs underneath her, faced him, and rested her chin on his shoulder.

"Still?"

He nodded.

"And I don't suppose your doctor has anything to say about this?"

He shrugged, lying.

**

Lexus sat on Dr. Renesque's couch, watching the empty space in front of his eyes, while the doctor busied himself with the riffraff on his desk — sorting loose papers into file folders, typing in brief spurts on his computer.

He cleared his throat and stood up. "Okay, Lexus," he said, "what should we talk about?"

Lexus stuttered, "Lexus, not Adam?"

Dr. Renesque gave him a deadpan smile. "I think we have more important things to deal with," he said.

Lexus waited, glancing at him and away, uneasy. He wondered if all doctors had this scientist and bug-under-the-microscope relationship with their patients.

"I guess."

Dr. Renesque sighed. "This'll work better with some cooperation."

"Well, I'm here, ready to start," Lexus said, tossing his pill bottle up in his palm. "How many today?"

Dr. Renesque sat close to Lexus, on the coffee table across from him, so that their feet were interlocked, knees an inch apart. He smiled again, patient. "Something's going on with you, Lexus," he said, "you don't seem … pleased about your little victory, just now —"

"It's no victory what you call me," Lexus said. He resisted the urge to squirm in his seat, to try to put some distance between him and Dr. Renesque.

"No?"

"No, of course not," he said, "I know who I'm not, as I've always —"

"But you don't, Lexus." Dr. Renesque shook his head — "You don't. That's why you're here, remember?"

He heard echoes of questions Sarah had asked him before. "To be honest, I don't know why I *am* here."

As the words had left his mouth, he regretted saying them. That's what Renesque wanted to hear, he knew — he'd given him an opening, like a confused and nervous defendant on the stand, blundering right where the slick prosecutor wanted him to go during his cross-examination.

"Why, Mr. Sam, you're revealing so much today. Maybe we can skip the hypnosis."

Lexus raised his eyebrows.

"You don't know *why* you're here? And yet, you came," Dr. Renesque said, like a teacher wagging his finger at his student. "That's interesting, isn't it?"

"Is it?"

"Let's go back to Adam Williams, or Lexus Sam. You say that victory is of no concern to you, and yet you've gone to such *lengths* to prove me wrong in the past. You refuse to book your appointments with my secretary as Adam, you won't let me begin until I start calling you Lexus … So you're not indifferent. And now you say you don't know why you're here, but you didn't finish that thought, did you, Mr. Sam?"

"What do you mean?"

"You meant to say you don't know why you're here *now,* Lexus. Today. This session. And why? Because something's happened to you; you've found some memories, real ones, perhaps that solidify this point of yours that you've been trying with such dedication to get me to acknowledge, which, of course, is by extension proving something to you."

Lexus smiled. It broke through everything he normally felt in this office. "That's pretty smart," he said, nodding.

A glimmer of something passed across Dr. Renesque's face. "So?"

"You're almost right," Lexus said, "but it's not a memory I found …"

Dr. Renesque raised his eyebrows. The gesture seemed fake. "Oh?"

With a deep breath he launched into it — into meeting Sarah, as he remembered her — almost — feeling the love for her as strong as ever — even admitting how she didn't remember him, how she had subtle differences from his memories — not living in California, not having the yellow rose tattoo — about how they were together now, a happy couple, almost perfect.

Almost perfect.

"But not?"

Lexus took a deep, steadying breath. He felt good. Emptied, but satisfied — like he'd just confessed some huge secret he'd held for too long.

"Well, we, I …," he hesitated.

"We've come this far, Lexus."

"It happens to everyone, I've read," he said, "but I'm not always able, with her, you know?"

"You're impotent."

He nodded, then shook his head.

"Well, which is it?"

"I … I am. But not always."

"That fits. Do you see a pattern, or something that all the times when you can't perform sexually have in common?"

"Sure, I do. Like I haven't thought about this," he said. "Sometimes it's all I think about. It's here, this, okay? I come back from this voodoo, and I can't fucking … fuck."

He knocked Dr. Renesque's legs out of the way with his knees as he jerked to his feet.

"And why is that, do you think?"

"These fucking pills, probably," he said, throwing the bottle across the room. He grabbed his coat. "You said we could skip our session today, so let's skip it."

"We can, if that'll help you to face it," Dr. Renesque said. "The answer's quite simple, actually."

Lexus paused at the door, hating that he did, that some impulse made him stop and wait and listen — just curiosity, he told himself; if the doctor had an answer that would fix it — him — then he'd listen.

"Is it?"

**

Sitting on his couch next to her, limp, he hated the twists of his thoughts — thinking about what Dr. Renesque had said — he was wrong, but it fit.

He had walked out of the office without taking his pills or going under hypnosis — with no complaints from Dr. Renesque — yet he still felt nothing.

Nothing.

**

"Our sessions are working, that's all," Dr. Renesque said, his voice cold and flat. "You've started to remember who you are. Maybe it's only subconsciously for now, but you are starting to recover bits of your personality. And, naturally, your true desires are at odds with this fantasy you've created and are trying to live out with that girl. Hence, you're impotent."

**

His record player reached the end of the last song on *Unknown Pleasures* and stopped with a loud, mechanical click. The control arm lifted off the vinyl as it slowed and swung out of the way. A faint hiss leaked out of the old speakers. It was punctuated by ghost voices from some radio talk show the unshielded speakers picked up — a warbling, muted sound, like people talking loudly in the apartment beneath him.

He made no move to turn the record over, put another on, or turn the stereo off. Instead, he listened to the garbled talk, picking out some words, filling his ears with something other than the echo of Dr. Renesque's explanation.

Sarah had dressed, threw her coat on, shoved her boots on, and left. She might've said good-bye — might've said a lot more than that — but he'd ignored her.

He didn't know why he did. And he regretted it now, in the near silent apartment with only the ghost voices to keep him company.

A few months ago, he wouldn't have noticed sitting alone in his apartment for the whole night. There were stretches of nights and days and more nights when he did without noticing.

But her company, just her *existence,* had changed him. It was like looking at one of those Gestalt images — once you saw the picture had two faces, in profile, you could never look at just the white vase without seeing them.

**

Sarah walked down the short hallway to the elevators and jabbed the Down button. The displays counted off the floors, sluggish; each elevator was reluctant to stop what it was doing to fetch her. She paced between them, glanced up at the displays, still counting down or up, slowly, and strode off to the stairs instead.

She banged the heavy door open with her hip and bounded down the stairs. The door slammed shut behind her, a loud boom that echoed in the quiet concrete staircase. After a couple of floors, she stopped mid-stairway and sunk down.

Because he tells me to.

That wasn't a reason. And the sessions weren't working. Lexus had said so. But he goes. Arguing wouldn't help, though. Fucking guys. Fucking nutcase guys. You always get here, to this point. And what'd you expect this time? With a damaged stranger armed with a fantasy about life together. With him, you expect a fairytale romance?

But he was so sure. So confident.

And normally, they just *fit,* like they'd grown up together. He'd read her so well. He knew when and how to make her laugh, when to listen, to be serious, when to jump her, even get a little rough — a perfect mesh, so symbiotic — beyond anything she'd felt before.

She dug her cell out of her purse, dialed Julia, and waited with it up to her ear, listening to the ring and feeling something she hadn't in a long time with a guy — unease.

This guy made her want him in such a way she was uneasy, she was scared to lose him; just the thought of losing him felt like death — this incomprehensible void of everything she felt now — a fear she'd known since her teenage years and still confronted.

Lexus. She feared losing him over something as trivially crucial as their sex life. Knowing this would pass, it happened, it was just stress or them moving too fast and moving in together before they were ready. It was just something outside of them and their impossible, crazy relationship that they'd solve. Together.

She listened to the phone ring on the other end, waiting for Julia to answer so she could vent and ask her what the hell she was doing with this nut, why she wasn't looking for something normal, where they'd meet and get to know each other and explore their pasts in the present while building a future instead of this mix of delusion and truth, this story they lived through that had enough truth in it to keep her guessing what else it'd say. She listened to the phone ring, but it didn't matter, she wanted their story to go on, turn the page, see what was next. Maybe whoever was writing it — or had written it already — would end it with something like "and they lived happily ever after."

Chapter Ten

Lexus stood outside the campaign headquarters for William MacTeague. The governor's oversized face was plastered over every inch of street-facing wall and window. A couple of different flattering photos were captioned with one of two slogans — "The Voice for YOUR Future" and "Together We'll Make OUR Future" — in big white letters.

He opened the door on a crowded, rectangular room with a few dozen people — mainly young volunteers — talking on phones or shouting stats across the room.

"Up five point eight, latest from Gallup …"

"… down three …"

"… appreciate the time you're taking to talk to us today, Mrs. Clements. And I think you'll agree …"

A row of cheap plywood tables with fold-down legs ran across the first third of the room, except for a narrow gap in the middle. More posters hung down the front of these, taped to the tabletops — so that an army of smiling governors faced the doorway. A few signs that read "Campaign literature, please take one" were stationed across the tables like turrets, just behind stacks of photocopied flyers.

One tired-looking young woman with straw blonde hair tucked behind her ears sat behind the desks to the left with a bank of phones in front of her. She glanced up at Lexus as he walked in, cradling one receiver on her left shoulder like a baby she was about to burp and spitting words into a wireless headset she wore in her right ear, rat-tat-tatting her words, a verbal machine gun.

He got only the one glance. She swiveled in her chair, turning her back to him.

Beyond the desks, a few filing cabinets stood with their drawers open, giant metallic dogs, panting in the heat, the folders and papers drooling out. A balding man with a black-and-white beard twice the size of his face rummaged through the black cabinet on the far left, shaking his head, without pausing the conversation he was having, in yells, with a malnourished, high-strung volunteer squirreling around the room with an open laptop in one arm and a cup of coffee in his hand.

For a moment he could only stand and gape at the buzzing hive of incomprehensible noise and motion. The stunning contrast to his quiet apartment — where the peak of its commotion involved Sarah having a seemingly frantic conversation with her sister — and to the pace of his life where the most he'd accomplish in a day was grocery shopping, making a few meals, and reading for several hours — kept his feet rooted two steps inside the room. Any closer to this swirling juggernaut, and he'd be drawn in.

He couldn't ride the subway without wondering where all the people came from, where they were going, why they were in such a hurry — but at least that activity, all that movement, was channeled and ordered in two directions: getting on and getting off, going northbound or southbound. This was like the foot traffic of a station stuck in a merry-go-round.

"… anyone got his latest schedule? Come on people, the itinerary …"

"… you'll agree that Governor MacTeague's stance on …"

"… no, Danny, you've got to go there yourself, *in person,* and get me …"

Of all the people — now that he looked, there was more like a hundred in the headquarters — he could see only one who was free — bored, slouched back in a plastic folding chair with her legs crossed.

He walked through the gap in the tables — the woman wearing the headset waved at him but didn't get up — and crossed through an aisle in the filing cabinets.

The bored woman looked to be in her thirties, but she dressed young — black tights tucked into mid-calf polished leather boots, strips of leather tied around her left wrist with beads and stainless steel charms hanging from them, a pair of necklaces hung around her neck, resting between the swell of her breasts. She watched the ceiling like most people did television — attentive but vacant — and didn't notice him until he was standing right in front of her, and then she just raised an eyebrow.

"Any chance I could talk to someone?"

"I'd say you are." Her eyes went back to the ceiling.

"About seeing the governor."

She gave him another look. "Press?"

"What?"

She tilted her head to one side. "I asked are you with the press?"

"No, I … I'm an old friend."

"That a fact?"

"I think so."

A small frown creased her forehead, just for an instant, but then she smiled — a small smile — and when she did, she seemed familiar. Not like remembering Billy MacTeague or Sarah. But close.

"I don't recognize you," she said.

"No? You look familiar to me."

She watched him until he felt uncomfortable.

"I could talk to someone else," he said.

"Forget it," she said, "they won't even let his own sister have an audience."

Leila. That's it. He looked at her with a fresh perspective and saw the girl he'd remembered, the troublemaker of the MacTeague family. He studied her and tried to place her in some scene — any little hint or clue that they had met before — but couldn't.

"We haven't met before," he said, as much to himself as her. The tabloids loved to spread photos of party-girl Leila around, heiress to her father's wine money and thorn in the side of her brother's political ambitions, so of course he'd seen plenty of her while searching for stories on the MacTeagues.

"You look disappointed."

He nodded and gave her a smile. "I am."

**

Lexus sauntered down a side street, not paying attention to which one, trying to find a bit of stillness. The sounds of traffic hemmed him in, but at least he couldn't hear any phones ringing or people yelling. Disappointment paced him. He didn't expect to walk in and see Billy right then and there, but he'd hoped he could make an appointment — or maybe catch him in passing — something, some excuse to get face to face with him and gauge his reaction, see if there's some glimmer of recognition.

Renesque would say I'm fantasizing again. I think I recognize the governor's face, I feel I have some memories of him that survived the amnesia, so I figure I'm actually related to the MacTeagues, that my long-lost family not only exists but are also rich and powerful.

Leila didn't recognize him. But neither did Sarah, and he still felt — was — right about her, despite the truth.

Remember the Pizarros!

He stopped halfway down the street, underneath a line of laundry strung up to dry between two closely packed brownstones, listening, convinced he'd actually heard someone yell out.

"Hey, frat boy," Leila called out. He turned to see her walking up behind him. She had added a big pair of black oval sunglasses and what looked like a vinyl coat to her outfit.

"You lost?"

He took in his surroundings — a dumpster up the road, fire escapes clinging to old brick walls, steel fire doors emptying onto cracked asphalt — and shook his head.

"Not really."

"This is a dead end," she said, pointing down the street, where it did end in a concrete post and steel railing barrier marked with a bright-red "No Entrance" sign.

"So was the trip over here."

She caught up to him and withdrew a packet of cigarettes from a coat pocket. She offered the pack — it looked like a packet of crayons, each cigarette wrapped in brightly colored paper — but he declined. She withdrew a long cigarette wrapped in yellow, lit it with a thin blue flame from a butane lighter, and held it front of her face, examining it.

"What do you have to talk to big bro about?"

"That's a weird story."

She nodded, inhaled; the pencil-thin line of glowing red ate along the yellow paper, and smoke curled up from the cigarette's tip to be carried off by the late morning breeze.

"Some people like weird stories."

He thought of Sarah and smiled. "I know they do."

She turned her face up to his — he couldn't see if she was looking at him or not, because her shades were too dark.

"Buy me a drink, then," she said. "I'll tell you about Bee Mac, and you tell me your weird story."

He smiled, hearing another little piece of trivia verified. "You call him that? Wasn't that an old college nickname?"

She nodded. "From football, yeah. Maybe I was testing you," she said, taking his arms and turning him around. "Bar's this way."

** **

Leila walked him to The Duke — a British-style pub in the basement of an old bookstore. A squat staircase led down from the sidewalk to The Duke's entrance, surrounded by a wrought iron fence, rusting and painted over in flat black paint.

Lexus pushed through the front door — covered in bright-red, chipped paint — and held it out open for Leila.

Inside, dim pot lights glowed from the low ceiling, spaced every few feet in long columns. Lexus paused a moment, just inside, as his eyes adjusted to the dim — like a pre-dawn morning, the light was a diffuse glow on the surroundings.

The furnishings looked plush but old — a long dark stained wood bar stretched the length of the wall on his left, covered in deep gouges and lined with a thick leather pad to rest elbows. A forest of brass taps sprouted from behind the mahogany, where a couple of bartenders sauntered between them, pulling taps, filling and passing pints, calling out orders — "Two pints of Guinness up!" — in heavy Irish and Scottish accents.

The Irish bartender, wide and blonde and freckled, hollered a greeting in their direction that sounded like one long word without pause.

"Leila-girl-bar-or-booth?"

"Booth, thanks," said Leila from behind Lexus. She nudged him, gently, and pointed him to a free booth halfway down the cavernous bar.

"Grab our orders," she said, squeezing past him, "I'll have a pint of Stella."

"Okay, sure."

He plunged his hands into his pockets and came up with a few bills. Leila slid her jacket off as she walked down the aisle between the bar and booths — catching a few looks as she walked, slowly, swaying from hip to hip.

He turned to the bar, found a gap, and squeezed between two solitary, early lunch drinkers. The Scottish bartender set a pitcher of Budweiser to fill and nodded at him.

"Aye?"

"Two pints of Stella."

He paid for the drinks, grabbed one in each hand, and walked over to the booth where Leila sat, sprawling, arms spread wide. She sat up, slightly, to accept one of the pints.

"Why, thank you."

Lexus set his glass down on the table before sliding in opposite her in the booth. The thick seat cushions were wrapped in soft, torn leather; the kind of cushions you could sink into more easily than you could climb free.

Leila watched him with a smile on her face, sizing him up for a silent moment. Then she shifted in her seat and picked up her glass.

"A toast, to unwanted guests," she said.

He thought that was a strange toast, but she was smiling, so he lifted his glass to hers, then took a shallow sip. Leila drank down half her pint and pushed the glass off to her left.

"Well, now. You really know Billy? You dodged that question earlier."

He smiled. "Can I dodge it again?"

She laughed and tugged her ponytail free. "Sure. Let's talk about something more interesting."

"Okay," Lexus said, sipping. "Like?"

She looked around their immediate space, leaned over the table, and spoke in a whisper, "Like why you were being followed." She leaned back, one eyebrow raised, in a silent challenge.

"What?"

"Didn't you see him?"

He shook his head, frowning, wondering. "Detective Rose," he said.

"Oh, he has a name?" She picked up her glass and gestured with it. "Friend of yours, then?"

"I don't know what he wants," he said. "Thinning red hair, average-sized ... blue sunglasses ... that the guy?"

She downed the last half of her beer. "Who notices that shit?"

"Well, you saw I was being followed."

"Only because I was following you too," she said with a grin.

He raised his eyebrows, unsure how to react, expecting some explanation, but she just grinned back, challenging again.

"At least he didn't follow us in here," he said, glancing around the room. "I wonder if he saw you —"

"I'm sure he did," she said, "I was leading you when we lost him, remember?"

"You were ...?"

They had taken a lot of twists and turns on their way to The Duke — passing several bars that looked open, jaywalking, and cutting through a hotel lobby — her arm linked in his the whole time, tugging and guiding.

She laughed. "Did you think we were taking a scenic route?"

"I've never ... ditched a tail before," he said, inexplicably embarrassed. He took a sip to distract his thoughts and avoid her eyes. He swallowed, looked back at her. "Not that I don't appreciate the company, but what are we doing here?"

She watched him for a moment, as if readying an answer, but just slid out from the booth instead. "Thanks for the drink."

And without another word or backward glance, she strode out of the dim bar, slipping her arms through her jacket sleeves as she slinked off in her black tights, some exotic feline on two legs.

**

Lexus sat for a long while, finishing his pint sip by sip. He took his time, not ready to go out in the day that was already too strange to make sense of.

He stood up, feeling pleasantly buzzed — it was still early, for him — and made his way, with slow steps to keep it from showing, to the bathroom.

When he returned to his booth, Leila was back, sitting in her spot with two pints of Stella. She didn't look up at him as he neared — but smiled as he sat down across from her.

"You're back."

She nodded. "I decided you weren't a reporter."

"Oh?"

"I called Billy — well, Billy's people at the campaign headquarters — to see if he'd gotten back to me," she said, watching a trail of condensation ease down the gentle curve of the Grail-shaped pint glass. "Someone called, asking about me." She looked up at him, eyebrow raised again.

"Detective Rose."

"The same."

"Really?"

"Really. I never lie to strangers," she said, "only friends and family." She stuck her hand out across the table. "Leila, by the way," she said.

"Lexus Sam," he said, shaking her hand. "I guess you can start lying to me."

"Almost. But I'll leave that to you, Adam."

He frowned. "You talked to Detective Rose."

She picked up her glass but didn't drink from it, only held it up to her eye and peered at it. "Do you know what he said?"

Lexus looked at his own glass, at the foamy layer slowly subsiding on top, sinking, melting back to beer like ice to water. "He's never talked to me at all," he said, "but he thinks I'm hiding under a false name."

She nodded. "Do you really have amnesia?"

"That part is true."

"But you know you're Lexus Sam, not this Adam Williams they've got you pegged for?"

Lexus took a drink, thinking. He wanted to answer with something honest and convincing, but it was hard when all you had was what you knew in your heart without much proof.

"For the longest time, I didn't," he said. He took another sip and then held up his hands. "Not the best answer, I know. But it's true. After waking up … I didn't have much to go on."

Leila's eyebrows were scrunched together, but she stayed still, silent, patient enough to hear him out.

"I have near-total amnesia. The doctors don't really know why — whether it was physical or emotional trauma that led to it. But what I *do* remember is pretty clear. Imagine living in a basement with no windows your whole life, seeing half-shapes and vague outlines in the darkness. Then imagine stepping outside, in the bright summer's sun …"

Leila reached across the table to pat his arm. "Okay, okay," she said, "let's not get too poetic. You don't take your memories for granted."

He stumbled in his mind, hiding behind his pint while he swallowed mouthfuls of beer. Okay. He started in again.

"Right, well, my memories aren't lost in the background noise. I'll leave it at that. So I have these memories. They seem so clear and pure and *true* to me, and then I have Adam Williams, this identity created for me —"

"What do you mean, 'created'?"

"I mean exactly that. Fabricated. Made."

Her scrunched-up eyebrows released and rose up her forehead.

"I can prove that, too," he said, "but let's stay ... somewhat focused. At first, all I had was my faith in my memories — and Adam Williams. I had to choose between the two —"

"Why? What's so wrong about Adam Williams?"

"Nothing, I guess, but he's not me —"

"How could you —"

"Know? I can't, really. That's why it's called faith, Leila. Let's just keep it at this: Adam's identity, based on people who claim to know him, are at odds with my memories."

She shook her head. "I still can't see how," she said. "So you remember, what, playing soccer as a kid, and Adam is a fanatical baseball fan? Maybe you just changed your mind."

He nodded, sipping his beer. "But I'm not talking about a hobby you can simply drop —"

"So religion, then? You're one of those born-again nuts who can't believe you didn't —"

"They say I'm gay," he said. He wanted to shout and whisper it at the same time. "Alright? I know I'm not, know what I feel, but Adam Williams has a boyfriend, a lover."

Silence stretched out — not just at their booth, but along the bar, too. All the stools in earshot hiccupped in their conversations.

He took solace in another gulp of beer and emptied his glass. The chatter resumed, the bar's sounds rushed back into the room's space.

"That ... that's something," she said, shifting her gaze. "Let's talk about your memories and my brother."

Remember the Pizarros!

He focused on what he knew to be true about the governor — his nickname, his rough-around-the-edges sister, his powerful father and seemingly non-existent mother — and nodded, confident.

"Not friends, really," he said, "but I remember things about Bee Mac ... more than just casual 'he's the governor, he's pro-choice,' that kind of stuff, more like what you'd know about a friend."

"You went to the same college?"

He shrugged and glanced over at the bar, thirsting for another. He never drank beer because of this problem — one led to another, which led to half a dozen.

"Maybe."

"That doesn't sound like your 'sun and basement' metaphor."

He paused in word and thought to listen to the truth of that. The memories of Lexus Sam and his life weren't all as clear and shining bright as he'd made them out to be — to Leila, to Sarah, to Renesque, to himself.

No. The divide wasn't that clear, always; and Lexus Sam, his personality, his identity, his life, was really a collage of true memories and false ones — of rare glimpses of the sun and dim, gray-filled days in the basement; of feelings and hopes, illusions and memories; fact and fiction that had been merciful, so far, in which landed where. Governor MacTeague's murder: fiction. Sarah living in California: fiction, too. But his love for Sarah, and hers for him: fact, now.

"It's not that I doubt the memory. I just can't place it in time. So these things I know about him, you, your father … suddenly I just remember them, like I got back some of my memories —"

"What do you know about me?"

He glanced at his empty pint glass, tilting it towards him to verify that, yes, it was empty, before looking up at Leila.

"That's a loaded question."

"Ah, so you assume what you know about me is negative," she said, finishing her pint, too, "so you're trying to be delicate."

He glanced at the bar again. "We'll need more beer."

"Is it my treat, again?"

"Aren't you rich — enough for another pint, at least?"

She smiled, but there was no warmth in it, and glanced over at the bar.

"Hey, it was just a joke —"

"Forget it," she said, sliding out of the booth.

He watched her over his shoulder. She ordered two more pints, left a crumpled bill on the bar, and ferried them back.

"Can I ask, why'd you come back?"

"I'm a sucker for reverse psychology, probably," she said.

"Not sure how to take that."

"Well, this Detective Rose says you're confused and dangerous, and I should stay away …" She looked around the room as she talked, distracted, lying, maybe.

"Well, now that you're here," he said, "maybe you can help me out."

"Besides the pint?"

He nodded. "I'm good for it," he said. "No, I was wondering, about your brother —"

"I can't do you any favors with him," she said, an edge to her voice, "or with my family or money or any of that usual shit."

"What?"

"You know how many guys I meet who are just looking for an in? You want to really know why I came back in here? Because you didn't follow me out. So if you want —"

"I can tell you exactly what I want," he said, his voice steady, sure for once. "I just want to remember who I am, Leila. That's all."

**

After their third pint, Leila seemed convinced that Lexus wasn't after money or an interview or a job on her brother's staff — or at least was less concerned — and she settled into the task of finding out how Lexus knew Billy.

They ordered a platter of garlic bread, calamari, and coconut shrimp, which the cook brought out on a thick wooden cutting board. Wedges of lemon were piled on one corner; several piles of coleslaw, packed in paper cups, waited in the middle, with cups of butter and tartar sauce.

The calamari was still sizzling, sending up sparks of grease and a waft of butter-and-squid-scented steam. They ate the garlic bread while it cooled.

Around mouthfuls, Leila talked about her brother — what she remembered of him in high school, the names of his friends and girlfriends, his jobs, the sports he played — in a disjointed narrative, running from tangent to tangent as she remembered more. Neither of them knew what to cover, since Lexus could know Billy from anywhere, any little story or fact might trigger that epiphany he chased.

They finished their lunch of appetizers, a fourth pint, and were sipping at some Scotch when Leila's mental momentum ran out.

"Well," she said, putting her glass down, "that's the most I've talked about Billy ... ever, I think. I usually talk about myself."

He smiled, gauging the distance to the bathroom from the booth but feeling too buzzed to get there. So he sat, swishing the Scotch around in his glass, watching it for a moment while he tried to consider all of what she'd told him. Most of it sounded familiar, but none of it stirred up an original memory, not even a glimpse, a snapshot of some scene he'd lived through.

"Nothing?"

He shook his head. "You've been very helpful," he said, "and patient."

"And trusting," she said. "Remember, the cops are after you."

"They're not *after* me," he said, taking another drink. "I don't know what that guy wants. He might not even be a real cop."

She raised her eyebrows.

"Did he show you a badge?"

"I just talked to him on the phone."

"He harassed my girlfriend, too," he said, "but never showed her —"

"This amnesia thing's just an elaborate pickup line, isn't it?"

Caught off guard with his glass tipped into his mouth, he swallowed too much at once. Coughing and laughing, he put the glass down on the table and blinked away some pleasant tears.

"I guess it is," he said, "I'm with Sarah —"

"Because you think you know her brother?" She grinned at him around her glass.

"Not quite," he said. "I remember *her*."

And because he couldn't resist, he launched into a rambling dialogue of his own — about how they met, what he remembered of her, the little things she'd done or said that made him smile and laugh and fall in love with her — the real her, not some ghost he carried in his mind.

He even talked about the yellow rose tattoo and all the other subtle differences between real and remembered Sarah.

"And this tattoo her sister paid for," Leila said, "is the same one you remember?"

He nodded. Undeniably.

"You didn't put her up to it?"

"Who, her sister?"

"Yeah, well, it sounds like the tattoo did it for her," Leila said. "She believed you, all of a sudden, and you just go at it —"

"It wasn't like that."

She rolled her eyes. "Of course not. It was very romantic," she said, "but the tattoo was the clincher. So if you found the sister, somehow convinced her …"

He downed the last of his Scotch. "Who'd do something like that?"

"Guys. And plenty of them," Leila said, shaking her head. "Some I've known, the shit they did … saying you remember a girl with a tattoo and then fixing it so she gets that tattoo — not too hard to imagine."

He scooped up the last few crumbs off their platter, not really hungry, but he needed something to help soak up the booze.

"Well, not me. That sounds crazy."

"*You* sound crazy."

Leila stretched out in the booth, arching her back in one long, slow and supple movement of spine and arms and chest that he sat and watched, feeling entirely cured.

"Why do you think you're together, then? She's not the girl you remember —"

"Sure, she is."

"Okay, but she doesn't remember you. So, she's not. The girl you remember would remember you back, right?"

"So?"

Leila's expression softened a bit, sympathetic, and her voice dropped. "Hey, listen, I don't mean to say you shouldn't be together ..."

"Don't worry about it."

"I guess I'm just too curious about all this. To me, this is really, really cool. Like how did you remember the tattoo *before* she got it?"

Sarah should have remembered him back. There was no getting away from that. Is it a delusion then? he wondered. Am I just pretending she's someone else, someone I remember?

But so much is true. Too much for coincidence.

"Lost in thought?"

He came back to the here and now.

"I don't know if 'cool' is the word I'd use," he said, holding his hands up to ward off another apology, "but you're right. Everything you said. And the short answer is, I just don't know."

She finished her glass and rose up out of her seat with the glass held high above her head, empty, rattling the few chips of ice left over in the bottom to attract the attention of one of the bartenders. She held up two fingers for him to see, smiled, and slid back down in the booth.

"Do your memories of Billy-Boy work the same way, I wonder," she said. "If we somehow got the two of you face to face, would he recognize you?"

"I doubt it."

"But you came down to see him; you sat through an hour of bad stories about him."

"It was worth a shot," he said, "like calling up different people named Williams in the phone book — I don't actually expect to find someone who had a relative disappear who matches my description, but I try anyway."

100

She turned to her side and rummaged through her purse. "You actually do that?"

"Wouldn't you?"

That struck her, and she seemed to really think about it, quietly, for a long, stretched-out moment.

"I guess I would do anything to find out who I really was," she said, "even though now ... *now* I do everything I can to get away from my family and friends. Fucked up, isn't it?"

"You can't waste having a family," he said. "They'll always be there for you —"

"Really? I can't even *see* my brother."

The Irish bartender arrived with two more glasses of Scotch, which he placed in front of them without a word. Leila handed him another bill — before Lexus could offer to pay — and he walked off with some of the empty glasses reclaimed.

"But your father," he said, drudging up some half-remembered story, "he still cares — he bailed you out that time ..."

She raised her glass to her lips but didn't drink. "What are you talking about?"

He took a sip of his instead of answering.

"Come on Lexus, what time? You're not dodging *this* one."

"With the coke," he said, keeping his voice low. "I read you bought some off an undercover cop, your dad bailed you out ..."

He rambled through it pretty quickly: she had tried to buy cocaine from an undercover cop, and her dad had managed to silence the whole thing and get the charges dropped.

It probably wasn't a story she wanted rehashed, so he expected a reaction — maybe she'd be embarrassed, angry, annoyed, something, about him bringing it up — but what he saw instead was nothing, really — a void where some emotion, some effect of the words registering, should have played across her face.

Chapter Eleven

Sarah's uncle lived in Cobble Hill, a part of Brooklyn, amid the restaurants and bakeries — mainly Italian — and tree-lined streets of old brick houses. She took her time walking to her uncle's, looking all around her, remembering the slow drive up she used to take in the back of her father's rusty old Jeep every Easter.

But it wasn't just nostalgia that kept her pace slow. Part of her regretted what she was doing — visiting like this, bringing this problem to Uncle L. without talking to Pop first — and worried about what'd come out of their little talk. She'd get a lecture, have to answer too many questions, that much was obvious; she didn't mind *that,* no, what she didn't want to hear was what she feared — almost knew, by feel — to be true: that this Detective Rose wasn't a cop, that the cops themselves had nothing on Adam Williams *or* Lexus Sam.

Detective Rose's visit at the school was strange, what he told her about Lexus even stranger, but it wasn't until weeks later, when she thought she saw him again, across the street as she walked with Lexus to the grocery store — it wasn't until catching that glimpse of a red-headed, bland cop face, turning aside too quickly to be casual — that it dawned on her what had been bothering her about Detective Rose and his visit to the school: he had never showed her a badge, identification, anything real.

She stopped outside a squat restaurant with a small patio next to the sidewalk and an open set of big, inviting doors. She pretended to read the specials chalked up on a sandwich board propped up outside the entrance and decided not to think about anything until she'd talked to Uncle L.

**

Sarah sat on her uncle's makeshift back porch in one of the kitchen chairs relegated to backyard duty for its split in the cushion and wobbly leg. The porch was made out of a dozen six-foot weathered boards run across four cinder blocks and painted white.

Leaning the chair back against the brick wall, with her feet on a stack of milk crates filled with bags of soil, seed, and birdseed, she looked over the backyard. The yard wasn't really a yard, anymore. Every blade of grass had been ripped up from every useful inch of soil and replaced with whatever would grow — tomato and pumpkin plants, rows of onions, carrots, and herbs, and a few dead stalks of what could have been sunflowers.

Her uncle sat to her left, on a big purple bucket turned upside down. At one point it had contained grape juice he'd bought to turn into wine. The basement was littered with them, empty bottles of every size, corks, stoppers, tubes for siphoning, and wine-soaked rags.

"Well," he said. He took a sip of coffee from the square, white mug he cradled in his two massive hands and shifted his gaze from the garden to her. "You have a problem."

She felt a pang of guilt for not visiting more, for making it so obvious to him that she was here for a favor, for help, and not simply as a niece visiting her uncle.

She didn't answer.

"Papa know?"

"No, he doesn't — well, I haven't told him. Sis knows, so, with her …"

He slurped the last drop of coffee out of his mug and set it down on the floor between his bare feet. "So it's *interesting,* then, eh, Fi?"

She laughed. "It's something," she said. "Listen, Uncle L., I'm sorry to just …"

He shrugged and gestured a little tumbling barrel roll with one of his hands: get on with it.

"I don't know; there's this guy —"

"And you come to me?"

"Well, it's not a *guy.* Not like that. This detective came to see me a while back …"

**

Sarah told Uncle L. everything she knew about Detective Rose, which wasn't much: just a description, how he never showed a badge, where she saw him.

Uncle L. listened, quiet and calm at first, with a fixed, stern look that spread across his face and into his eyes, like frost growing on a window. His nods became slighter, less frequent. His eyes never left hers.

When she stopped, he cleared his throat, told her he'd be right back, and went inside to make a call that she could partially overhear through the screen door and across the language barrier.

This is my *niece,* he had said, in Italian, and then hung up the phone.

His face appeared in the screen door, entirely changed, relaxed and warm again. "Dinner?" he asked.

She smiled. "I'd love some."

Chapter Twelve

Lexus shuffled down the steps to The Duke with his breath streaming out behind him in white puffs. He could hear music and the shouts and calls of a loud, boisterous crowd leaking out from the bar's front door. He pulled on the door, opening it against the wind, and the noise of the crowd spilled out onto the street in an avalanche of voices — all loud, each trying to outdo the others.

He trudged into the bar, trying to knock some circulation and warmth back into his legs. He'd gotten off at the wrong stop and walked a lot farther than he'd planned.

Not that he'd *planned* on coming here, on seeing Leila again, really, but her message didn't give him much choice.

"Lexus, it's Leila," her message had said. "Meet me at The Duke tonight at eight. Things have gone crazy."

He waded through a sea of argyle sweaters stretched across wide chests and thick arms, vests atop bright dress shirts, and black-shirted waiters who split the current of bodies with apologies and loaded-drink-tray gestures. Lexus squeezed and eased and pardoned himself through The Duke's rows of tables and booths, scanning the faces for Leila. He spotted her in the back corner and made his way over.

Things have gone crazy, she'd said on his answering machine. And he'd heard, then, at the end of the message something in her voice — something like unease, nervousness, that brought him here on a Friday night instead of going with Sarah to Uncle L.'s.

He reached the corner and saw her waiting, sprawled in the booth with her bare arms spread wide, a couple strings of thick beads draped over her chest, maroon, almost dark brown, lipstick absorbing any of the pale light that reached her lips.

He smiled and tugged off his scarf and coat, hung them on a post between the booths, and dropped in opposite her.

"Things have gone crazy?"

There were two pints already on the table, beading in the warm, stifled air, perched on thick white coasters. She slid one across the table at him.

"You haven't heard?"

He shrugged.

"I guess Pop's plan is working, then," she said. She picked up her pint and held it raised in a toast. "You called it."

He clinked his glass with hers, took a shallow sip — determined to pace himself this time — and put it back on the coaster.

"Called what?"

She just grinned.

"Seriously," he said, glancing between her eyes and his coaster, "I don't know what you mean."

In the background, the song ended, and one layer of noise quieted, but the crowd's roar filled in the empty spaces of silence.

"I can't decide if you're full of shit or not," she said, not angry.

"I'm not," he said, raising his voice to be heard. "Not that I understand what we're talking about here."

She gulped down a mouthful of beer. "My coke deal gone wrong."

He waited for her to continue.

"No 'I told you so'?" she asked. "You were right. You called it, and it happened."

"But that was a while back —"

"Was it?" She raised an eyebrow.

"Well, I remember hearing about it, somehow," he said. "It must've been before my amnesia, and that's been … over six months."

"But your girlfriend's rose tattoo, that should've happened six months ago, too."

Sudden insight drained the reality out of his world, the bar, like it was all inside a television and someone had just fiddled around with the picture settings, turning the contrast up, the color down.

Things have gone crazy.

"It happened again," he said.

She nodded.

"So … you … this happened since we met?"

"The day after I met you."

"Not before?"

"Nope."

They watched each other, then, like a pair of conspirators who'd just agreed to kill the president or something — something they both understood, agreed on, but couldn't actually put into words — and now they waited, quiet, for the other to break the silence first, to renege or maybe rationalize and explain it away, molding it from the incomprehensible to concrete terms.

Leila downed her pint.

"You know what's crazy? Well, all of it is," she said, looking at the empty bottom of her glass, "but … it was on my mind, at the time. I couldn't go to my regular guy, so I asked around at this bar where people know me …"

She shrugged.

"Normally, I'd never buy off someone I wasn't introduced to," she said. "Never. That's how you get busted. But after you told me what happened, I was thinking, like, yeah, what *if* I get busted? Would Pops do anything to help, I wondered ..."

She cleared her throat.

"Not like I got caught on purpose. And it's not like, like you caused it, got me busted ... you didn't. I don't blame you, really. But ... in a way ..."

He nodded at the similarities to what Sarah had said about her tattoo. "In a way, I did."

"Don't apologize or anything."

"Well —"

"Man, I'm kidding."

"No, I know," he said, "but ... you're okay, then? Dad came through, you're free —"

"Almost. Cops dropped the charges. I think the press is out of the loop for now. But I made a side deal with my father."

"What kind of deal?"

"I couldn't help talking about you, about this," she said, leaning forward to prop her elbows on the table. "It's just too cool to resist. Like, what else would you get right?"

**

"Alright, enough, Lexus," Leila said, rolling her eyes. "You either remember this or you don't."

They'd spent the last thirty minutes going over exactly what had happened. Lexus asked for details. And more details, comparing, searching her descriptions for the spark. He shifted his gaze from her. Over her shoulder, the band took the stage —

six sweating kids who played a blend of Irish folk and punk rock music as loud as their amps could go and The Duke's speakers could take. The anorexic-looking singer, with more tattoos on his skin than clothes overtop or flesh and muscle underneath, leapt from the crowd and onto the stage, kicking off the back of a large black-shirted bouncer. He grabbed the mic and shouted, and the band launched into the second half of their set.

The music crashed onto their table like the surf over sandcastle ramparts, drowning and washing everything clean, and with the jumbled noise his skeptic's voice failed.

"I remember," he said, his voice lost in the music.

Leila leaned in. "What?"

"I do," he said, raising his voice. "I remember this."

Leila grinned and shouted back: "Cool!"

Cool. Like it was a magic trick.

"But you were arrested," he shouted.

She shrugged and said something he couldn't hear.

"What?"

She stood up from the booth, grabbed her vinyl oil-slick coat, and urged him up with a wave. He downed the sudsy remnants of his Guinness, mouth salivating against its bitterness — like black coffee, inviting and harsh — and followed her to the back wall. She opened the black unlabeled door between the men's and women's bathrooms and traipsed down the brightly lit staircase leading to the sub-basement.

He followed more slowly, with one hand on the railing. The air was cooler and calmer, like an underground cave. The band's raucous medley upstairs flattened, the treble highs filtered out by the door as it slammed home, so he could hear only the bass and drumbeat.

He squinted until his eyes got used to the ultra-white light the bare bulbs gave off.

Leila rounded a corner to the right and disappeared. He followed a moment later and entered a small square room, with two tables pushed against the walls to the right and left and an empty space running up the middle in which Leila stood, arms spread wide.

"VIP room," she said, a smile on her lips. "Not bad?"

"We're VIPs?"

She picked the table on the right, pulled out one of the chairs, and sat down. "Well, I am," she said.

He sat opposite her and listened to the ringing in his ears.

"Okay, so you were right about the drug bust," she said, "but now what?"

His eyes wandered over the wall just behind her head. They settled on an old dartboard in a small wooden hutch pockmarked with errant darts. Two darts stabbed the faded red bull's-eye. He traced his eyes over the painted cork of the board, trying to picture all the darts that had been thrown into it and what it took to put each one there — all the variables and all the luck or chance or fate that went into each.

"I'm not a fortune teller," he said.

If you were intelligent enough to deduce and name all those variables, and observant, armed with the most precise instruments to measure all those variables — instruments to rival God's omniscient eye — could you then predict where each dart would strike? Could that prescience exist? And if you could, *when* could you make that prediction? After the dart was in the air? As the player readied his throw? Even earlier?

"Probably not, no," she said, "but it's like you were saying …"

But to make a prediction in silence proved nothing. You'd have to voice your deductions and call the shot for it to mean anything; to verify your ability.

"… memories you do have are amplified in your mind. You pay more attention to them than the rest of us — so what if …"

110

But as soon as you said something, like "You're going to hit double twenty," you'd unbalance what your God's-eye instrument measured: you'd add to the equation a prejudice in the thrower's mind — he'd minutely adjust his aim either towards or away from double twenty as his eyes focused in on that small band on the dartboard.

"... you're drawing conclusions, ones that turn out to be true, not because of some psychic power bullshit, not because of something you have that the rest of us don't ..."

Okay, so you don't call the shot out loud; you write it down and leave it on the bar, where everyone can see it, but no one can read what you wrote. The thrower's mind isn't prejudiced, then, by knowing where his dart is supposed to go — it's back to all those variables you deduced and measured.

"... but because of what you don't have, a lifetime of memories to clutter your thinking ..."

But that wasn't entirely true, either. He'd know he was being watched, know someone was guessing his shots. He'd still, deep down, maybe not even consciously, have some prejudice. He'd either want you to succeed, call it right, or not. And even if he didn't know what number you called, he'd try to figure it out, irrationally or rationally — he'd aim for a common target, thinking you picked one he was likely to go for, like the bull's-eye, or where his last dart had landed, or opposite where the last had landed because it was less likely to hit the same spot twice, or, or, or — an infinite chain of "ors" would stretch out.

"... I can't imagine what you'd remember about me or my father that'd make you figure out I'd get myself arrested ..."

It was like one of the psych books he'd read, wandering through behavioral studies, that mentioned a group study on light levels in relation to worker productivity: there was a control group, with a constant level of lighting, and a study group who had to work under dim light or ultra bright light or some level in between. The two groups were office workers, performing the same everyday tasks they performed routinely. They weren't told *what* was being studied, only that some consultants were studying their office. At first, the results seemed inconclusive — they couldn't confirm their hypothesis that low lighting conditions would detract from performance. Even the control group's performance was higher than expected. And then it dawned on someone why. The workers were being watched. And they *knew* they were being watched. They worked harder and harder each day, regardless of the lights, because, naturally, they assumed their performance was being reviewed and good performance meant a reward.

"… Dad doesn't really see it my way, though. He's too superstitious. You probably don't know *that* unless you really are psychic — he keeps it pretty hidden …"

So a flawlessly true prediction would have to take into account this prejudice, somehow. The God's-eye instrument would peer into the psyche of the person throwing the dart and figure out how knowing his shot was being called affected his shot, adjust the prediction accordingly, and come out with the right answer again and again, for any thrower with any dart on any board.

"But that can't work," he said to himself.

Not with free will.

"Lexus?"

Aside from the obvious practical problems — making this God's-eye instrument to see and measure all — with free will, without an explicit fate — preconceived and written, immutable, in the ethereal fabric of life — then there'd always be a *chance* that any prediction would be wrong — and you'd be back to guessing where the dart landed, just like someone without the God's-eye instrument.

"You can't write down fate," he said. "Nothing I knew about you, or about anyone, could tell me what they'd do next."

"And what happened to me? Your girlfriend's tattoo?"

"I was calling my shots out loud."

**

Leila fished out of her purse a flask of something strong and bittersweet tasting — fluid, flaming licorice, candy napalm that burned all the way down. They shared it, passing the flask back and forth between nips, as Lexus put his dart-guessing theory into words.

"That's all it is," he said, "the power of suggestion. My telling you about the drug bust got you thinking about what would happen *if* you were arrested. Same with Sarah. I told her about a yellow rose tattoo on her shoulder, she started thinking about it, started to like the idea of having one there ..."

He lapsed into a comfortable silence, content that he'd made his point. He accepted the flask from Leila and shook the liquor in the bottom to gauge how much was left.

"You can finish it," he said. "You're almost out."

She took it out of his hands.

"Suit yourself." She took another sip. "You won't mind settling this business with my dad, then," she said. She took another sip, and her face relaxed somewhat. "I tried to keep you out of it, you know, I just ..."

He's too superstitious. You probably don't know that *unless you really are psychic — he keeps it pretty hidden ...*

That sounded like the opposite of what he thought he knew about the elder MacTeague, steely-eyed frontiersman turned business leader turned community leader turned politician.

But you've been wrong before.

And that thought made him smile.

"You enjoying this? I don't ask for many favors, okay," she said, "so if I seem ... I don't know; it's just a lack of practice."

He shook his head, but didn't explain; he wasn't going to bring up his false memory of Billy's murder or the relief he felt in confirming for himself that it was false.

"You don't have to ask," he said. "What's your father want?"

**

Leila slumped in an old club chair that had supported too much weight for too long. The plush seat cushion had long since given up the ghost, and she sank deep into it.

It was an awkward way to sit, and she felt a knot that her masseuse would have to work out later start to form in the base of her neck.

Considering she was in a police station, the chair was pretty comfortable. Because she was a guest of the police, she didn't have much choice but to sit in the chair and wait for the effects of her one and only phone call to reach her, here, and wash her away like a beach umbrella before a tsunami of pulled strings, called-in favors, and plain, old-fashioned bribing and bullying.

She looked around the office. Not the police chief's — she was only a governor's sister, and an unpopular sister of an unpopular governor, at that. No, she waited in some middle-rung detective's office. A lieutenant, maybe. Did the cops have lieutenants? Or was that just the army? She wondered where they'd gotten the blow. It wasn't a prop — the undercover had let her taste some first. She'd rubbed some into her gums, above her front teeth — probably the last hit she'd get for a while.

114

The middle-rung detective's office looked like an office cubicle, except with real walls and a frosted glass window in the shitty painted-over particleboard door. It was probably better than those open desks where some of the narcotics boys sat. You couldn't sneeze out there without someone saying "bless you," and what little personal shit they brought in was on display — hey, cute kid; hot girlfriend; who's that, your brother? That'd be the worst. Here, at least this lieutenant detective could shut the door and pretend to work while he mourned the remnants of his life in a world where a little bitch like Leila could get caught, mouth off the whole way down to the station, the whole time *in* the station, and then just stroll out of here like she'd just been visiting the zoo to see some apes who actually worked for a meager living.

That detective is probably beating up some perp in a holding cell, right now, in the guise of sweating him down — playing bad cop without the good cop hanging around fucking up a perfectly good frustration-venting hard-on.

It was a nasty thought. But it was too perfect, a caricature of hard-boiled detective stories. And she was feeling nasty.

Billy had wanted to be a cop, growing up. Not one of the poor bastards riding through gridlock on a bicycle in the dead humid haze of August, but a detective, like this pent-up-rage one who'd dragged her in here by the chain linking her two new shiny bracelets together, unshackled her, and pushed her into the seat.

But he never did. It was what he'd wanted — and that's the main reason it never happened. She had to sympathize, a bit. All the focus of their parents on him — extremely opinionated parents who sacrificed a lot to get him the opportunities he didn't exactly want. And boy, did they remind him of those sacrifices, every and any time he showed any initiative, any hint of going against the parental grain — the groove set down in stone before he was old enough to walk.

**

"He doesn't want much," Leila said, watching her hands, the way her nail polish ate the light, like a little dead star waited at the end of each fingertip. "Like I said, he was spooked. So when I mentioned you remembered Billy too, he … he wants to know *how*."

She could see him shift in his seat, his face turned to hers, watching; he was a beige oval in the top of her vision.

"And you told him how we went over that, right? How I have no idea where I know your brother from?"

She glanced up and nodded — that, at least, was true.

"But he didn't believe you?"

"You didn't go all the way down to the campaign headquarters the other day without some clear memory."

**

The door opened behind her. She left her head tilted back against the chair's rest, staring at the ceiling, and waited for the detective to launch into some other tirade.

But he didn't say anything.

The silence stretched.

What was this, the silent treatment?

She waited.

Her father's face filled her field of vision — gloomy and backlit, looming.

"It's time to go," he said.

**

She heard Lexus say, "I can't tell you anything real."

"Tell me what you're hiding," she said, "so I can tell Pops and he can do a rain dance or have a séance or do whatever he thinks he can do."

**

She knew it was bad when he came to collect her in person. Not an aide, not the butler, not their chauffeur, not any one of the countless little serfs running around the family's kingdom.

Her father wasn't a big man. But he was still fit and physically powerful, arms taut and wiry from their countless days in the fields, working the vineyard — watering, pruning, picking, crushing, pressing — at one point or another, he'd done every single job related to raising grapes and turning them into wine. But his strength was belied by a slim frame, neat moustache, silver, trim hair, and a pair of bifocals that aged him ten years.

Still, he had this way, this argumentative streak that would run over any obstacle, or beat itself against it again and again until it was dust, that was so consuming, so complete and exhausting, that he made people do things.

And now, with it, he made her tell him everything.

And she did, including Lexus and his weird premonition about her getting busted, that her father would come and bail her out — it also included how they met and what Lexus was doing at the campaign headquarters in the first place.

"So what does he know about Billy?"

"I don't know."

"Why not?"

"Because we tried to figure out how they knew each other —"

"Does Billy remember him?"

"No idea. The prince doesn't return my calls."

"So you don't know what he knows about Billy?"

"Nope."

"Find out."

"Why?"

"Because. He was right about you."

She looked at him for the first time in their winding route home. He drove, slowly and methodically, like his arguments, letting other drivers cut him off, stopping for yellows. The model driver. She sat in the passenger seat massaging her neck and switching the radio stations every few seconds, just for something to do.

She could never read him.

But he was probably serious.

"It was a weird guess or something."

He laughed. "Don't be naïve."

She frowned. "I don't get it, if you don't believe me —"

"I believe you."

"You said I was being naïve."

"You are."

She sat back in her seat and left the radio alone for a moment. She'd have to puzzle that one out while New York City's streets crawled by her window.

"You don't think it was a guess. But you ... you believe me. You think he was right about what would happen to me."

"Absolutely."

"So you think he'll be right about something else," she said, "something that'll happen to Billy."

"Absolutely."

**

"He really believes I … I know something?"

She could hear the disbelief in his voice.

Fuck.

This shouldn't be this hard.

"Do you remember something about Billy, Lexus? Come on," she said, "seriously. Don't worry what it is, just tell me."

**

"But you don't believe him," she said. "You can't."

"No?"

"No, of course not," she said. "I'm not *that* naïve. You think he predicted that bust? No way."

"You *can* still think," he said, easing the car to a stop. "Of course he's not psychic. That's bullshit. But that doesn't mean he didn't predict the bust."

She frowned, watching the traffic cross in front of them, and thought about that for a moment. By the time the light went green, she understood.

"You think he rigged it."

"Right. And why would he bother? To get our attention, Leila. And he has it now. So find out what else this bastard thinks is going to happen. Whatever he says, it's a threat. You find that out — think of it as your parole — and I'll figure out how to deal with him."

**

119

"Okay, okay," Lexus said. "It sounds nuts, though. It is nuts, completely not real, utter bullshit —"

"Lexus. Spill it."

He drummed his fingers on the tabletop, timed with the drummer upstairs, took a deep breath, and let it out. Sighed. Stalled.

"Anything else to drink?"

"You're drunk enough."

He laughed. "Alright, well …"

And she listened, fingers laced together and resting in her lap, keeping her face slack, feeling it go red — digging her fingertips into her hands to keep from fidgeting or from punching him out or from pulling her hair out, whatever felt best.

Pops was right.

If the point of Lexus's threat was to scare Leila, set her running back to her family all teary-eyed and panicky, the dumb fuck didn't do his homework, didn't gauge her very well — although he was bang-on about her drug habits. Well, whatever. This was a mistake. She wasn't scared and panicky. No, she was pissed right the fuck off because this smiling, handsome wolf in lost-lamb clothing just sat there, threatening her brother in some twisted, veiled way, in that calm, almost apologetic voice, because he made her know-it-all father right, because she liked him — liked that he was a bit of a weirdo, a bit damaged, like her in a lot of ways — and that meant, or she thought that meant, she could just relax around him and be weird and get drunk and not worry that he was worming his way into her pants or the family.

No, this fucker wasn't worming. That's for sure. He was bulldozing; he was bludgeoning his way through to it by painting a picture of her brother's death — getting shot at his next rally.

He got that detail right, too.

The next scheduled public rally was on the steps of the library.

Fuck.

And he was still apologizing. She barely listened, now. But he was laying it on real thick. Of course this didn't mean anything. Of course it was a false memory. Of course her brother was fine and would be fine. Of course her drug bust was just a weird coincidence. Lightning doesn't strike the same spot twice, right? She nodded. He smiled. It was a good smile. This guy is ice cold. Must have had a lot of practice.

She cleared her throat. "Is that all?"

She didn't look at him. Couldn't.

"Yeah, I think —"

"I mean, it seems to me …" She let the sentence die and tried again: "If you remember all these details, I'd think you'd remember who was after Billy, you know? Who wanted him dead in this false memory."

You work for someone, she thought, so tell me and don't be cute about it. Tell me outright so I can get out of here.

"Well, I did hear someone shout 'Remember the Pizarros' just before the shot."

She almost laughed. That was too good. Her regular guy used to brag that he was connected to them. She used to think he was just another dim-witted punk who figured being a big bad mobster goon — or even just knowing a lot of them — was impressive.

But then the other day he tells her he's out. He was never out. Not once, for the years she'd been buying off him. But just after Lexus fed her that crap about her getting busted, he's out and gives her a reason to try her luck with some stranger that turns out — of course — to be an undercover. What a coincidence.

And like a good little pigeon, she predictably tells her father the whole thing, the load of bullshit she swallowed, gets his attention and gets here, listening to more bullshit that she'd have to regurgitate like an empty-headed messenger.

And all of them — her dealer, Lexus, even the undercover who busted her — were probably working the whole time for the Pizarros: Billy's publicly sworn enemies, the targets of all the crackdowns he'd demanded statewide, and, rumor had it, the same bunch of goons who backed and funded his career in its early beginnings when Pops realized even the MacTeague's wine money wouldn't be enough to buy their way into New York politics.

Chapter Thirteen

Lexus lay on his back, feeling the beat of his heart, listening to Sarah's deep breathing beside him, awash in ecstasy and a sweaty, satisfied tiredness. The muted light of the mid-afternoon sun seeped through the blinds on their bedroom window that were drawn shut to satisfy Sarah's modesty.

"You've been feeling better," she said.

He shifted his body weight, twisting slightly toward her, pivoting on one hip. A noncommittal answer of body language to her gentle dig at a subject he'd rather ignore.

He had improved. It was obvious. To Sarah, it was a drastic, black-and-white difference from impotent to potent, where the dividing line was the day he had stopped seeing Dr. Renesque. But to Lexus, the truth was a little more complicated. Although he hid it, his condition didn't completely reverse itself when he stopped taking Dr. Renesque's mighty pills.

Weeks later, and he'd still have moments of horror, when even the slightest touch from Sarah — a hug, a back rub — repulsed him, moments he couldn't explain, couldn't rationalize away, and all he felt was an intense desire to get away from her. Those moments came on sudden and fierce, a migraine of the libido, the heart, that'd clench his teeth and screw his eyes shut. He'd hide his face, make an excuse, and leave the room, desperate and frantic to get away, scared.

Since they happened sporadically, without a pattern he — or Sarah — could see, he didn't think she noticed, and to her, he was fixed.

He was getting better, the moments fewer the longer he went without seeing Dr. Renesque, taking his pills, going under hypnosis. Better. But he didn't see the sessions as the cause, the impotence the symptom.

Maybe it's only subconsciously for now, but you are starting to recover bits of your personality, Dr. Renesque said in his memory, reminding him of what he wanted to forget. *And, naturally, your true desires are at odds with this fantasy you've created and are trying to live out with that girl.*

There had to be a third option.

"I am Lexus Sam."

"No, you're not," Sarah whispered back, in his ear, before kissing him. "We'll figure you out, one day."

He shifted, snuck his arm under her, and hugged her close.

"Just something I say."

"I know," she said, "and I still love you, too."

**

The next morning Lexus was by himself in the apartment, cleaning up from the breakfast he'd made for Sarah — eating the leftovers, scrubbing the frying pan — and making a list in his head of other chores he should do today.

Hunting for more records and books was his first thought. He had a lifetime of reading and listening to catch up on, and the music and stories and ideas in them, the feelings they evoked, the associations he formed, helped his recovery, helped him find his personality and who he was — maybe just as important as finding a name, his real name, with childhood stories and pictures in a family album. Every time he hit on something, like listening to Joy Division or the Stone Roses for the first time, it felt like a galaxy in his mind expanded at the speed of light, dazzling, finite, but with dimensions too large in scope to really comprehend — and what wasn't there a moment ago, what had been a void of no-thought, of inexistence, was filled, like that, with creation.

Every time it happened, every new favorite he found, he felt a little closer to something important. He felt more whole, more him.

But if he was out, going from shop to shop, he'd end up at the main branch of the New York Public Library, at Billy's rally.

It shouldn't matter.

If he went, he'd stand and gawk like all the others and watch as nothing out of the ordinary happened — the governor would make a fine speech, shake verbal fists, even take a few jabs at whatever punching-bag cause his aides figured made the most popular target, thank everyone for coming, wave some more, smile for some photos, maybe, and leave with the secret service.

It'd be like every other rally he'd held throughout the election, whether Lexus went or not. So not to go, to hide away in chores and busybody work, was ridiculous superstition.

Remember the Pizarros!

He piled the washed pots and plates in the drying rack. Just another ordinary rally. No reason to go. Nothing to see that he couldn't catch on the evening news without wasting a day standing in the cold. Right. Only today wouldn't be just another rally. It *would* be all over the news, but not for the sound bites in the governor's speech.

He knew it without knowing why.

It just had to be. Because it'd be wrong if it wasn't, it wouldn't fit — like Sarah's bare shoulder without the yellow rose tattoo.

Leila knew it too. Somehow. Her reaction when he told her, disturbed, tensed, angry, even. She left abruptly, didn't say good-bye, didn't say anything, just up and left — she must suspect it, feel it.

He turned the taps off, dried his hands on the front of his jeans, and went to his closet. He opened the door, pulled out a weatherworn pair of leather-lined and leather-treaded boots, and pulled them on.

He glanced at the clock on his way out of the apartment. Ten in the morning. The rally wasn't for hours. Plenty of time to get there. Plenty of time.

He stopped, hand on the door handle, and leaned into the door — pressing his forehead against the painted wood for one last moment of quiet, clear sanity.

**

Climbing out of the Grand Central Terminal, his foot caught the lip of the next step and his mind caught some edge of a memory, and both stumbled.

He steadied himself on the railing to the right. And slowed, to look, to watch the stream of people that walked beside him, passing in either direction, hurrying, sauntering, hands on the railing, in pockets.

This isn't right.

Or it is, but shouldn't be.

Next comes —

— a tall, lean man in a wool trench coat who glances down at him —

— right on cue. Then the kid in a hurry, with the —

— puffy bomber jacket hopped up the steps two at a time —

— and finally the redhead —

— beside him put up her faux-fur-lined hood. Her pale face disappeared within.

Where am I?

He stopped midway up the staircase.

Climbing out of Grand Central.

A voice barked, "Watch it, buddy," in his ear.

Lexus reached the top of the stairs and walked, following something like the groove in a record, heading to the library and the rally, just like before, the needle in this groove sounding out the same song he'd heard before.

He walked along the sidewalk with a string of stores on his right. He passed a jewelry store, its glass tinted dark, and looked in at the small display of rings and necklaces sunk into black velvet and lit in brilliant halos of halogen.

He stopped. *Sarah's ring. Right there.*

He stared at it while the reflection of the crowd behind him, some carrying bright neon bristol board signs, flashed by like a pinwheel.

A few bodies back, he saw him — not tall, not too big, with square shoulders and a narrow, dimpled chin. It was the red, thinning hair, his hairline like a reforested patch of clearcut forest that Lexus recognized.

He looked away and ducked, hiding his face.

Detective Rose. The detective that questioned Sarah about me. He must be following me. But why bother? They must know where I —

— Jesus Christ. This is the dream, he thought. *I wrote this down.*

He stepped on a newspaper, still folded and held by a blue rubber band. Part of the headline peeked out from underneath his boot, enough to make him lean down and pick it up.

The paper was crumpled and old, the headline the same now as it was the morning he'd read it, waiting for his pizzas to arrive.

"Governor MacTeague Pledges to 'Correct Our Mistakes.'"

He read it again, louder.

"Governor MacTeague Pledges to 'Correct Our Mistakes.'"

He threw it away and started walking.

The noise of the crowd drew him on more than anything — a rising and falling tide of individual conversations that flowed like sewage down the streets.

The police had shut down 5th Avenue between 40th and 42nd with dull gray barricades. The crowd was penned in like cattle between them, shifting and swaying — spectators at a faith healer's show, waiting for a miracle.

Lexus turned up the collar on his coat and trudged through the wind and the crowd, drifting along the current of bodies that streamed into the middle of the block; he moved shoulder to shoulder with rosy-cheeked supporters, carried along with their pace, quiet and unnoticed, like a glitch in the film, there and not there.

*

"Governor!"

Everyone was yelling something.

"MacTeague for office!"

Cheers and slogans trying to lift above the rest — "Mac-Teague, Mac-Teague, Mac-Teague" — and reach the governor, who stood a dozen feet away, halfway down the library's front steps, talking into an aide's ear.

Someone pressed against Lexus's back.

He looked around — a pair of women held hands to his right — taking an inventory, comparing what he saw with what he'd seen before — the Latino to his left — shifting his gaze from right to left and back again.

He glanced at his watch. The governor's speech was scheduled to start. He looked up, saw the governor approach the podium, felt the moment sync with what he remembered in his apartment's hallway, and knew it was happening. Now.

"Hey, Bee Mac!"

Look at me, goddamn it.

He yelled again.

Billy shifted his gaze up from his notes — déjà vu drenched his senses like a bucket of ice-cold water dumped over his head — oh fuck, it's now, it's going to happen now — and he panicked, lunged forward — I'm too late — security personnel, like bouncers with guns, saw him, reacted — Billy's pleasantly surprised face changed to shock — his mouth formed that round *O* Lexus had seen before, right before — he spun, too late to reach the governor, faced the crowd, saw a gun in the hand of a bland, forgettable blonde-haired man who stood just behind the cigar-smoking Latino.

He ran, dove, shouldered the little man out of the way, reached out, and grabbed the gunman's wrist just as the gun went off. The noise of the first gunshot was almost lost in a moment of shock and disbelief. But Lexus recovered quickly — he'd seen it already.

Momentum carried him forward, his shoulder rammed the gunman in the crook between his chest and raised arm, and they stumbled.

An arm reached across his back, a strong hand clamped down on his left shoulder and tugged, pivoting him on his off-balanced feet, so that he ended up in a headlock, with his back against the gunman's chest, a bony forearm under his chin, pressing against his neck.

"Remember the Pizarros!"

One moment the governor was falling down — Lexus had seen this, too — and in the next, his head burst. Maybe because he'd seen it before — and reacted, then, in horror — the small firework of gore that went off in place of the governor's face didn't startle him.

Half the crowd had dropped to their knees in shock and fear, while the other half was running, exploding and scattering away from the source of the gunfire with the same sudden, chaotic burst as Billy's skull.

But Lexus didn't even flinch.

The killer's arm around his neck relaxed. The chest drew away from his back. Lexus pounced. He grabbed the man's gun arm, just above the elbow, stepped back into him and thrust his elbow, hard. He hit something that felt like a rib. Heard a grunt. The man's arm was tightening again on his neck. The gun pivoted as the man tried to bend his elbow and aim it at Lexus.

With his free arm, he grabbed the short barrel of the gun and kept its end pointed away from him while bringing the killer's hand that held it close enough to his mouth. He lunged forward — the man's forearm squashed his windpipe shut — and bit the fleshy part of the man's thumb.

The arm around his neck disappeared.

He focused only on the gun, on wrenching it free—

Pain came sudden and fierce — dull and hard, jarring even his teeth with a pain that was like biting down on a fork. Everything let go at once. His hands relaxed, legs folded, eyelids dropped shut, and he fell.

A trailing thought streamed out behind him like exhaust from a passing, speeding car on a cold autumn evening — shifting vapor trails that dissipated before they formed any real, definite shape — and for an instant, he remembered.

Chapter Fourteen

Erik had been made. It happens. There was only so much they could do with just him and Elle. Even the dumbest, most unobservant pigeon strutting around out there would start to recognize the same tail at the grocery store, his bar, strolling down his street time and time again.

And Adam Williams *did* recognize Erik. He'd been standing outside a jewelry store near Grand Central, studying one of the rings displayed in the window with the intensity of a doctor peering down a throat.

Most of the crowd was going to the rally, so it was hard for Erik to blend in with the traffic. He'd had to cut across it to keep Adam in view — and that's when Adam looked up and recognition splashed across his reflected face.

So Erik turned away, crossed the street, and let Adam go. The last thing you wanted to do, in this business, was tail someone who knew you were tailing them — that's how you got yourself in trouble.

The girl, Sarah Easter, must've said something to him, too. Visiting her had been a mistake. She had that look, like Elle sometimes got after he drove home a little tipsy and claimed to have had only a couple of drinks — an I-don't-believe-you look that, on Elle, came with a kind of bored indifference; with Sarah, it came with a cagey nervousness, like a doe downwind of a hunter, smelling the blood of others on his hands.

Had he been carrying a badge instead of just pretending he was, he'd assume she was hiding something, try to bluff her into thinking he'd haul her in for questioning.

Sure, it was that kind of thinking that turned his old shield into a plastic knockoff with his alias, Detective Rose, written on it. But he was more discreet now, had to be. But he could only be *so* discreet. And it wasn't enough.

The gig was probably done, now.

It had been weird. For sure. Well paying, strange, boring — rookies would even say pointless. But rookies were rookies because they didn't know that the trick of this business was to make money and stay alive and stay out of jail, in that order. Sometimes the boring, pointless gigs were the career-makers — the paydays you could bank some downtime on so you weren't desperate, so you could show a little discretion in which jobs you took and which you left for the action junkies who never lasted long enough to be anything but rookies.

He never knew why he was following Adam Williams. Or was it Lexus Sam? He wouldn't know the answer to *that,* either. Or why they put him onto Sarah Easter — she was just a girl he met, it seemed, no significance there.

Ah, well. Having a fat bank account and a healthy and free body were better than having a satisfied curiosity keeping him company in jail.

Erik reached his apartment, a squat, five-storey building in Manhattan that showed its age in a charming way — creaks and groans on the stairs, a worn polish down the middle of the wooden hallways.

Elle wished there was an elevator — something she exclaimed nearly every time she carried groceries up the stairs to their top-floor apartment — which, to be fair, was only once or twice a month.

He was just doubling back on his thoughts and had reached the very thought about jail — *better than a satisfied curiosity keeping him company in jail* — when he'd climbed enough stairs to see his floor and a pair of dark-blue-jean-clad legs sprouting up from the hardwood outside his apartment door.

The dark-blue-jean-clad legs of someone waiting for him. Because Elle was home, so the visitor either didn't knock or chose to wait outside. If the visitor didn't knock, it meant they knew he wasn't at home. And if they did but were waiting out in the hallway, it meant they wanted a word in private.

It wasn't a social call.

"Come on up, Erik," a familiar voice said, "instead of skulking on the staircase. I'm just here to talk."

That voice belonged to his old partner, Jack, who retained a real badge, not a plastic fake like Erik's.

Someone's complained.

"Hey, Jack," Erik said, climbing the rest of the stairs, "what brings you out?"

"Oh, you know, the usual," Jack said, meeting him in the hall, halfway to Erik's apartment.

They shook hands, measuring each other up like two old combatants meeting on the outside — relaxed, to a degree.

"Keeping it together?"

"You don't even know," Jack said.

Jack kept his back to Erik's apartment door. He blocked the hall with his wide-shouldered bulk, a steady gaze, and a constant smile.

"Who's making trouble now?"

Jack laughed. "You are," he said, shaking his head. "Jesus, Erik, you didn't recognize the name 'Easter' when you railroaded that poor young lady?"

"She's connected?"

"Yup."

Figures. Sarah Easter wasn't part of the original deal with LM Industries — at first, it was just tails and taps on Adam Williams and Greg Redfine — so when they threw a bunch of money at him to include Sarah Easter, he skipped his usual due diligence — the background checks that reassured him he wasn't pissing in anyone's sandbox, or at least no one who could cause too much trouble.

"Her dad is in the force?"

"An uncle, Detective Rose, an uncle."

"Ah."

They stood in silence for a moment.

"I've got to back off the girl," he said.

"You've got to back off the girl and her boyfriend …"

"Adam."

Jack frowned. "Name I got was 'Lexus.'"

"Adam Williams, Lexus Sam, same thing, same guy," Erik said. "Long story."

"Well, whatever. This job: drop it."

Jack's cell phone rang before Erik could agree. He frowned at the display.

"Duty calls."

Erik nodded.

Jack worked in homicide now, as one of their lead detectives, and part of that job was getting called at any time.

Erik walked to his apartment door, thinking back to that look on Sarah's face, the instincts he'd felt, then, to can it and walk away. But the rep at LM Industries who was sending him his pay was so damned insistent that he find out what he could about Sarah …

That guy cost me some steady pay.

Erik fished his keys out of his pocket and had them in the lock when Jack grabbed his arm.

134

"It's the governor," Jack said, his voice tight. The easy tone that reminded Erik of some movie star doing press was gone. "I need to know everything that you do about this 'Adam Williams.'"

Chapter Fifteen

Lexus lay in his hospital bed, staring at the ceiling, an IV in his hand and a dull ache all over his skull from a firm pressure on his temples, the corners of his jaw, his eye sockets, like a pair of thumbs kneading, grinding.

The ache made it hard to concentrate on the questions the police detective was asking him or what he was answering — on distinguishing thoughts, pain, voices, speaking. I'm just here to take your statement. Okay. Name? Adam Williams. And you still live on 7th Street? Yes. And what do you do, Adam? About what? What do you do for a living, I mean. Oh, I'm on disability, I guess. Insurance pays me an allowance. Okay, Adam, mind telling me what you saw? A man with a gun. In the crowd. What did he look like? Blonde hair. White guy. Maybe five ten. I don't know. Thirtyish. Clean shaven. I didn't really look. The gun. I should've stopped him. I should've done more. Pain rumbled under the sweating skin stretched too tight across his forehead. He shut his eyes. He was just so bland. That's what made him stand out, even more, with the gun in his hand. He should be the bartender at a forgotten bar. Or the guy who takes your tickets at the movies. Some face, some person, you see, interact with, but never really feel is there. A mannequin with a pulse. But that gun. It was like a clown on the subway, in full face paint and floppy shoes, clutching a dozen balloons. Out of context, wrong element.

Adam? Yes? You didn't answer my question. Sorry, my head.
What question? I said, What did you do next? After you saw the
man pull the gun. I tried. There was no time. I wanted to warn the
governor, get down, run, something, but it was so loud, everyone
was shouting his name. I ran at the man instead. I grabbed his
wrist, but the gun went off. It was so loud. He flinched at the echo
of its memory. The pain in his skull tightened. His teeth felt too
big for his jaw. He yelled, then. Remember the Pizarros. And he
fired again. Two shots. We fought. He was strong. You saw the
gun before you heard the shot? Yes. I was looking behind me, at
the crowd. I saw it. He looked at the IV bag hung up beside him
on what looked like a steel coat rod on wheels. Tried to remember
where Sarah was. Sarah. She was on her way now, probably. Have
they called Sarah? Pardon? I'm just wondering if they called
Sarah, if she's coming. They, they've called someone, yes. Your
emergency contact. Now when the second shot was fired, where
were you? Tangled up with the man. I was trying to fight him off.
After that, I don't know. He must've hit me on the head, got away.
Oh no, we caught him. You caught him? Running up 6th, I think.
Who was he? Let's just get your statement finished. The doctor
said you need rest. He was tired. He shut his eyes. And saw blood.
The governor's face. Stay awake. He looked at the IV again.
What's in there? He tried to feel it drip down, into the lines, into
his veins. Tried to imagine it work its way through his body. Don't
sleep; don't dream.

**

When his head cleared, a bit, Lexus noticed he was talking to a
different police officer. A second detective, older, gruffer,
bigger, with bloodshot eyes like cracked marbles, squinted at the

statement Lexus signed, at Lexus, and then at his watch. He looked like a movie star, in a way, broad, handsome, sure.

"Let me tell you what I know, Adam," the detective said. "I know what you've signed here is accurate. I know there are facts in your statement that, when we check against other eyewitness statements, will line up … And that's all good. I think, thanks to you, we got the son of a bitch who murdered our governor.

"But I think you're leaving something out. I think you could tell us more about what you were really doing at the rally, about how you found the shooter *before* he fired, yelled his threat … I don't know. What else? You could tell me why you sometimes go by 'Lexus Sam.'"

Lexus felt worry stir in him as he watched the detective, waiting for him to go on. But he didn't. He tried to think. What bothered him? He didn't sign as Lexus Sam; on the statement, he'd scrawled the name 'Adam Williams' in a rough approximation of the signature on the back of Adam's license.

He signed as Adam because, as far as the police, the government, anything official was concerned, he was Adam Williams, and the middle of the investigation into the governor's murder didn't seem the best time to get into the whole Lexus-Sam-versus-Adam-Williams argument — how Adam Williams was an alias, a fake name someone had constructed — and poorly, too, if—

Oh, fuck.

The detective seemed to smile. But his expression did not change.

"I think you could also tell me why you were at Governor MacTeague's campaign headquarters recently. Or maybe try to explain what you talked to Leila MacTeague about? Was it a death threat against her brother, Governor MacTeague?"

Then, shock. What, no, that can't be — and more dread — but she *asked* me, she practically dragged it out of me — he tried

138

to take a breath — and she knew it was just, just a dream — but he couldn't, he was panting like a dog — a dream that came true — a dog in the pound, about to be put down — and in hindsight, that dream looks like, like a prophecy. He sunk deeper into his hospital bed, but that didn't help any more than the howls of a doomed canine facing his last needle.

Underneath him, the room rolled, like a ship in a bad storm, threatening to crash, to beach him on foreign, hostile shores with no real hope of getting home.

He had to say something, but "What?" was all he could manage.

"You *were* talking to Leila MacTeague," the detective said. It was more of an order than a question.

Lexus nodded back, dumbly.

The detective waited for more, so Lexus cleared his throat and tried to say something, anything, helpful; something that'd amount to more than the frantic braying of a rabid dog being put down for society's good.

"She, she misunderstood, completely," he said. "I, okay, yes, I said I'd … *dreamed* about … this. But if she took that as a threat … It just wasn't. Look, I thought I'd remembered reading about her getting busted for buying coke off an undercover cop —"

"She told you about that" — that smile was back — "did she? Well, she was never charged."

"No, she didn't, I —"

"Then how'd you know?"

The detective's eyes hardened again, and they watched each other for a moment.

"Leila, she … she *confirmed* it," Lexus said, "but I, listen, this is nuts, but it's important. When I first talked to her, I mentioned it — her bust and her dad getting her out of trouble — and she went all pale and weird on me. Then, a week or so later, it happened. Ask her. And now it's happened again."

139

**

Erik had some time to kill while Jack talked to Adam Williams. Or Lexus Sam. Whatever. He was only talking, for now, not questioning. Talking was casual. Questioning was official.

Erik picked up enough on the ride over, after he told Jack about Adam. The police had a dozen eyewitnesses who all saw the same thing: Adam lunging for the gun, fighting with the shooter, and ending up in a bloody pool with a concussion after losing that fight while the shooter made it to the end of the block, where a pair of uniforms brought him down.

Pretty brave.

He'd almost stopped the shooter.

Almost saved the governor's life.

Almost.

So was there something in that 'almost'?

Maybe. Maybe it was a choreographed dance.

Fuck. Or he was a citizen who saw a murder happening and tried to stop it. Pretty fucking brave. Or stupid. Or both.

Erik had come face to face with a guy with a gun, once, when he was on the force. And what did he do? He blinked. He got shot. He did *not* jump the guy, point-blank, and wrestle the gun away while the bullets were flying and the blood spilling.

Not your case, though. Don't get your head too wrapped around it. Make your calls. And then catch a cab back. Get out of everyone's hair.

He fished around in the pockets of his coat until he found what he was looking for: his cell, a notepad, and a pen.

He called Elle first, told her their case was done. They were splitting from LM Industries.

"Suits me," she said. "That whole setup, you know?"

They had never met a representative in person, their contracts were signed with a serial-numbered rubber stamp, and their payment was deposited electronically through a subsidiary. Telltale signs that LM was up to something if not illegal, at least improper — something they didn't want linked to them or to anyone in their company.

"Right, well, no more cloak and dagger with them ..."

"What do you think they really wanted with Adam and Greg?"

According to the contact at LM, Adam and Greg were both outpatients participating in a highly controversial and experimental program. They needed to be monitored in their homes, work, and social situations because changes in behavior and habits were relevant to the program — whatever it was.

But Elle was used to thinking of her and Erik as the good guys, public defenders, doing good for people who had suspicions but not enough to get the police involved. They were busting cheating spouses, employees who were robbing from their employers, con artists who went from town to town, running their scams time and time again.

Occasionally, they went after completely innocent people — the few cases where the suspicions were unfounded, the spouse wasn't cheating, the door-to-door salesman was really just selling door to door, or whatever — those were the times Elle hated the job.

Adam and Greg seemed like two ordinary people living their lives. If they were part of some controversial program, it certainly didn't *look* all that controversial at face value — Greg went to work, visited Adam occasionally, met with friends for drinks, the usual, while Adam did even less.

So it seemed like they were innocent people being spied upon. And that bothered Elle. It bothered Erik, too. But he couldn't let it show.

"What it was, it's done with now."

"No, it isn't. LM will just hire somebody else."

Erik took a deep breath. "That's true."

"We should tell them."

"Come on, Elle," he said, "we'd never work again."

Now it was her turn to pause. She sighed. "You're curious, too," she said. "I know you are. We don't have the full story with these two."

Sure, he was curious. He wanted to know the whole story to every case, the answer to every question, and that side of him rarely listened to rational objections like "you'll ruin your career, break the law, get arrested," and so on.

"I think I might be able to get to the bottom of Adam, at least," Erik said.

"Oh? So we're not quitting?"

"No, we are. But I bet my old buddy Jack will investigate Adam," he said. "Maybe I can stay in the loop … Anyway, let's hear your rundown on Greg, and then I've got to go."

He flipped his notepad open, palmed it, and with his phone cradled in his ear, started to take notes as Elle listed what Greg had been up to during her spot checks. It seemed pretty routine, as usual, except he hadn't visited Adam in over a month now.

"Thanks, great, babe; talk to you tonight."

He hung up and dialed the 1-800 number LM Industries had given him. It connected to a switchboard he imagined was buried underneath a glass monolith full of cubicles and workstations, where phones and data jacks were routed and rerouted in a crocheted mess you'd never untangle without undoing the whole thing — anonymity through sheer size. He'd tried his usual tricks, reverse lookup directories, calls to the telcos hosting the lines, but wasn't able to pin down an address to the number he called — let alone the full name of his contact.

He gave his name and current serial number, reading it off of the plastic fob they'd couriered him. It was about the size of his thumb, encased in a hard plastic shell with a faded readout like a first-generation digital watch, which spat a jumbled string of numbers and letters that changed every minute.

The operator confirmed his serial number and connected him to his contact, Dale. After going through Dale's secretary, he finally got the voice he answered to. Erik ran down what was going on — how Adam went to see Leila MacTeague, the rally, what the police knew, and Greg's fairly mundane behavior.

"Listen, this has to be my last report," Erik said, clearing his throat to override whatever Dale was about to say, "the cops are all over Adam now —"

"Well, I don't expect he'll go very far, then," Dale said, "so your job should be easy."

"Some are even saying that he shot the governor," Erik said, lying, but it was a good cover, "so the security's going to be tight. They see me lurking and loitering around his room, they'll ask me why I'm there, which will lead to who I'm working for …"

"Fuck."

"I know, it's fucked up."

"The program isn't anywhere near finished," Dale said.

"Well, you can pick it up once the cops are finished with him."

Silence on the other end.

Erik glanced up as Greg Redfine walked off the elevator at the end of the hall.

"Listen, Greg's here now. I doubt he'll recognize me, but I have to go."

**

Lexus didn't hear the door open, didn't realize there was anyone else in the room but him and the detective's two narrowed eyes, until Greg cleared his throat.

"Is he under arrest, officer?" he asked.

The detective snorted and shot back: "For what?"

"How would I know?" Greg's voice snapped.

"Lexus and I are just talking, son —"

"I haven't been anyone's son since my parents passed away. So unless you're charging him, you should leave now. The doctor's furious, but too polite to come in here. He needs his rest."

He needs his rest.

Greg's voice echoed, strangely, in his ears.

He needs his rest. That's what —

— four pills in his palm. He swallowed them one by one. The doctor stood, just inside his field of vision, pacing, warming up for the little ceremony —

— but I was in the hospital.

Waiting for Sarah.

Greg came.

Sarah. But I —

— Greg walked into the room, in short, quick strides, like he was late. He smiled, waved to Dr. Renesque. He looked at Lexus, sitting on the couch. His wave stopped. His smile lessened. He watched for a long moment, turned to Dr. Renesque, said something. Argued, maybe. Lexus couldn't hear him. Couldn't hear anything.

Greg stepped closer. The light fell on his face, highlighting a yellow patch of skin under his left eye, where a recent bruise was healing. The look on his face was a mix of —

— one of the tiles on the hospital room's ceiling was discolored, a brownish yellow, like a black eye starting to heal —

— but he couldn't see anything. Just grayness. A thick fog wreathed his head.

Greg's voice came out of it: "What's he doing here?" he asked. "Did you get our appointment times mixed up?"

"I asked you to come, now," Dr. Renesque said.

"I told you what happened last —"

"I know. I know, Greg. But that was … well, that was something we need to —"

"Need to what? Talk about? Can he even talk, now? Or hear us?"

— a young woman's face peered over his, indistinct and out of focus, a flesh-colored blur capped by a streak of black —

— he could see again, in Dr. Renesque's office, while Greg and the doctor argued. Greg looked upset — at times mad, at times on the verge of tears — while the doctor kept his damnable clinical composure, punctuating his sentences with a gesture towards Lexus — a nod or an outstretched hand.

The heat drained out of the argument.

Greg looked at Lexus for a long time.

And —

— another face, a blurry outline, joined the young woman's. He recognized the ER doctor he'd seen earlier. He swept a penlight back and forth across Lexus's eyes, then both faces disappeared from view. Lexus stared at the ceiling and its discolored tile, while he heard the frantic sounds of the room. An alarm screamed —

— Greg eased himself forward. He moved slowly, poured himself off the coffee table and onto his knees. He rose up in front of Lexus, between his thighs, slow and sinister, a cobra responding to its master's tune —

— the alarm stopped, replaced by a content, repetitive chirp. Another face peered over his, different from the other two —

145

— can't be happening. He felt like screaming. Maybe he was. He still couldn't hear. Or move. Greg could. And did. His lips were warm and moist on his neck, moving up to his ear —

— came awake and aware, sudden and fierce, leaping, falling, scrambling to his knees. Doctors and nurses scattered like pigeons disturbed, lab coats like white-feathered wings. His IV drip ripped free with a slight prick of pain.

He vomited in his lap, heavy and warm through the bed sheets. The taste of blood was thick in his mouth.

Voices were yelling.

The detective was gone.

Greg stood in the doorway, his face a mixture of different emotions fighting for space. Something like concern gave way to relief. He rushed forward, his arms reaching out.

Lexus fought forward, kicking free of the sheets.

"You sick little bastard!" Lexus yelled. "You fucking *rapist,* you stay the fuck away from me. You *stay* the *fuck* away from me."

Whatever words he still had rattling around in his head were lost to the snarling static of rage and anger vented with every bit of air in his lungs.

He grabbed Greg by the throat, pinned him hard against the door, and shoved his fist through his skull. He cocked his hand back to strike again, but someone grabbed it and his legs gave out.

He crumpled to his knees, one arm held up and behind his back, coughing, streamers of blood spraying from his mouth like confetti thrown at a wedding that married his delusions and desire.

Book Three

As long as people have free will, they'll ensure that very little is immutably fixed, creating an unknown — the future — and what we call the present is just the time it takes for that unknown to crystallize into the past.

Chapter Sixteen

Lexus stared at the small television pinned to the far wall of his shared hospital room, not watching, while the laid-up bicycle courier in the bed next to his flipped the channels every few seconds, complaining about what he saw on every channel.

A football game, a soap opera, and two channels of commercials flashed in front of his vacant stare while he counted up to one hundred, idle, in time with his pulse — twenty-two, twenty-three.

"Well, Lexus," Dr. Renesque said, "we've got a real problem now."

He turned his head, slightly. Dr. Renesque stood in the doorway in a worn suit and tie, hair tied back, face blank, stare almost vacant as Lexus's as it took in the hospital room, Lexus on the bed.

"It's not Thursday."

Dr. Renesque smiled reflexively, without warmth — a disposable gesture — and walked into the room. He kept his arms behind his back. In an absurd flash, Lexus imagined he was hiding a bouquet of flowers back there, waiting to flourish them.

"Think of this as a house call," he said, and cleared his throat. "Greg visited you?"

Greg: lips warm and moist on his neck, moving up to his ear — stop. Greg's throat in his hand, lips warm and moist — stop. A hospital aide, talking: he's not going to involve the police. Restraints binding Lexus to his bed — holding him to the couch, transfixed — Greg moving closer — stop remembering. The police. Not going to involve the police. Was it a death threat against her brother, Governor MacTeague? Greg eased himself forward — no — raised up between — stop — slow and sinister. Remember the burst of blood — the Pizarros — a flash of color, bright — the red carpet at his feet, underneath Greg, kneeling, rising — the blood — a red flash.

Flashes. Just flashes. Rape. Murder. A terrible car accident. Footprints in the snow. Flashes that were a few frames from a film, a few lines from the script. Read your lines — telling Leila, warning her, not enough, reassuring her — hit your mark — the gun in the crowd, his hand on the wrist holding it, struggling, failing — meaningless actions — the blood, the screaming — the gun, he almost had it pointed away — but it was just a prop that had to go off.

"I'm not here because of Greg."

Lexus nodded, eyes back to the television — an ad for laundry detergent, children running, laughing, grass stain aftermaths — seeing Greg, the governor, footprints in the snow, overflowing with blood, bright on the white.

"No?"

"No," Dr. Renesque said, moving his hands from behind his back and revealing a worn, red-covered spiral notebook, its cardboard cover creased, dog-eared pages browned. "Get dressed, Lexus. We should talk in private."

**

Sarah waited in the lobby with several bags of groceries at her feet. She watched the floor numbers above each elevator, willing them to change. They were all frozen on the top floor.

She pressed the call button again.

Dammit.

She left her groceries by the disobedient elevators, walked out to the front door, and tried buzzing their apartment. The intercom rang and rang, but Lexus didn't answer.

Oh, well.

She retrieved her grocery bags and headed for the stairs.

The door to the stairwell opened as she approached. Jill, their neighbor, stepped out and greeted Sarah with a big smile.

"Hey, Sarah," she said. Her smile caused a few wrinkles to appear at the corners of her eyes — the only sign of age on her young face. "Lexus has a friend staying with you or something?"

"Uh, no, I don't think so."

"This afternoon I rode up to our floor with this older guy," she said, frowning, "I'm nosy enough to know everyone in the building ..."

Sarah laughed and rolled her eyes.

"... so I noticed this guy go to yours."

"Really? He went to ours?"

"Yup. Had a key, too. Let himself in."

Sarah shifted the weight on her feet. One of the bags had a bag of flour in it and was starting to get heavy in her hand. But she had to know if this older guy was Detective Rose, harassing them again.

"What'd he look like?"

Jill looked up, blinked a few times. "Oh, well, he was middle-aged," she said, "bit of a saggy face, like too much skin, you know? Black beard, balding, long ponytail. You know what really got me? He dressed in this maroon, striped three-piece suit, like a fifties banker or something."

**

Lexus and Dr. Renesque sat at a small round table, just big enough for two seats, in the hospital's cafeteria. Lexus sat with his back to the bank of windows on the south-facing wall that let a flood of light in. His dream journal was spread open on the table, exposing the pages of tight, slanted script in blue ink telling and retelling the dreams — memories — stories — he heard echoing through his days.

"You've been diligent," Dr. Renesque said. "That would have helped our sessions —"

"I'm not coming back."

"And I'm sure I could've helped you with this ... dangerous manifestation of —"

"They're just nightmares," Lexus said. He took the book up, fanned the pages, and shut the notebook. "Nothing dangerous."

Dr. Renesque raised an eyebrow. "I've read it, of course."

"Of course."

"May I?" He held out both hands, palms up. Lexus surrendered the book. "Thank you. Now, certainly, most of these fall under regular categories of dream interpretation. I have a colleague who specializes in this field, if you'd like. But *this* dream, concerning Governor MacTeague's public address ..."

Lexus didn't listen. But it was hard not to *hear* the words, physically, have them register. He tuned the doctor out and focused, instead, on the chitchat and gossip coming from a pair of young nurses who waited in line and grasped their trays with both hands.

Still, some of what Dr. Renesque said made it through the audio smokescreen. Just individual words, each a clump of pollen, the wind-blown seeds of weed-logic that'd replace the thoughts, opinions, and perceptions he'd carefully planted in his mind's backyard.

"… I know, right? He's the worst on-call we have," the blonde nurse said. "Like, why even bother if you're …"

"… it could be viewed as a fantasy, of course. In the wrong hands. The District Attorney's Office, for example, might be interested …"

Words. Just words.

"Christine! You're too funny," the chubby nurse said, laughing. "Shit, if you only knew …"

"… for your own sake, sure. But not just for yours, if you think about it …"

Just words, but he heard them.

"Funny isn't enough," the blonde nurse — Christine, he guessed — said, "unless I get somewhere beyond friends with Mr. Bartender …"

"… assume for a moment you have these fantasies of violence. You don't believe you do, I know. But if you allow the possibility that you *do,* well …"

He heard them. And started to listen.

"… still hasn't sent a clear signal, one way —"

"Oh, he sends signals every day," Christine said, laughed, "but I sound crazy listing them all."

Lexus gave up on Christine's bartender dilemma and surrendered his attention to Dr. Renesque's weed-logic — why he needed to turn himself in, not to the cops, but to the doctor's personal care.

"Like an asylum for the insane?"

Dr. Renesque shook his head.

"What then?"

"Think of it as a retreat. There's an empty apartment in my office," Dr. Renesque said. "I used to work with a mental health hotline. We'd put up the borderline cases there —"

Lexus snorted. "Borderline what? I'm not going to commit myself."

"Of course not. I'm not talking about anything official. It's just a retreat from all of this."

Lexus flipped through the pages of his dream journal. He skimmed — a path of footprints, little craters in the sheet covering the hard ground, trailed away in a gently curving arc over the horizon — seeing each clearly — the road was cold and hard and forested with boots and legs — remembering the dream or recalling the buried memory.

**

Sarah said good-bye to her neighbor and piled her groceries by her feet. She tried the door. Locked. So their mystery guest had locked up after himself. How nice. She put her key to the lock, imagining things she shouldn't, some mural of barely remembered nightmares and choice horror flick scenes — blood on the floor, a psychopath waiting just behind the door, his eyes wide and staring and too white, his breath held in soon-to-be-released ecstasy …

Stop it.

She unlocked the door and shoved it open — a little too hard — stooped, gathered up her groceries, and stepped into an empty, normal apartment. She dropped the bags off on the kitchen counter and took a quick walk through the apartment. Maybe Lexus had left a note.

The kitchen was clean, dishes and pots dry in the rack, leftovers whisked into the fridge. Just like Lexus. His usual morning routine. He'd stuck around after she left.

She sifted through the clutter on the coffee table. No note.

She tidied the papers that had fallen onto the floor and stuck her head into their bedroom.

And felt something, something bad. Like a ghost calling your name from the other room. Too quiet to really hear, to dread. But enough to sense. To make you uneasy.

All their dresser drawers were pulled open. Some socks were spilled onto the floor. The nightstand table had been swept clear. Even the closet looked disturbed. Rummaged through. Like Lexus had looked for something he'd lost, almost frantically, and hadn't cleaned up after — Lexus or some fifties banker with a ponytail.

She shook her head, those things she shouldn't imagine creeping back in, and started to tidy up. She tried to see what was missing. Money, passport, jewelry, everything valuable was right where it belonged. We weren't robbed.

Those unthinkable imaginings stirred, grumbling like a subway passing beneath her feet.

There's an explanation. There is. Lexus had given his key to someone. Sent him back here to get something for him, from the bedroom. The guy had to look around a bit, couldn't find it, in a hurry too. Or something. We weren't robbed. He had a key. Nothing's missing. Nothing's wrong, then. But someone had been here. Going through everything. He pawed through all my stuff. She shut her eyes as the thoughts conjured up goose bumps with their black magic.

She hurried to the door and locked it. But they had a key. Fuck. They could get in whenever they wanted. Even now. When I go to bed. What 'they'? The stranger, singular. Older, balding. Probably harmless. Still. She fit the chain across the bar, ignored all the scenes she could remember of men — cops or burglars or murderers — kicking through the same kind of little chain.

**

"There's Sarah to consider, too."

Lexus looked up at Dr. Renesque, watching, testing.

"That's right, Sarah. You care about her," Dr. Renesque said, "which is … what it is. We differ in our opinions on that point. The police were told you made a death threat against —"

"No, I didn't." Lexus shut his eyes. "I didn't. Leila, she misunderstood —"

"Maybe, but that's not important. Not to Sarah. Someone thought you were a danger, and they told the cops," Dr. Renesque said, tapping the dream journal, "and then there's what you wrote in here. Was this what you saw, or what you made happen?"

Remember the Pizarros!

"I didn't —"

"But is it so hard to believe you could be a danger to others? If you do have repressed feelings, emotions — memories, even — could they progress to violence? Are you willing to risk her?"

**

Sarah rushed to the phone, spilling the open book on her lap to the floor. Her heart beat a little faster. She was mad and worried and already a bit relieved even before she could answer the phone to say, "Hello," or hear his voice and his lame apology and the *story,* the what-happened, the who-the-stranger-was, the explanation that would make sense of the apartment.

"Hello?"

"Fina!" Julia's loud voice sunk Sarah's hopes. "How are you doing with all of this?"

Her thoughts stuttered. "Fine … All of what?"

"Have you seen the news?"

"What? No," she sighed, "Julia, listen, this isn't —"

"Who'd have thought your weirdo boyfriend would be, like, a hero?"

"What?"

"It's on CNN, Fi. You haven't...?"

She snatched the remote from the coffee table, flicked the TV on. The picture took a moment to appear — a moment filled with Julia talking unheard — and when it did, she switched to CNN.

"He's been on and off it all day."

"GOVERNOR MACTEAGUE ASSASSINATED" ran in bold capital letters across the bottom of the picture.

"My God ..."

Julia kept talking, saying things like "amazing, isn't it?" "so brave," and "he caught the guy, on his own," her hyper recap just a little faster than the bullet-point summaries, graphics, sound bites, delivered with photogenic deep looks.

Sarah just listened, processed, while the fearful magic cast more shivers down her back and goose bumps across her arms like strings of firecrackers bursting. There he was, face covered in blood, police and paramedics, the crowd, reporters; it was just a clip, two seconds, walking, an arm around his shoulder, latex-gloved hand prodding his temple. Just a clip. The blood though. The blood stayed. It stayed while the news went over it. She changed the channel, but it was still there. The governor dead, assassinated. Gunned down. Lexus the Boy Scout who had stepped in. Gripping television.

"He's hurt."

Her tone cut through to Julia. "Oh, hey, Fi, he's okay. Really. Just a bit of a bump on the head."

She nodded, alone and feeling it, in the apartment. "But he's not back yet."

"I was just calling to —"

"Where is he?"

She heard a muffled commotion on the other end of the line.

"We'll go see him now," Julia said, her tone snapping into an imitation of the calm, airplane-captain way of speaking their dad adopted a lot, "I'm coming over."

**

Sarah sat on the curb because she didn't know what else to do and she didn't feel like standing anymore. People were arguing around her. There were police officers asking questions, using deep voices, and her sister, somewhere, yelling. Everyone seemed confused about a lot of things. Except they all agreed Lexus was supposed to be in his bed resting, but he wasn't. He was gone.

Chapter Seventeen

Greg woke up with a start and a scream. He flinched and threw his hands up, protecting his bruised face from some dream-glimpsed blow — but it was too late, the blow had already landed, the damage done, here in reality, in the past.

And it still hurt.

He rolled out of bed, stretched, and dropped to the floor, legs straight, palms in close to his chest; up on his toes and fingertips he started his push-ups, one, two, three, breathing in time with them, out on the push, in on the drop. He finished, rolled over on his back, breathed deep, once, twice, started his crunches — mindless excursions for his body.

He finished, rolled to his feet with grace, and headed for the shower. He slipped off the Jockey shorts he slept in before he left the bedroom.

His bruised reflection waited in the mirror, passing with him as he walked across the bathroom tile to the shower, coaxing him to look, but he didn't. He knew what he'd see.

It was awful, but at least it settled a question he should've answered, on his own, months ago. Greg'd been with some assholes before, rougher types that he didn't mind, but Adam wasn't just domineering or distant — two types he could handle — he was, well, what? Bipolar. Manic depressive. Something. Fucking crazy.

He turned on the cold water tap, didn't touch the hot, and pulled the plunger to divert the water from the faucet to the showerhead.

He stepped out of the way of the first spray of water, braced himself, and stepped under the ice-cold spray. He held his breath and rubbed himself in the cold.

His doctor had told him it was good for his circulation, which was extremely poor — he was perpetually cold — so he took cold shower after cold shower.

Adam felt like a cold shower. But worse. Worse than any analogy he could come up with. He remembered Adam as a perfect guy. But then one night when he'd gone over, all Adam would talk about was some car accident. What car accident? He couldn't even hold Adam's hand. He acted like they'd never met, just like that: in one moment, they were perfect strangers.

Adam was nuts.

Had to be.

But.

But there *was* something about Adam Williams that lasted in his mind; something he couldn't explain to friends, to himself, to his shrink — a feeling that was stronger than the memories of them together, stronger than the common sense — his and the advice from friends — that said he was in a bad relationship, an emotionally, and now, physically abusive one, a one-sided affair that wasn't even fucking acknowledged by his other half.

How fucked up is that?

You wake up one day, and your boyfriend denies even dating you? You can't respond to that. It didn't make any sense, could never be rationalized with the usual post-breakup comfort words and logic — but then could any breakup, really, be rationalized? If you were dumped, you were dumped. It didn't matter, really, how or why or when. You could indulge in some tears and some

160

pouting, maybe, or you could vent and shout, or go on a fucking spree, or whatever, but at the end of the day, you were alone again and you'd better get that into your head.

But moving on wasn't easy when some draw kept bringing you back to the guy over and over — sitting outside his apartment like a fucking puppy — God, he hated that he did that for so many weeks — actually feeling happy — no, thrilled — that the hospital called — not thrilled that Adam was in the hospital, but pleased all the same that he was listed as the emergency contact and when they'd asked Adam if there was anyone he wanted called, he'd said Greg Redfine and gave them his number.

I mean, if that wasn't a mixed signal ...

He toweled himself dry, wrapped it around his waist, and turned his attention to shaving — a delicate, more difficult task, now that half his face was bruised.

And after he called you to the hospital, he called you a rapist.

And broke your face.

**

Greg took a taxi to his doctor's appointment. He knew, if he looked it up or asked around, he could figure out a subway route that'd probably take him from door to door, but he liked riding in cabs, talking to the driver, watching Manhattan out the window, trying to imagine where everyone else was going, if they were late, if today was a good or bad day for them.

All of it was empty daydreaming — imagining other people's lives and errands, or hearing about the driver's, whichever — but it prepared him for a session with his shrink. He felt it balanced his mind — thinking, hearing about others to cancel out all the self-indulgent talk, the inane details rehashed under hypnosis.

The cabbie wasn't particularly talkative today.

"How are you today?" Greg asked from the back seat, smiling at the reflection he saw in the rearview.

"Fine, yes."

"Has it been busy today?"

There were a few questions he relied on to get a cabbie talking: ask about their day, if it's busy, or talk about the traffic and good routes to take.

"Usual."

The cabbie's cell phone rang — loud, metallic tunes over the constant chatter of the dispatch — and he answered it, ending the chitchat.

People watching, then.

Traffic crawled along. They were in the right-hand lane, skirting into the left to steer around particularly wide parked cars, next to a sidewalk and a line of low-rise apartment buildings.

Next to his window, a young couple walked their black Lab. They generally kept pace on the sidewalk — the taxi would leave them behind for a moment, until the next red light, backed-up stop sign, or general congestion forced them to stop.

The woman had one hand buried in the man's jacket pocket. She kept looking, smiling up at him. He paid more attention to the bouncing, bounding leaps of the Lab — yanking back on the leash every other step — than he did to her. But she kept smiling. He was talking, saying something funny by the way she was laughing.

It's all an act, he thought. A delusion. She's clinging to him. She knows — or at least thinks — she can't do any better, even if he does like his dog more than her. Why? Because her self-esteem told her she didn't deserve any better?

Stop it.

They're just a happy couple out walking their dog.

You're projecting.

He looked for another target while the cab drew closer to the doctor's office and another dose of pills and hypnosis, courtesy of Dr. Renesque.

**

Dr. Renesque ushered him into his office with a concerned look — raised eyebrows and a long, silent, searching gaze — and invited him to sit down with an open-palmed gesture to the couch.

He was dressed impeccably, again. Today he wore a three-piece suit, somewhere between navy blue and charcoal gray, with a watch chain dangling from his vest pocket. Simple, tasteful cufflinks pierced his light blue French-cuffed shirt. His tie was diagonally striped, dark purple and pink, separated by thick black lines.

Greg already felt self-conscious in his jeans and untucked, off-the-rack dress shirt. He smiled and shuffled over to the couch.

"You shaved."

Dr. Renesque smiled. "It was time," he said, and scratched absently at his bare cheek. It was thinly carpeted with stubble, like the concrete foundations, reminders, of homes in a burned-out town. "It grows back too quickly to keep it neat."

"I have a really light beard, so it's easy to shave," Greg said. "I got lucky, I guess."

Dr. Renesque's painted-on smile remained. He hovered by the door while Greg stalled, on the verge of sitting on the couch and starting their session.

163

Just tell him.

Dr. Renesque watched. Eye to eye, waiting, silent like always. He presided in his office like a judge holding court, and you never knew the verdict until the gavel came down.

Greg felt like he'd come home with an obvious hickey or something to stare at, which demanded attention and an explanation but would never be verbally questioned.

And now Dr. Renesque was staring at his bruises, making all these calculations in his head, forming theories of when and where and how Greg got them, why he got them, why he hasn't mentioned them yet — or if he did mention them, why he felt compelled to talk about it.

Tell him and get it over with.

Greg sighed and sat down.

"You don't have to tell me," Dr. Renesque said, sitting behind his desk, "but if you *want* to talk about it …"

That was the only prompt he needed. Greg told the whole story — getting the call, finding Adam in the hospital, his fit, or attack, whatever it was, then Adam waking up, accusing him of rape and attacking him, punching him, collapsing.

He could feel his mood improve the more he talked, the more he let it out — a bloodletting that drained his mind of the grief and anger and hurt. But it was replaced with emptiness, a tiring void that made him grateful for the hypnosis as a break from waking thoughts.

"You'll need five pills today," Dr. Renesque said, flipping a page in his ledger to check something, "but we'll start only if you're ready. We won't be talking about this under hypnosis."

"You know, Doctor," Greg said, smiling and shaking his head, "I think I'm ready to move on."

Dr. Renesque nodded. "Well, we can talk about it."

Chapter Eighteen

Leila sat cross-legged, back to her couch, the TV on but muted, patterns of colored light falling on her face, flashing across her blank stare; a digital kaleidoscope in her eyes of infomercials and talking heads.

The blinds were open to the night. The skyline — jagged, blocky teeth of light — blurred with the TV and the lit candles that burned and flickered from every flat surface around her. All the light refracted through her tears, painting rainbows on the back of her skull.

Did Billy ever see a rainbow? *Really* see one? Stop and watch it, marvel at it, childlike, or chase it, try to find its end. Was he ever a kid like that? Free and wild and silly and pointless and innocent? Or was his birth, even, so devoid of miracle that it became another line item for the books, part of the eighty-year plan — a cog in the machine of flesh and souls Dad had designed, a weird kind of architect who drew plans with lives — a cog that had to fit to work, to help that plan, to benefit the machine and its designer and maybe the cog itself.

You had a choice. You did. But you liked being part of that machine. Working in it. For it. Whichever. The same. The things that machine did with you churning away in it were now the sound bites they've reduced your career, your life, to in the mourner/voyeur pieces CNN and Fox News and everybody else ran. They were real results, thanks to that machine. But now you're gone. And only those results are left.

She picked up her guitar from the floor beside her. It was a battered old acoustic with several faded stickers plastered to its body — album covers for Radiohead's *Pablo Honey* and Pink Floyd's *Wish You Were Here* plastered side by side with a few for Nine Inch Nails. She strummed idly, going through the intro to "Wish You Were Here" while the kaleidoscope spun and her tears broke it all down into rainbows that Billy never saw.

Her cell phone rattled on her kitchen table for a few rings. Then it switched to a ring tone, a cheap proxy of "Electric Feel" that she'd kept far too long. She let it ring. No phone calls. No visitors. No sunlight for days of sleeping and nights of drifting on her introspection; that was her new regime.

The funeral was today, finally, after, what, a week, of bureaucratic paperwork, forms and officials, of preparations made by the same machine, the same organization, that ran his campaigns and did his ads and scheduled his appearances — one last appointment to keep.

She looked at the clock mounted above the bookshelves to her left. It was late. The service had finished hours ago. The wake would be closing down, too. MacTeagues from all over drinking and commiserating while the head of the household surveyed his ruined machine like a child's set of Lego strewn across the floor.

She finished the song. Or what she remembered. Strummed the last few bars over and over again, trying to pick up on the fleeting melody, fragile and beautiful, like a butterfly caught so long ago.

**

Lexus paced in his room, a small square carpeted in worn beige stained dark at the side of the bed where he planted his feet every morning. Rise and shine. How many mornings? Windowless and without furniture, it felt like a prison cell. But the door was open. Free to go. Now. Yesterday. Tomorrow. But he never did. Yet. Once he was ready, he'd leave. Go back and look up Sarah. Tell her he was better. Explain why he'd left. He had to. Why he never called. Well, I will call. Soon. Tomorrow. There's a phone downstairs, I think. I'll ask Dr. Renesque. And then I'll call Greg and — Sarah. I'll call Greg. Sarah. He frowned, rubbed the bridge of his nose. Another headache formed behind his eyes, temples; storms in his mind.

He fished the bottle of Advil out of his jeans, dry swallowed two, thinking he'd had two already, today. Or was that …? He had lots of headaches, lately. Because he didn't have those hospital-strength Tylenol that Greg used to get him. He lifted them, I think, although he always said they were free samples.

He shook his head.

What?

Headaches … Advil … Greg.

Get some sleep. More sleep. I'm always sleeping. Damn. He started pacing again.

"My name is Lexus Sam," he said, "and I still love you …"

**

Leila strummed some idle chords, not really playing, not a song or even a tune, just chords, hands moving on their own. Separate. Apart from the rest of her body. Her thoughts. Everything. They didn't know grief.

They just played.

**

Lexus walked out of the room on feet that didn't seem to touch the ground. He drifted above the carpet, down the stairs, numb and ethereal, just a lost soul.

He shook his head. Blinked. Focused. It was the damned pills and the headaches and the sessions, the unending, constant sessions with Dr. Renesque.

Where am I?

**

Eventually her tired hands returned to her and she became aware of what she played, the intro to "Wish You Were Here." Eyes shut, she listened to what she played synch with how her ear heard the original. She moved passed the introduction, into the first chords, strumming.

All the times she'd heard this song, played it, connected somehow, strung together through time.

**

Lexus wandered out of the squat walk-up and down the short path to the sidewalk without a second thought. But which way now? The question snared him. He turned around, looked back at Dr. Renesque's offices. Such a deceiving building. All the times he'd come here before, he'd assumed it was full of offices — or empty offices, available for lease — and no bigger than a couple of townhouses mashed together. But stumbling out now — against the strictest of orders — and looking back at his voluntary prison, he tried to mesh his knowledge of all its rooms and beds and the kitchen inside with the view of its exterior — tried, and failed, like integrating the two halves of an optical illusion.

He blinked, shook his head, and turned left.

There has to be a pay phone nearby.

**

The pay phone's earpiece was greasy, the booth vandalized with at least three different tags, and most of the phone book's pages had been torn out. His skin, eyes, related these details to his brain so preoccupied with what he was going to say, how he'd say it, and imagining Sarah's response that he didn't notice, at first, when the phone stopped ringing on the other end.

**

Lexus didn't say a word. He couldn't. He placed the receiver back, gently, with exaggerated caution — desperate not to disturb anything, to make this any more real. Just hang up. He hung up. Okay. Breathe. He exhaled. Took a deep breath. It couldn't be. Maybe it was. That's weird. Okay. It's just weird. He fished another quarter out of his pockets and tried dialing Sarah's cell phone again.

This time Greg answered after one ring, obviously still right by the phone.

"Hello?"

His voice sounded a little annoyed, now. But it was definitely Greg's voice.

"Who is this?"

**

She sung out in a forced tone, words from memories untouched by this feeling, this now. Her throat was thick and aching. Tears spilled. She let go of the guitar, and it slid off her lap, from her limp hands. She pushed it aside, drew her knees up to her chest, and hugged them.

**

Lexus walked the couple of blocks back to Dr. Renesque's place, not sure where else to go, not trusting his legs to carry him anywhere else — not trusting his memory of *where* anywhere else was — not really walking, just shuffling, a prisoner ensnared in ankle cuffs, forced to stutter in a slow, hopping trot down a bleakly lit death row while the other inmates catcalled and the guards looked on grim and officious, not looking at you, not making eye contact, but not looking away either …

He looked up at the squat building. His new home. He knew how to get back here, at least. He walked up the front path and tried the door. Finding it still unlocked, he pulled it open and half-turned to look around him — I could just walk away, even if I don't know where to go, even if every time I tried to get back to Sarah, to follow her footprints through the snow-covered plains of my delusions, I ended up at Greg's doorstep, well, I could still try, I could still turn around and retrace my steps and try again, determined.

But you're not.

He put his back to the outside world, opened the door fully, and trudged inside, slow and deliberate, the condemned man choosing his steps to the gallows.

**

Lexus stared at his reflection in the bathroom mirror. A bare bulb hung just beyond his right cheek, glowing bright. It obscured half his face in the reflection and cast most of the other in shadow. He could see his sweat, beads gathered on his forehead, hair slick against his temples longer than he realized it'd gotten.

The bulb's radiant warmth kissed his cheek. But he felt cold. Chills. A fever. Dehydrated, too. Dizzy all the time. And the headaches. He stared at his face. Tried to focus. But his vision was split; he was seeing double. Adam Williams. Lexus Sam. He saw them both in the mirror.

"I am Adam Williams."

Nothing.

"I am Lexus Sam."

Still nothing.

"And I still love you …"

Greg, he finished silently. Nope. Sarah. No, still nothing. Neither, then. I don't love you. I don't love. I don't feel.

Dr. Renesque described what he felt with Sarah as a delusion, a powerful, conscious, learned desire to find a girl, get married, have children, and grow old together — a cultural, societal mandate implicitly pressed upon every Western child raised by saturated media and reinforced by the perfectly natural tendency for human beings to desire *belonging,* to fit in with what they learn over and over is good, normal.

But it was conscious, learned — a fantasy he played out while his subconscious reacted with disdain at first, manifested in repulsion at intimate touch and then anger and violence. He shut his eyes. And remembered. Billy. The gun. The blood. Greg. Greg's neck in his hands. I could have killed him, too.

171

Choked him to death. With my bare hands. My hands — Sarah's hands, holding them, walking down the beach, miles from home, going nowhere, really, but getting there, too. They were laughing. Enjoying each other.

Looking at her smile. Greg's smile. Greg. Distant, but there. Birthdays. Seeing The Cure play Madison Square Garden and singing along together. Unpacking after the move. Passing him dishes to put away — dark plates with a ring of white around the edge. Greg picked them out. And they were still at the apartment. His apartment that he shared with Sarah. Greg. The chain of memories pulled him down into the murk, showed him —

No. I'm not Adam Williams. These thoughts I have — The Cure, skating and hot chocolate, Vegas — are his. Not mine. Adam's. Sarah's a fantasy, but Greg is an alibi, needed only for Adam to exist, to corroborate what Adam knew, to make him, them, real.

But.

I have these thoughts.

The chain of memories was barbed, wrapped around so many mundane thoughts and sights and smells of the day — like reliving a dream over and over after you woke — so much was tied to Greg.

He turned from the mirror and dropped to his knees, just in time. He wretched into the toilet, the bowl already freckled with dried and rotting bits of half-digested meals; he coughed, spat, and hit the plunger. The toilet flushed. The water swirled. He could feel it stir up a cool breeze against his sweating face.

He pushed himself up, tottered, and grabbed the countertop edge. Weak. Dizzy. He tried to spit the bad taste out of his mouth. Okay. Eat breakfast. What time is —

— breakfast?

Greg slipped his slender arm around his waist, nuzzled close, head on Adam's shoulder.

"Smells good," he said, his voice a cat's purr.

Adam smiled but kept focused on the skillet. Crepes were hard enough to make without the added distraction of —

— Sarah's arm eased off his waist. Her hand reached around —

— "… but you should come back to bed," he said, she said, emphasizing the point with his hand, her hand, massaging, rubbing, stirring his lust with the simplest gesture and the unspoken promise of what could — would — come next.

In his twin memories, he grinned the same grin at Greg and at Sarah, shook his head, and said, "These'll burn," pointing at the crepes with his spatula.

Chapter Nineteen

Leila sat on the floor in front of her bed, candles burned down and snuffed out, sat in the darkness, the silence, guitar on the floor next to her, a can of warm beer in her right hand and an unlit cigarette in her left. Tears dried on her cheeks. Snot dried on her upper lip.

She had nodded off out of exhaustion, boredom, eyelids sliding closed, head drooping; loose hair had fallen into her face, screening it from the empty apartment full of ghosts — the picture of Leila and Billy, smiling in their early twenties, snow-capped peaks in the background, that hung next to the front door in a lacquered black frame; the copper and bronze chess pieces he gave her for her twenty-fifth, so large and elaborate she used the opposing kings, queens, and knights as art pieces around her place, handmade sculptures of antiquity without the telltale seam most pieces had, meaning these had been sculpted individually, truly one of a kind, without being formed in a two-piece mold like most sets; the black leather ottoman, too, a Christmas present, a reminder, a ghost.

The knock on her front door woke her. She sat up a little straighter, tilted her head to her left shoulder, then her right, stretching her stiff neck. Another knock. She put the warm beer down on the floor and rolled her shoulders. Another knock. Fuck.

She stood on bare feet, stepping on the legs of her loose, flared jogging pants, and walked out onto her balcony. She shut the sliding glass door behind her, muffling the sound of loud knocks. Someone's fucking eager, she thought, lighting her cigarette with a white Bic lighter she found resting on the balcony's railing.

The artificial grass she had installed over the balcony's concrete kept her bare feet warm. An oversized beige sweater, loose knit and three-quarter length, draped over the chair to her left. She put it on, switching the hand holding the cigarette to pull her arms through, but left it open. The tie that cinched it close hung down each leg from the sweater's belt loops.

She smoked in peace.

She finished the smoke, flicked it off the balcony to twirl end over end in the darkness, ember glowing as it spun out into the empty air and down out of sight, and pulled the sliding door open.

Head down, hands in her sweater's pockets, she walked inside, the door open behind her, the cold refreshing, releasing the smoke-scented warm air of spilled beer and tears.

Inside, a lamp was on.

Inside, someone waited for her.

She tensed, fists clenched, heart thrashed a frantic beat; her head snapped up just as her legs froze, feet planted.

Her father waited for her in the middle of the room.

"Shit." She let out her breath. "Fuck, Dad. What are you doing?"

Her dad watched, black suit jacket with a subtle pinstripe, over a wide-collared white dress shirt, gray jeans pre-stressed and faded to seem well worn off the rack, hands at his sides, jacket open.

"I knocked," he said. "You didn't answer."

"So?"

He held up one hand, holding a key ring with a single key and a plastic fob on it. "I have a key."

"Of course you do," she said, pulling the folds of her sweater around her middle. She grabbed the cloth belt and tied it closed. "Coffee?"

"You missed the funeral."

She walked into her kitchen, to the sink — a deep, stainless steel one, with faucets labeled Cold and Hot in black, cursive ink on white enamel buttons. She spun the Cold one and let the water run.

"I said good-bye here."

"I'm sure you did," he said, turning to face her, "but you missed the funeral."

She looked at him, cold water running. "I don't think Billy cared," she said before turning away. She found her stovetop kettle, filled it, and placed it on a burner. She switched the heat to high.

"No," he said to her back, voice steady and slow, "but your mother needed you there —"

"I already told her I wasn't coming," she said, over her shoulder. She plugged in the glass-topped digital scale on the counter to the left of the stove and zeroed it out.

"You should've come."

She measured out two tablespoons of coffee beans and placed them on the scale, adding and subtracting until it read twenty grams, then gathered the beans up, dumped them into her grinder, and flicked it on.

The electric motor whirred to life; the concealed blades reduced the beans in the hopper to a powder that gathered in the grinder's doser, a small, clear plastic bin underneath the blades.

She watched, waited for it to finish, ritualistically.

The pitch of the grinder changed, went higher, signaling that it was empty of beans, so she switched it off and pulled out the container of grinds, their aroma potent, fresh.

She turned back to her dad with the container in her hands. "What are you really doing here, Dad?"

"The media was there."

She rolled her eyes and turned back to her coffee prep: she selected a small, round paper filter from the stack she left by the grinder, wet it, placed it in the plastic cap, and set it aside.

"And you can be sure they noted your absence, Leila."

"So?"

She dumped the grinds into the bottom of her AeroPress — a thick plastic tube with a plunger, like a syringe without a needle — set her timer, and poured the hot water in. After a minute she screwed the filter on, upturned the press over a mug, and slowly, with even pressure, pressed down on the plunger, squeezing out a light brown, almost amber coffee.

"We need to talk, Leila."

She picked up her mug, turned, and leaned against the oven's handle. She smelled the coffee. And waited, watching her dad scratch just above his eyebrow, stalling, thinking.

He walked up to the breakfast bar that divided the kitchen from the living room and put his hands flat on the granite. Here it comes, she thought, getting down to it. The pitch.

"You know, I used to pay for this place out of my own pocket. Utilities, rent, cable, every month." He looked down at his hands. "But the money's been tight, lately. The winery isn't performing, a bad year, some bad reviews. Manhattan is expensive. And so is politics. With your brother up for reelection, I had to free up some room, so I made some calls and got these expenses for your place on the campaign's dime. That means we can dip into whatever the fundraisers come up with

177

each month for this place. Wrote it off as the per diem for a bunch of staffers."

Dread, then.

She felt dread because of what he was saying, what he might be about to say, and what that'd mean about Billy's death — that it wasn't just a murder, a savage act, a message writ in blood and tragedy — no, she could handle that, was handling that truth — but if in some twisted way it was justified in their eyes or anyone's eyes, *caused* by money or the MacTeague's debt, then it was so much worse; dying for nothing, a senseless, stupid death was hard. Dying for a bad reason, a shitty, cheap, mean reason, no, that was too much. That was too unfair.

"Dad, listen." Her voice wavered. Her hands trembled. "When you say money's tight —"

"It's been worse."

She set her coffee down to keep from spilling it. Her voice neutral, monotone, she said, "Okay, but I have friends out there who say you had to go back to them" — he'd know who they were — "because we needed more. Some even say you missed payments. Lots of them."

Her dad's expression changed, then. Nothing anyone who didn't know him very well would notice. But enough for her to know she hit close to something. His eyebrows drew closer, just a slight frown, and the slight curve to his mouth, a thin line drawn in pale lips, disappeared.

"Gossip."

"You can't lay that on me," she said, tears in her eyes. "Okay? You just can't. If you think I'd take your money for this place if it meant going back to those —"

"No, no, you're all turned around. The money just means this: the campaign pays for your place, here. At least for another month, which means you *work* for the campaign."

178

"Like Billy?"

He sighed. "Just do what I say, okay? Jesus." He withdrew his hands from the countertop. "This isn't easy, but we have to be seen as a family, in public, in the spotlight. If you won't do that out of — let's call it 'familial obligation' — then think of it as a *job*. Like I was saying, you *are* getting paid for it."

She nodded. "Okay."

"Okay?"

"Yeah, sure," she said, picking up her mug and taking a sip. "What's the next appearance?"

"We're going to church on Sunday. A car will pick you up, downstairs, at nine thirty."

"Nine thirty on Sunday," she said. Her dad nodded and turned to leave. "Wait, Dad. Listen, do you know what happened? I mean not the shit on the news, but the real story." Her eyes teared up again. "Why did they do it?"

He looked at her for a long moment, the frown pulling his eyebrows together. "Because they're animals," he said, finally.

"But if Lexus was really threatening —"

"It was. Your brother and I responded."

"But then why'd they kill him?" He started to say something, but she talked over him, for once. "They go through all that effort to get our attention, like you said, just to kill him anyway? That doesn't make sense. Do they tell the banks which branches they're going to rob, too?"

His frown deepened. "You finished?" His voice flat, deep. "Remember, downstairs at nine thirty. Sunday."

"When you say you responded —"

"Leila," he said. Not shouting, but loud. "It's none of your business."

"He was my brother!"

"And *my* son."

179

They faced off, then, across the breakfast bar.

"Something happened," she said. It wasn't a question. She knew. She knew her dad, knew Billy. "Lexus wasn't threatening Billy, he *was* trying to warn us."

"That son of a bitch."

"Shit, Dad, I went to the cops with your ideas. He could be in jail —"

"Fuck him."

"Dad! Hasn't there been enough trouble? If he had nothing to do with —"

"That son of a bitch *caused* this. One way or another, warning or threat, he set this in motion. How else was I supposed to respond? These greaseball punks think —"

"I thought you *and* Billy responded," she said, shutting her eyes. "Jesus, Dad, it wasn't even his idea, was it? Whatever you did."

"Don't forget Sunday," he said, his voice back to normal. Not loud, but monotone, assured. "Nine thirty."

**

Sarah sat in the back of the cab, hugging her purse, watching the neighborhood slide past her window, trying to remember what simple, calm happiness felt like — and not getting much further than thinking of the last breakfast she had with Lexus — and then that started its own tumble of linked thoughts that were everything but calm and happy; a disordered jumble of anxious worries, imagined — and real — fears, a frustrated sense of helplessness and unfairness. Trying to remember his smile. Their first date. Their first time. It had been five days now, only five days, five whole days. Five days wasn't *so* long. It didn't mean the story couldn't have a happy ending.

But he was gone. No sign of him in the hospital. He was gone. AMA, they said: against medical advice. One minute the cops were talking to him, and the next he was attacking some guy, Greg — they said Lexus *attacked* him — and then he was gone. For days. Reporters called. Cops called. Lexus didn't.

She thought about that roller-coaster-upside-down-but-standing-still feeling that inverted her world when Julia came over with her birthday present: a yellow rose sketch and the money to tattoo it. *The* tattoo Lexus remembered. He couldn't, really, know she was going to get that tattoo any more than he knew what her old room looked like at her parents' place or what their beach house in California is going to look like — but he did.

Adamantly.

Her rose tattoo. The governor being killed. Lexus and his nightmares — waking with a start, sweating, crying, stumbling out of the bed and into the bathroom to rinse his face and repeat his mantra over and over, oblivious to her calls if he was all right.

Nightmares.

I keep dreaming about Governor MacTeague, he told her once, one morning over breakfast.

Really?

Maybe I knew him. Maybe some real memories are coming back.

Nightmares about the governor. And he would've written them down. In his dream journal. She finally realized what had been taken: that red spiral-bound notebook. Did Lexus take it? The police? Lexus wrote about the governor being shot. And then he was. And someone knew. They knew. And now the notebook was gone.

And so was Lexus.

181

She blinked away a pair of tears wrung from her by the stressful, endless pace of this insanity she'd tumbled down like Alice, chasing a man instead of a white rabbit — a stranger who had her heart before they'd even met, an ideal true love, fated love. Drawn together and ripped apart, an ebbing tide that rushed onto the beaches of life only to withdraw soon after.

After a while, she got the cabbie to circle back to the empty apartment.

Chapter Twenty

Leila found the detective's card in the bottom of her purse, folded and bent, one cold hungover morning, walking, ignoring the cabs that slowed, honked, ignoring the people who walked around her, the herd, looking for her cigarettes but pulling the card out instead. Crumpled in her hand, she slowed, flattened it, read the number over and over, thinking — about Billy, about her father, what he'd said, what he'd probably done, what may have happened — and debating whether it mattered, now, whether any of this shit mattered now that Billy was dead and Lexus Sam and his weirdness was out of her life, his part played, whether cast as villain or victim, martyr or murderer, she didn't know.

Of course it didn't matter.

It was over.

But.

Lexus hadn't been threatening Billy.

He was trying to help. He *was*.

Fuck.

She took her cell out and dialed the number before she changed her mind.

It rang a few times before a far-off voice answered amid the sound of radio and traffic.

"This is Leila MacTeague," she said, and the music on the other end cut out. "You gave me your card, in case ..."

"Yes, Ms. MacTeague," the detective said. "How can I help?"

"It's Jack, right?

"Right."

"Jack, I've made a mistake, I think. It's about my brother, about what happened."

There was a pause on the other end. Then, "I'm in my car, now, but I can turn around and pick you up. Or meet you at the station, if you'd like."

She shook her head. "No, I don't want to come in." She turned her back to the road. "I just want to talk. Nothing official."

"Well, we can do this over the phone, or you can come to The Duke, this bar on —"

"I'm there too often," she said. The Duke. Figures, she thought, the epicenter of all this weird shit. Where she'd first heard Lexus Sam's story. The yellow rose tattoo. Her bust. Dad bailing her out. Calling his shots out loud, he'd called it. "I can talk now, then. There's not much to say, really. It's about Lexus Sam."

"You mean Adam Williams?"

"No," she said, switching the phone to her other ear and cradling it with her shoulder. She fished her pack and lighter out of her purse. "That's not his real name."

"You sound convinced."

"I am."

"Why?"

"Because he's been right about everything else."

Near silence on the other end. Traffic. A distant horn honking. She lit her cigarette, inhaled, and blew smoke skyward.

The detective cleared his throat. "Okay. Say I believe you," he said, "because I've been doing some digging of my own."

"What'd you find?"

"Can't comment."

184

His final word on that, it sounded like to her.

"But?"

"Like I was saying, say I believe you. What was he doing threatening you and your family? He had to know we would check him out, his background."

"But if he *wasn't* threatening us?"

"Is that why you're calling me? To change your statement? Because anything on record has to be down at the station or at least recorded, written and signed, something. Something more than just a phone conversation I supposedly had with someone who was supposedly Leila MacTeague."

"Are you going to arrest him? Because of my statement?"

"Can't comment."

"Okay, but you can listen," she said, and took another drag.

"I can."

"That was my father's idea," she said, "that he was threatening Billy. Lexus was right about something, something he could have no way of knowing unless, unless he fixed it to happen that way. That's how my dad saw it." She dropped her cigarette on the ground and put it out with the toe of her boot. "And I believed him, his explanation. It was the only one that made any sense."

"This is about your coke bust?"

"Yeah."

"Lexus, he mentioned that. I told him there was no record —"

"My dad fixed it."

More silence on the other end. The noise of traffic was gone. She heard a car door thud shut.

"Okay," he said, "that verifies one thing he said, at least. Can you tell me anything else?"

"I was wrong about Lexus. I don't want what I said to get him in shit, that's all."

**

Leila browsed through her call history until she found his number, thumbed it, and held the ringing phone up to her ear. It rang five times before it went to voice mail.

"You're probably not taking any calls. That's fine, just listen. Try to get to The Duke, that pub on 7th, north side, between 3rd and 2nd. There's a detective there, Jack," she paused, glanced at the card in her other hand, "Lawrence. He knows something about you, has some reason to think you're not Adam Williams. Not sure if it matters, but he told me he was investigating. You should talk to him, try to get the truth out of him."

She paused.

On the other end the voice mail was quiet, empty.

Waiting.

"I know you were trying to help," she said. "I wish I saw it that way, did more ..." She blinked away some tears. Fuck. She took a deep breath. "I probably got you in some shit. So, I'm sorry for that. I want you to know that ... that we're cool, okay? Okay, that's it. Bye."

**

The Duke was subdued. Only Jon, the Irish bartender, was working the taps, calling out greetings and orders like an old-fashioned train conductor bellowing out the stops.

Erik sat at one of the few round tables scattered in front of the bar's rickety, squat stage like breadcrumbs before the pigeons. He kept his back to the washrooms and faced the frosted glass front door. A half-drunk pint of Heineken waited in front of his laced fingers, the beads of condensation

186

collecting on the glass matched by the beads of sweat on his forehead.

Jack was late. By thirty minutes. He glanced at his watch — no, forty-five now. But he was working a big case. The biggest, probably, he'd get. Doing a fine job too, if the grapevine could be counted on for anything.

I should go. Call him, meet later. He's busy. But. He had news. Erik needed news, some new angle to see this shit with Lexus. Elle was *right*. He was curious. Too damned curious to let the thing drop. So he was sitting in the old hangout, nursing his second pint, waiting when he should've left.

But his coaxing, hinting, had worked. Jack had looked into Adam Williams as part of his investigation. And why not? It wasn't too much of a stretch. There were allegations that he'd threatened the governor's life. Leila didn't testify to that. But some of the MacTeagues's people did. And he was at the rally, right beside the shooter, as Adam Williams. Did he not expect anyone to connect the two? That Adam and Lexus were the same guy?

"There's enough question marks to go digging," he'd argued. Not that he believed Lexus or Adam had anything to do with the shooting, but he knew something was going on.

The TV above the bar was on, turned to CNN. They were still talking about the murder. Assassination. Whatever. Packs of roving reporters, pundits, experts, reenactments, and eyewitnesses came on air by the dozen, all talking, analyzing, rehashing — gratuitous coverage that had a disturbing way of glorying the event and turning the reality into a soap opera.

But they didn't talk about Adam Williams, much. There were mentions, of course. There had to be, given all the accounts of the good Samaritan seemingly risking his life in a futile attempt to blah, blah, blah. But he was never interviewed by the press. As far as the coverage went, he was taken to the hospital, questioned by police, and released. Calls to his home went unanswered.

That much seemed true. Erik had tried a couple of times from different pay phones. Just out of curiosity. Man. He was suckered in easily. This guy was just a gig, a paycheck — one he was told to lay off of, too — but he was still working it. After quitting. Before it was work. Now it bordered on an obsession. Stalking.

He took a long swallow from his pint. It was halfway to room temperature. He waved at Jon and held up his glass.

"Sure-nothers-coming," Jon said, in his signature slur.

He finished the pint before it got any warmer.

"Its-up, pint."

Erik got to his feet. On the way to the bar he saw Jack come in, his quarter-length coat overtop an open blazer and dress shirt.

"Can you put in an order of fries, too?"

"Right."

He flagged Jack down, who waved back. He walked through The Duke's lobby — a square room lined with coat hooks and carpeted in a red plaid that had faded through the years to a slush brown and gray — running a hand through his black, thinning hair — combed back, away from his forehead to a receding hairline. Along with the streak of white shot through his hair just off center, like a lopsided skunk, the pockmarks freckling his cheeks from a bad bout of chicken pox, and the frown and smile lines creasing his brow and the corners of his eyes, Jack looked every bit the part of a weathered police veteran, steady and sure. He had the kind of face you'd trust your virgin daughter's safety to, a face to put on the televisions of countless New Yorkers searching for an explanation, a photogenic face, Erik admitted every time Elle brought it up, teasing. "It's rugged, like a beleaguered actor," she liked to say.

The movie star cop strode up to the bar, his eyes downcast, watching the little screen on his phone, one hand diligently fiddling with the tiny buttons of the fancy tech gadget, the other hand stuffed in the pocket of his new overcoat.

Erik caught Jon's eye and jerked his thumb towards Jack as he walked up.

"And whatever he wants on my tab."

"Good God, I'm thirsty," Jack said, pressing one last button on his phone before he slid it into his overcoat's pocket with the same practiced ease with which he holstered his weapon.

"A pint of domestic," he said to Jon.

"Bud?"

"Sure."

He turned to Erik and stuck out his hand.

"I'm late, I know."

Erik shook hands with him, grinning.

"You've been busy," he said. "I get it."

He nodded at the news running on the TV above the bar. They watched for a moment, a quiet, perfunctory vigil, like grace before dinner at most tables. Something about the news of the governor's murder demanded these quiet observances whenever his name was mentioned. It reminded Erik of seeing flag-draped coffins coming back from the war. Except the governor was such a public — and popular — figure; he was everyone's neighbor, in a way, someone whom you felt closer to than you really were.

"It's pretty fucked up," Jack said, looking at one of the cell phone videos of the crowd running after the shots had been fired. "You know there are still people confessing to us?"

"Confessing to what?"

"To the murder. We've a dozen confessions on our hotline. 'I did it, I killed Governor MacTeague, I'm so sorry.' That kind of shit."

Erik took a sip of his pint and cleared his throat. "That is fucked." He gestured with his pint at his table. "Let's sit down."

"Right, sure."

They walked over in a comfortable silence, both waiting for it to start — another recap session, just like old times — both content with letting the other get the ball rolling. Nothing had changed between them, really.

Jack pulled his chair out, put his pint down, and climbed out of his overcoat gingerly, one shoulder at a time, like an old gladiator taking off his suit of armor, feeling his years, his new wounds, and the weight of repetition — the knowledge of every other battle he'd fought becoming foreknowledge of those still to come.

He gave Erik a look, just a glance, before turning his attention to his pint. Erik saw the challenge, the pride, and the envious longing in that look; because Erik had what Jack wanted — peace, a steady girl — only by giving up what they were both built by God to do. Only someone who'd worn that armor knew how heavy it could really be — and understand all they'd have to give up, like Erik did, when they left.

"Alright, say it," Jack said, lifting his gaze, "I look fucking old, right?"

Erik raised an eyebrow but didn't answer.

"I feel it, too."

"It's just the case."

That was a lie. A merciful one. They both knew it was never just the case. It was what the case said about life — theirs and the lives of the people of this city whom they were out serving and protecting. But most of all, it was what the next case would say. Because crime had a way of progressing, like everything else in life.

You see your first body, first stabbing or shooting victim, only once. And after that, you know, in your heart and soul, that people kill each other. Sure, you'd always known murder happens. You hear it on the news and read about it and see movies and TV shows about cops and their murder cases. It's a given. But you'd known that rationally, and that's a big difference from knowing it firsthand, seeing it, the body, the victim's tear-stained family, the blood, the cold morgue afterimage of a life, like a beautiful sunspot in your eye that clears and disappears forever before you really see it — you get just a fleeting glance of beauty, the unshaded, naked sun, the victim's smiling face in the photos you inevitably see in their room or have shoved in your face by some sobbing parent demanding you do something, just a fleeting glimpse, and you turn to look.

And, gone.

Knowing this, feeling it, is tough. So you tell yourself, well, it's just the case. Life's still good. I'm still good. It's just the case. But then another case, and another, shows you that people kill children, women, grandfathers; that sometimes the murder is just an incidental, an afterthought; or others show you how the taking of life is just a start — the means to an even darker end — and you start to realize that whatever the case shows you, however painful, there'll be another that's worse and worse, and it's just as terrifying to think about that next one as it is to deal with what the current one means. So where does this leave you? You can't look forward, so you put on your armor every day in the morning and shrug it off in the evening and hope nothing gets through it too deep.

Jack smiled, wearied but determined. The old champion still saw a shower of roses in his victories. And that was the biggest difference between them. Jack kept smiling. And meaning it, believing there was reason to smile.

"Right," he said, his grin in place, "and my hair's growing back, too."

191

Erik tilted his head down and pointed at his thin covering of red wisps. "Compared to me —"

"Compared to you, we *all* look better."

"Must be why I have so many friends," Erik answered.

"Friends," Jack scoffed. "People slowing down as they pass the car wreck."

Erik laughed. "Alright, fuck. If I wanted this abuse, I'd stay home with Elle."

"If you ever want to spread her abuse around ..." Jack winked at him.

"Oh, fuck off. Get your own."

Jack was ready with a reply, he could see it in that damned movie-star grin of his, but he just sipped at his pint instead.

Erik cleared his throat, again. "So. How's it going?"

"Good, good," Jack said, running his hand through his thinning, skunk-striped hair, "but nowhere. On one hand, we've got the shooter, the gun. No confession, but we don't need it. But we also don't have any motive and certainly no connection to the Pizarros — except for a couple of testimonies about what the shooter yelled out before he pulled the trigger."

One of the cooks, who looked too young to drink, shuffled out of the kitchen with a wire basket full of fries balanced in one hand and an old wooden toolbox stuffed with condiments and utensils in the other. He placed both on their table without a word and darted back to the kitchen.

Jack scooped a handful of fries out of the basket and dropped them into his upturned mouth, one at a time, like a baby bird being fed worms.

"But you still think the Pizarros were behind it?"

Jack finished chewing, dabbed the grease from around his mouth with one of the brown paper towels stuffed into the wooden toolbox, and scooted his chair closer to the table.

"Well, there's some facts and some rumors," Jack said, his tone serious now. They were into it. "Fact: you know the task force on organized crime?"

Erik nodded. "DeSilva's squad?"

Jack shrugged. "Sort of. DeSilva's out. Made a mess of some cross-border thing with the OPP. The team's the same, but Richard's running it —"

"He's that new kid from Oakland?"

"Forty's getting old for a kid, but yeah, that's him. He ran a lot of the Angels out of Oakland and figures the mob in New York is next."

Erik arched his eyebrows. "Ambitious." Erik grabbed a handful of fries, cradled them in one palm and picked at them. The first bite reminded him why people kept coming back to The Duke for their fries. Damn good. "So what's he got to do with this shit?"

"His squad got the order to shove through some warrants on guys they were sitting on," Jack said. "Instead of waiting for something big to come through, they go in, classic cowboy style, and take down half the Pizarros's captains in pre-dawn raids."

Erik tried to think, rattling through his memories of the past week's worth of news, looking for some mention of the raid but coming up dry. "This raid — it didn't make the news."

Jack leaned in close. "Brass wanted to keep it quiet because of the … pressure. Word is the order came down from the governor's office — maybe from the man or his old man himself."

And like that, his attention, his thoughts focused and everything sharpened. The predator was on the hunt again. The scent of blood was in the air. And it made him grin. Or sneer.

"Before?"

Jack nodded.

"So the rally, it was … fuck. It was a fucking retaliation, wasn't it? The governor already owes the Pizarros money —"

"Just the facts." Jack held up his hands.

Erik rolled his eyes. "Right, well. Hypothetically, they owe money," he said, talking his thoughts out loud, brainstorming. Getting ahead of himself — way ahead — with only half a mind to where it was leading. "They have some truce worked out, right?" he said, cutting Jack off before he could voice his protests. "Speculation too, I know. But then the governor locks half of them up?"

Jack downed the last of his pint, wiped the foam off his upper lip with the crumbled, greasy paper towel, and leaned even further in, practically climbing over the table to whisper in Erik's ear.

"And they get to him," he said, his voice strained. He snapped his fingers. "Like that, they get to him. Jesus fucking Christ. Who runs this town? Really. Fuck. It's enough to … to …"

He let the sentence die and eased back in his chair, deflated.

Erik plowed ahead with his version of the events, his story: it gained momentum the more he put it into words, the longer it was out there, outside his head and unchallenged, implicitly seconded by Jack.

"But the governor knew he'd fuck up the task force's ongoing investigation, with a just-do-it attitude like that," he said, eyes on the ceiling, "so … so this bullshit about Lexus threatening his life must be real. Right? Whatever he said was enough to get MacTeague pissed and arrest half the Pizarro family —"

"And that got the governor killed," Jack said, nodding.

Erik ran both hands through his hair and held them at the back of his head, tensed, waiting. Maybe hoping for a breakthrough. Jack's by-the-book thoroughness couldn't get anywhere with rumors and no confession, no link to the Pizarros at all.

Erik listened for the old magic. What could you do? If you were Jack and you *knew* it was the mob, knew why. "It's enough to make you old," he said.

Jack laughed. "We'll see. But what did he say to Leila? And why?"

"Did you ask him?"

"I'd love to, but the bastard's gone. He's a bit of a mystery, too, this mark of yours."

Chapter Twenty-One

Lexus sat on the couch, popping pill after pill, counting them like change in his palm, paying for something he didn't really need or want — the dosage Dr. Renesque read out from his ledger like a judge's verdict. Five little pills today. He swallowed the last and took a sip of the coffee that Mandy, the doctor's new secretary, brought him in a black-and-tan ceramic mug. Hazelnut. Always reminded him of winter nights avoided in crowded cafés, the kinds with too many papers cluttering countertops or stuffed between seat cushions. Like their first date. Greg was already waiting for him inside.

No. That wasn't right. I met Sarah for coffee. Sarah. After the … grocery store. Asking her out in the frozen — no. No, that was Greg. Adam and Greg. Not me. Adam. Then The Cure concert. "Friday I'm in Love." Singing along. Melodies, moody. Greg's voice.

His mind was a train diverted to the wrong sets of tracks. Down new pathways. The wrong way. Unavoidable. He tried to think where it switched, why it did — what hand was on the lever? Mine? He looked at his hands. Empty of pills. He traced the lines on his palms, one by one, the tracks. He turned his hands over. Took a breath. Breathe. He found it hard to exhale, lately. Starved for air. Breathing faster, too fast. His lips, numb, tingled. He slowed his breath. In. Out. He tried to breathe all the way out to the bottom of his lungs. But he couldn't. Couldn't. He felt like laughing.

Dr. Renesque talked to someone outside his office. His muffled voice soothed, calmed. It sounded like the tail end of an argument — the point where you've spent your anger and are ready to listen. Who listened? Dr. Renesque's voice sounded strange. Beyond soothing. Repetitive. Sing-songy. It sounded like the voice he used during their sessions, the voice Lexus heard on the tapes, just before …

He sat at the breakfast table, coffee mug in hand, reading the transcript, going into the trance. The trance. The same words, now, echoed what he read with what he heard. He remembered. Greg beside him, at breakfast, body still damp from the shower. Lexus looked up. Blinked. Greg stood in the room, here, now, in Dr. Renesque's office. A healing bruise stained the flesh around his eye socket, a tinge of yellow under the faded tanning-bed brown, like a puddle of watercolors.

Breathe.

I did that.

In a bad dream.

Breathe.

Just attacked him, punching and grabbing, yelling, shouting …

Breathe.

He remembered — the feel of Greg's throat in his hands — the ridges of his windpipe as he tried to crush it — tried to stop what had happened, what will happen, with raw force and aggression.

He stared at the healing bruise. It happened. It was real. But if that dream was real … That dream. Was real.

Breathe.

He looked back at his hands. He saw them around Greg's neck, squeezing, the feel of his tendons wire-taught, the ridge of his throat like a corrugated pipe buried in pliable flesh. He saw his hands, balled into fists, too, felt bone against his knuckles.

Breathe.

But.

Breathe.

But he saw them massaging Sarah's shoulders, the two of them in bed, her hair pulled to the right off her shoulders, neck, her skin warm, the two straps of her dark navy-blue tank top off and loose, with her arms pulled through they trailed down like limp streamers on the handlebars of a bike at rest.

Breathe.

Dr. Renesque stood behind Greg, hands on his shoulders, leading him forward, pushing, physically, verbally; they both watched. Dr. Renesque encouraged him, "Go on, really," while Greg protested, half-heartedly. "Say you're sorry."

"I'm sorry," Lexus said.

Breathe.

He looked back at his hands. Felt them in Greg's, walking, aimless, while the foot traffic of the city streamed around them, pushed past, blurred headlights in a time-lapsed video. And then those hands were in his. Warm.

Breathe.

Greg knelt in front of him on the bright red carpet, the throw rug like a bucket of fire-engine red paint upturned, spreading out. Greg's hands were over his, eyes full of tears, angry, happy, dazed.

Breathe.

Sarah. Her hair brushed aside.

Breathe.

Greg. Here.

**

Greg sat at his kitchen table, sifting through his mail, opening bills that were more than two weeks old, the phone cradled against his ear with his shoulder, his sister's voice soft and gentle, waves lapping at the shore of his melting certainties, like a beach of sugar, dissolved bit by bit with each salty caress. He didn't know what to feel. And she was picking up on that, echoing it, strengthening his unease.

"What does your doctor say?"

He put his Amex bill down, giving up on tracing its too-high balance into the financial stratosphere, and focused on their conversation, his dilemma.

"He's pretty supportive, I guess," Greg said, frowning at the tone of his voice. I sound like a stereotype. "Adam is being treated, too —"

"You are not being *treated*," she said, the emphasis there even in her doeskin voice. "Greg, you just went to him out of curiosity."

Dr. Renesque had advertised on Craigslist. A simple statement: "Are you unhappy, in some way? I can help." It lured Greg, whose love life seemed perpetually painful, to write back and explain his source of unhappiness.

That was a year ago.

And then he met Adam, and he was happy, completely. But he kept seeing Dr. Renesque — at his urging — despite it seeming that his problems were over. But now, maybe they weren't. Or never were. Shit.

"I know, but, well, he *was* helping, even with Adam."

"So he thinks you should stay with this guy?"

"Yes."

"I just don't know," she said, an unspoken thought lingering on the line.

"Neither do I."

"Honey, if you don't know, maybe you really do."

He picked his mail up again, the unopened envelopes that had been piling up underneath the mail slot in his front door throughout the listless week he hadn't wanted to face — even by opening mail — any more than he wanted to see Adam in Dr. Renesque's office.

But you did; you saw him.

And Dr. Renesque was apologizing for Adam, talking about breakthroughs; the day they'd hoped for seemed to be here — Adam was remembering. And because he remembered, bits at least, he wanted — needed — to start over again. To try again.

It sounded too rehearsed. Too perfect. Unbelievable. And Adam wasn't doing much to sell it, either — he just sat, chastised, staring at his hands, turning them over and over.

"What do you think of him?"

"Of Adam?"

"Yeah."

It was so weird. He'd walked up to him, thinking that, that Adam should be groveling, begging for me to take him back, glad to even see me, to be in the same room after —

I'm sorry.

That's all he'd said.

But then what happened? Jesus. I wasn't me anymore, after that.

"Well, it's hard to say, hun," she said, teasing, "since you keep him squirreled away."

Thinking about what had happened in Dr. Renesque's office, he didn't catch what she meant.

"Yeah …"

At first.

"… well, you can say you don't like him. It's okay."

"I really can't say. Beyond what you've told me."

"But before, when you met him …"

"I don't think I have."

He laughed. Or made himself laugh. He didn't really know why. He could barely feel it, his laughter, or hear it, or anything other than a deafening rush that filled his ears, like the sound of him leaving his body and falling into a giant seashell.

No one's met him, he thought, sudden and fierce and a little hysterical. No one. He laughed at it, the idea — to think somehow he'd imagined it all, to think this romance was built up out of nothing. It was funny. But not. Because. It was a real possibility. Because how else could his sister not have met him? Everything started to feel like the other day in Dr. Renesque's office: like scenes out of a movie, one he'd just walked into. They didn't have context. He talked and acted, but it all just seemed to happen — he couldn't remember feeling or thinking or even *doing* these things.

"What's so funny?"

He swallowed his laughter.

The feeling drifted, storm clouds blowing over but not far enough to clear the horizon. He felt them there, still, in the back of his mind, like the depression he'd originally seen Dr. Renesque about.

Depressed, lonely, not in the day-to-day sense, he had plenty of friends, plenty of company, but they were all couples, both his sisters were married, everyone around him was with someone, happy, and he wasn't and hadn't been for so long that he was forgetting what it was like to be happy in that way. He had crushes from year to year that broke his heart, each in different ways. Some were too indifferent, brushing him off before he had a chance. But the worst were the ones who were too nice, who became friends, close, who'd call him just to talk, who'd smile and hug him whenever they met for drinks, coffee, whatever, who laughed at his jokes and genuinely cared for him, felt his absence … as a friend. Who cared, but not enough. Who missed him, liked him, but not enough. You pay for those kinds of crushes; like a running tab at a club. Sure, you're having fun at the onset, laughing, everything is right with the world. Just because you enjoy his company, you tell yourself, but there's a part of you that's keeping a secret hope that every laugh, every bond, everything told in confidence is really bringing you two together, and one day … but one day never comes, and instead your fragile, secret hope dies with the realization he's not for you, and every scrap you've built that hope out of turns to needles, and you bleed; everything that makes them great, that would make the two of you great, hurts.

Those crushes, the nice ones, he knew he'd pay for them, bleed for them, but he just couldn't stop. He'd take their calls, make plans; he'd jump at chances to spend time with them. Hopeless. But not caring until the bill came.

Dr. Renesque said he could help.

And he did.

Or did Adam just come along, instead, like fate's sleight of hand trick?

What's so funny?

"You never met him," he said, his eyes wet.

He sat up straighter. Thought back. How long had it been? When did Adam meet his family? Christmas? Was he there? They had spent Christmas together. But, no, they didn't. He went north; Adam went … Adam went.

"Greg, you okay?"

"Yeah, fine…"

When did they meet? The details of how was easy — that little scene remarkably clear in his mind. Just *thinking* about relationships, his mind jumped on its own, it seemed, to their first glances, smiles, to replaying those adorably awkward, first verbal steps they took as a couple.

"Hey, Sis, someone's at the door."

He hung up the phone, then, without waiting for her good-bye, and confronted his memories, as empty and silent as his apartment.

Adam and I were together. Are together. His amnesia. He just doesn't remember, like I do.

I don't know what you want from me.

He just doesn't. But he's starting to now, right? He was sorry. We were together. He, well, I, but he didn't — Jesus, he just *let* me.

Get the fuck away from me.

Adam used to be the forward one, the aggressive one — remember, on the subway. Only the two of us in the car. Just grabbed me. Can still get a hard-on riding late at night.

You sick little bastard.

I remember in the back of a cab, coming back from … somewhere …

You fucking rapist, you stay the fuck away from me.

But when was that?

You stay the fuck away from me.

He tossed the cordless against the wall and brought his arm down and across, sweeping the bills and torn envelopes and half-read flyers off the table. The cordless hit — the envelopes and paper fluttered — its plastic shell split open, the batteries sprayed out.

Adam just doesn't remember.

I'm not who you think I am.

203

But I do.
I remember.
Adam and I.
I can't be someone I'm not, you know?
Adam and I?

**

Lexus sat on his bed, knees drawn to his chest, and cried. Sobbed. His cheeks were wet, vision blurry through tears. He saw a small room, his new prison without a lock. It didn't need one. He could leave. But couldn't. Wouldn't. He'd never get free of what happened here, what was happening, this stain, his storm cloud to walk under. Didn't ex-cons say the same thing? You never leave, never got free, truly.

This *was* prison.

I just sat there. I was just sitting, waiting. I could've ... the hospital. Like the hospital. Dr. Renesque's office, Greg kneeling on the carpet, red, like a pool of paint. Two reactions to the same thing — two reactions wildly different. Which was real? Both? Lexus and Adam, both in here, with me, somewhere. Is there a real me? I wanted it to happen. I sat there. And it ... I remembered other times. Lots of them. The Cure. Skating. Walking up 5th. They all felt good. I remembered them. I couldn't stop remembering, seeing, feeling, wanting. So. I just sat there.

I wasn't angry. Not like in the hospital. So angry, then. Pure rage. Rage acted upon. Put into an outburst. A thrashing. But this time, the real time, I just sat. Paralyzed, but not. Why wasn't I angry? Why didn't I at least try to ... to... But. The memories. The chain. The sensations — like a drug, pleasure and joy, addictive, an impossible high. I didn't want to. I didn't want it to stop. Didn't want it to go on.

That means something. It has to. I remember Greg, me. I just *remember*. I know. The memories — Greg's "good morning" in that low voice — that came — the bump on his collarbone, "broke it falling out of a tree" — from all corners of his mind. He remembered, knew them. But Sarah. That's not just a memory. Maybe it is, now. He shut his eyes against the tears, but they forced their way underneath his eyelids and flooded his hands, cupped to his face.

His throat ached.

The flood stopped, ran dry, as quick as it came. And he sat for a quiet moment, raw, lost. Something was happening in him. His mind was working. Again. Bewildered and harassed, assaulted, but working. Working. He felt ... a defiance growing. Like all those days alone in his apartment, going through the phone book, calling Williams after Williams, stubborn, determined, never answering to Adam, never seeing himself as anyone he wasn't. That person, that determination, might not be Lexus or Adam. That might be *him,* the real him, the one before all of this ... and *he* was stirring, thinking, reacting. He blinked away the tears. Okay. Concentrate. What was it about remembering ... about the hospital, the office? Both of them taken together ... Concentrate. Think. Greg, kneeling, rising up, a cobra with warm, moist lips. He tried to remember. In the office, the hospital. He compared them. They were the same. What he saw or dreamt or just knew and what had just happened were the same thing. Okay. Okay, so it happened the way he'd pictured it in the hospital — not a memory, but a glimpse.

A glimpse.

Yes.

Fuck, that's it. A glimpse. Enough. Okay? Enough. You've been hiding from it, not thinking, not acknowledging. But it *was* happening. The future. You see it, bits of it. The future happens. Sarah's tattoo. The governor. Greg. And they all came with a vivid knowing, like some pivotal flashbacks in the film of his life that explained to the audience, filled in the blanks and brought them up to speed. Only the flashbacks were reverse, flash-forwards, and he was the audience — the fourth wall not broken down but replaced with a mirror, so he looked out and in at once.

There was one left. The car accident. With Sarah. He nodded. Got off the bed. Paced. That's right. The others happened. So would this. Morbid, maybe. He grinned, felt the thrill of being on this track. Nothing he remembered or thought he remembered or was *told* he remembered — made to remember — about Greg, none of it was as real as what had just happened between them or the governor or the car accident that was coming.

These dreams. Flashes of fate. He wouldn't see them if they didn't happen. And so, in a way, they *had* already happened.

They had already happened.

His pacing stopped.

I can't remember what she looks like. Her face. He thought back and saw Greg. Everywhere. Every memory he thought was Sarah was now Greg in his mind. Like the cuckoo, laying her eggs in another's nest, usurping.

When did that happen?

How?

Wait. No. Not all — the car accident, her face turned to his in the last instant. Sarah. Real. Sarah, not Greg. That stayed untouched, as clear and as strong and impossibly real as the first time he woke up yelling out Sarah's name in Adam's strange apartment. The governor. Greg. The accident. Two down, one to go. And it will. It will. Has. Which means, has to mean, Sarah's real.

Sarah's real.

He laughed out loud. A few tears sprung up in his eyes. Laughing, he bent over, laughed more, harder, gasped for breath. She's real, though. Real.

And I'll see her again.

Even if it's just to say good-bye.

Chapter Twenty-Two

"Well, here comes trouble," Erik said, his eyes on Sarah Easter as she walked into The Duke.

Jack was right in the middle of telling him about Adam Williams. His disappearance. His falsified information — even his Social Security Number was bogus. But whatever else he was going to say was lost.

Dammit. I don't want any more trouble with this. I'm already in too far. This case was turning into his *Chinatown.*

Jack peered over his shoulder. "She's cute."

"That's helpful."

"Relax. You didn't follow her in," he said, lowering his voice. "She doesn't have a restraining order against you."

She was heading for the bar when she saw them.

Great.

"Detective Rose?"

He glanced at Jack to keep him quiet. "This is just a bad coincidence," he said. "I'm sorry, but we were just talking."

Jack turned in his seat. "It's true, Miss …?"

"I'm Sarah Easter," she said, "and your friend here …"

"I heard all about that," Jack said, "but he's off that gig. He was made to quit."

Erik glanced up at her expression and caught her eye.

"Well, okay," she said. She looked pretty upset, still, but her voice was calm and even. "I'm sorry if that cost you, it's just …"

He smiled and waved the apology off. "It was getting too strange for me," he said. "I like cases that add up."

"And his didn't?"

Careful.

"No, but I can't talk about it," he said, firmly. "I'm sorry, but I really can't."

She nodded, glanced at the door. "I don't see why anyone wanted him followed, or me …"

"I really can't say, sorry."

She nodded and turned to Jack. "You're Detective Lawrence, right? You've been all over the TV. What did you and Lexus talk about in the hospital?"

Jack answered with his "can't discuss ongoing cases" reply, well-worn, like the middles of hardwood stairs, polished smooth by all the feet traveling up and down them through the years.

"It's just that you were one of the last people to have spoken to him …"

Erik shot him a look, but Jack ignored it.

"… and now you're here with Detective Rose —"

"My name's Erik," he said, while Jack dismissed their meeting as another coincidence.

"If neither of you has an idea about what happened to him or where he went …"

"I, we, don't," Jack said, getting out of his chair. "I'm sorry, Miss, but there's not much for us to go on —"

"His ID was fake," Erik said, loudly enough to interrupt their conversation. "Driver's license, Social Security — all forged."

Jack half-turned, just enough to look over his shoulder and glare, his eyes narrowed to that trademark squint he used to sweat perps down in the interview room.

Erik just winked. "Hey, I'm not a cop. I can comment all I like."

A smile flickered across Sarah's face, just for a moment, at his help. But then what he just said caught up to her, and it was pulled under a deepening frown. "His …"

"And that's a crime, of course," Jack said, "so …"

"But he was right. Lexus was right," Sarah said.

"Pardon?"

"Adam was just a name. He always said 'Adam' was an identity someone had invented."

Something stirred in Erik. That feeling of being drawn in, towards some dark center, like the bottom of a whirlpool, inexplicably, while you knew you should be getting out.

An identity someone had invented.

Jack was steering the conversation back from conspiracies to facts, to things he could write down in a report or tell the detective in charge of his case — if he even had a case.

"We really are looking for him," he said, soothing. "Officers canvassed the hospital. I'm sure they've checked the security cameras, without turning anything up. The trail from the information he left at the hospital led to a fake Social Security Number, and from there, it's all been faked. So what leads do we have?"

"How about an older man, late fifties, balding, with a ponytail and black hair?"

Erik took a swallow of beer. Thinking. Balding, black hair, ponytail.

"He went through our apartment," she said, "before I got home."

Erik was pretty sure he knew that man. And as he listened to Sarah, he started to put the pieces together. And the more he did that, the deeper the hook lodged in the part of him that chased leads, wild and reckless — every bit the rogue officer they'd branded him as when they'd turfed him.

210

Chapter Twenty-Three

Lexus looked at the pill bottle in his hand. Orange hardened plastic with a thick, white, childproof lid. He held it up, squinted at the chalky pills inside, examining them like an appraiser would diamonds. But he could only squint and wonder — not as an appraiser, a learned, educated individual, but more like an ape at the foot of a sheer monolith, his mind aware of some significance, power — magic, even — contained within. But he'd have no way of knowing how to harness it for his own ends — even if he knew what he wanted from the magic medicine. So in his head he shrieked a dumb beast's animalistic reaction to the unknown, while his body stayed slack and still, listening to the sound of Dr. Renesque's tranquil voice.

"I want you to relax, to hear only the sound of my voice …"

** **

Greg didn't have to wait long in the lobby before someone left. He caught the door before it shut and walked inside, eager for some closure, a resolution to the question that grew and grew the more friends he talked to and the more memories he searched.

He rushed into the lobby. Eager but nervous. He thought about what he could find. And stopped. Just on the other side of the lobby door, a voyeur one step inside a haunted house, wanting and dreading the same thing — to see, feel, hear — to *know*.

He pushed forward and pressed the button for the elevator. He stepped back to watch the readouts as the elevator dropped, slow, as it slunk down to the ground floor, to him, like a huge metal spider descending on a steel web.

For some reason, he pictured the movie scene where the elevator doors open and release a flood of blood. Haunted houses and horror movies, strange imagery that fit; he came to see if this apartment housed just ghosts, his ghosts.

The elevator in front of him reached the ground floor and disgorged a pizza deliveryman, his bag empty, and it waited, doors open. He walked inside — the voyeur abandoning the periphery, in sight of the exit, heading inside to confront and confirm fears.

**

"Try to think back to your father," Dr. Renesque said, sitting across from Lexus, who was prone on the couch. "Not just the *word* 'father.' Think about where you'd see him."

Between them, on the coffee table, a handheld tape recorder ran. The slow turn of the plastic teeth on the cassette's spools were the metronome for the session.

"I can't …"

"You *can*. Just not yet. We're going to tie thoughts or feelings, subconsciously, to your father, like little reminders. This works. It will work for you. You will remember, one day. When you're awake and your conscious mind runs into one of these little reminders, it'll trigger a hypnotic suggestion — like a voice whispering in your ear, reminding you, prompting you.

212

And you will remember, if we put the right reminders with the right hidden memories."

Dr. Renesque paused to take a sip of water.

The cassette's spools slowly revolved.

**

Greg walked down a strange, familiar hallway. With the ghosts. Strange. Familiar. They didn't feel contradictory, now. He remembered the wreath on one door. The mat underneath another. He passed these details before. He remembered them. Familiar. But everything was strange — like those first moments waking up in a new city, a new bedroom, where nothing feels right because you feel you're in your own bed, old town, despite what your senses are telling you about the difference. This hallway was like that. But it lasted, stretched on and on with each step.

He reached the right door. The one he remembered. But didn't. Not really. He knocked and waited for the feeling to pass or envelop him completely.

**

"Think about birthday cakes. The taste, the sweet, fluffy texture of the cake, licking icing off your fork. All these sensations. Concentrate in your mind, on the sight of burning candles. Your childhood was full of birthdays and birthday cakes. When you eat cake, think of the others you've had. Remember your birthdays. Did your mom bake you a cake every year? Did you go out for an ice cream cake? These two feelings are linked: cake and growing up. Your birthdays. You're just going to remember, okay? One day you'll be eating a piece of cake, and when you do, your mind, thoughts, are going to focus on your birthdays and your childhood. You can't eat cake without thinking about your birthdays, your childhood. The two are linked. You'll eat some cake, it's sugary and fluffy — and you'll think, instantly, about your birthdays. The two are linked."

**

A young woman answered the door. She looked older than she probably was, aged by the tired look that started in her dulled eyes and stretched across her face in lines of worry on bloodless, paled skin. But he could see that she was quite attractive; he could see it in the polite smile she fixed on him, in her bone structure, like the foundations of a ruined castle, piles of quarried rock and walls that were proof of what once stood — and what some could see, plainly from these few bits of wall, if they had the right eyes, Greg saw in the narrow chin, razor-straight nose, gentle forehead. Foundations of beauty.

She was the kind of girl a lot of guys would go for.

He smiled back and introduced himself.

"I'm a friend of," he said, catching the name 'Adam' between his teeth and biting down on it, "of Lexus. And he's been —"

"And who are you?" she asked. Something in her face, her stance — one hand up on the edge of the door, ready to slam it shut — told him he'd already said something wrong.

"Greg Redfine. I, well, I've known Lexus —"

"Do you know where he is?"

He hesitated.

"Then leave me alone, please," she said. "There have been enough questions and well-wishers for today." She started to shut the door.

"Wait, no, please," he said into the narrowing gap between the frame and door. But it shut with a slam. He raised his voice and talked through the door. "I knew him as Adam Williams, if that means anything …"

He paused to listen, but it was quiet on the other side. Whoever that woman was, she wasn't going to make this easy. But the ghosts hadn't shown themselves, yet. He couldn't walk away thinking Adam or Lexus or whoever he was might just be a name he read off the television. Too many conversations came back to him, standing alone in this strange familiar hallway, too many to just shrug and walk away without some answers.

Recent conversations, doubts, came through the ether of memory, gaining substance, weight: *I remember you talking about Adam, sure…*

**

Dr. Renesque reached out, some jungle cat slinking forward with one paw, probing, oozing like a shadow, eyes narrowed on the prey. His hand snaked through the air above the coffee table, while the rest of him — save his mouth, still talking about cakes and childhood — sat perfectly still. Still, while the hand moved, descended on the tape recorder.

He reached it and pressed stop.

The cassette's spools froze.

He relaxed, relinquishing some rigidity in his spine, posture, to slump back and exhale and pick the handheld recorder off the table. He ejected the tape, put it on the coffee table, and pulled another out of his breast pocket. He popped the second tape in, cleared his throat, and hit record.

"Okay. Now we can begin."

**

Greg knocked again, harder.

"I'm a patient of Dr. Renesque's too," he said, "and I think something's wrong. I'm sorry, but I have to talk to you, to *someone* ..."

He stepped back from the door, mind working. That was it. His trump card. He hadn't admitted as much to himself, yet, but now that he'd said it, through a strange familiar door to a strange familiar apartment guarded by a woman who knew Lexus but probably not Adam, who both validated and invalidated what he knew because she didn't fit with what he knew or thought he knew — didn't fit at all — but now that he'd said it, he felt it — knew it — was true.

Doubts crystallizing into certainty.

He could hear the results of his rampage through his contact list, calling, seeking, failing; so many friends, colleagues, family, so many people, someone had to have met him, met Adam Williams, saw them together. So he'd called.

And called.

And now he couldn't help but remember — *I don't think I've ever met him, Greg ...* — and know: something's wrong.

A bolt slid open.

Dr. Renesque's name did it. But why? Was she a patient too? Are we all in the same maze?

Adam Williams? Really? That *Adam, the one on the news?*

She opened the door but didn't step aside.

"Is that how you know him?"

He shook his head. "No, we met ...," he sighed, "we met earlier."

I remember one night that he was supposed to show, but he canceled at the last minute, I think ...

She watched him, waiting for his explanation, his pitch, like a homeowner humoring the door-to-door salesman with promises of cheaper heating bills.

"I was already a patient, so when I mentioned what happened to my … to him, Dr. Renesque offered to treat him."

"So you knew him before the amnesia?"

He nodded.

The woman, still frowning, stepped out of the way.

"Come in," she said. "I don't know where he is, though."

Greg stepped into the apartment. A lot had changed since the last time he'd been up. Too much. The furniture, new pictures, new paint. It startled him. Had it changed? Or was it never like what he remembered?

Adam? Sure, you talk about him …

Greg hesitated by the front door as she shut it behind him.

"What's his real name?"

"Adam Williams."

She frowned. "You, too?"

"I know what he thinks, but he's …"

He could still hear the past conversations.

I don't think I know his last name. Did you mention it?

"… he's confused."

I remember you describing him, sure. Tall, long hair … Me? No, I've never …

"The police told me that was a false name. All of Adam's identification was forged, so are they just confused, too?"

**

"Tell me what you remember about Sarah Easter. From your dream. What did her face look like?"

"She was … pretty," Lexus said, his voice slow and soft. "It always looked like she was blushing."

"What color were her eyes?"

"Light brown … with … with flecks of gold in them."

"You're sure?"

"Yes."

"But that's the color of Greg's eyes, isn't it?"

**

"I don't know … something's not right, and I think —"

"Lexus has disappeared" — the woman threw up her hands — "so of course something's not right."

Greg shook his head. He barely heard; he was on the right track, he was convinced, of something — not the whole picture — that he couldn't see — but maybe enough for him to know and feel the closure he needed to live again outside this demented maze he'd wandered into, unaware after responding to the doctor's ad.

"It's that doctor," he said.

Yes. It was. He'd pretty much made up his mind, then, standing just inside this woman's apartment. Dr. Renesque. It came back to him, to whatever he was doing; his maze twisted a storyline through the real and the imagined, truth and fantasy, like a magician's unending handkerchief. Misdirection and invention.

"Why, what's happened?" She watched him with gentle green eyes.

What he thought sounded ridiculous, too strange to put into words — like convincing someone the magician *really did* call your card or put the quarter in an unopened pop can or whatever.

But she seemed sympathetic. Did she want to believe him? Did she suspect?

"I don't know, for sure," he said. He cleared his throat. "After I started seeing him ... it's like, some things I remember aren't real — I'm mixing up dreams for memories."

She nodded. "So you have amnesia too?" she asked, and swept her arm toward the living room. "Here, sit down."

He slipped his shoes off.

"I don't have amnesia. I — it was this ad," he said, his socked feet padding over the hardwood while past and present — or imagination and reality — combined, surrealistically, in his eyes and mind. The last time he was invited in and walked over these floors, Adam was still settling in — there were boxes everywhere.

Or did he just abduct that memory, that scene, from some other boyfriend? Robbie's condo looked pretty similar. So similar, actually, that he stopped just in the periphery of the couch and made the comparisons. Robbie's. Adam's. This one. It was like seeing through an optical illusion — now he couldn't *unsee* the similarities or be unaware of the little jumps his mind made between Robbie and Adam. Robbie. How did we meet? A grocery store. The frozen foods section, right?

**

"When you see Sarah's eyes, you are really seeing Greg's. When you remember Sarah, you remember Greg. You lived with Greg. You love Greg. Do you remember meeting him?"

"Yes ..."

"Tell me about it."

"It was ... where ... it was at the grocery store."

"That's right. You met Greg at a grocery store. Say that back to me."

"I met Greg at a grocery store."

"Yes, you did."

"I noticed him as soon as I walked in …"

"That's right. He looked familiar, didn't he?"

"He did. Like we knew each other from … before. School, maybe."

"High school?"

"Yeah."

"Where did you go to high school? A. D. Strong Secondary?"

"Yes … I … well, I don't know …"

"Because of your amnesia, you've forgotten."

"Right, yes … I've forgotten …"

"But let's get back to the grocery store. Imagine yourself there."

"Okay."

"Imagine all the little details."

"Okay."

"Describe it to me."

"It's cool. I'm in the frozen foods section."

"That's right. You met Greg there. In the frozen foods section."

"Yeah."

**

"You said there was an ad?" the woman prompted.

Greg blinked to clear his eyes — but Robbie's condo, the packing boxes in varying degrees of unpacked-ness strewn around, all of it stayed in the forefront, like an overlay to what he was physically seeing.

"It was just on Craigslist," he said, and sat down. "He was looking for new patients who were unhappy about something — anything. He said he could cure it."

**

Greg leaned further back into the plush cushions stacked against the headboard of his king-sized bed — needlessly big for just one. And it'd been one for so — but that was okay, that'd pass — but it's *not,* it just isn't and it won't — and he felt that ache in his throat again.

He cleared his throat. "You can *cure* it?"

"In a sense, sure. The perception of it — of anything, really — is controllable. And when it comes to things of the psyche, perception is reality," the doctor said, his voice a little too excited, like a salesman's. "It's like a fear of spiders, say. You see a spider, you feel afraid, an overwhelming and irrational feeling of dread —"

"I don't think I'm being irrational," Greg said, switching the cordless to his other ear.

"It doesn't matter. I'm just citing an example."

"Okay, sorry."

The doctor paused to gather the thread of his little speech.

"Okay, so we have this patient who can't fall asleep if he's seen a spider in his bedroom, can't kill them, all because of this phobia and what it makes him *feel* and *think*. It's an association. Spiders and fear, dread. But if we could make it so that spiders remind him of camping, which he enjoys, or his family's cottage that he loves visiting …

"It doesn't matter what associations we make, as long as it's not that fear. And like that, the patient isn't afraid of spiders."

Greg laughed, nervous, relieved that something he'd struggled with for so long could be … Just like that. He laughed. It felt like a reprieve. The doctor with your blood work, the test negative; just a shake of the head, and you were free of that weight, that certainty.

"But … you're not talking about pills?"

"No, there's some medication involved during the trials, but once the associations have changed, you won't need them anymore."

Greg nodded in his bedroom, alone.

"Interested?"

"Of course, but …"

"You wonder if this is really a cure?"

"Yeah, I mean. Isn't it like …"

"It's not like anything. There are no parallels. This is mind over mind. A cure."

"I just don't see …"

"Think of our patient," the doctor said, his voice hardening. "His phobia makes him feel afraid, and that fear impacts his life. When we block that, the phobia doesn't make him feel, it doesn't impact his life. If he's not afraid of spiders — which, now, he isn't — how can you say he has a phobia? And if you can't, he doesn't, and if he doesn't, he's cured."

**

"At the grocery store, in the frozen foods section," Dr. Renesque asked, "what are you buying?"

"Frozen dinners," Lexus said. "I'm looking at their calories, trying to find the healthiest one."

"That's right. So whenever you go into the frozen foods section …"

"I think of Greg. And meeting him."

"Or grocery stores?"

"Greg."

**

"So what happened with the doctor?" the woman asked.

Greg shrugged.

"It seemed like it was working." He stood up and paced between the coffee table and television. "It's just that, what I remember ... I think I've known Adam for over a year, I'd say. Then his amnesia ... and he doesn't remember me. But *then* I start to think maybe I never knew him, you know?"

He cringed on the inside, just saying it, admitting the possibility that he'd imagined all the little scenes playing out like snippets of a movie reel, made them up — is that why they *feel* like movie scenes?

"I don't understand," the woman said, "you said something was wrong, something about Dr. Renesque."

Greg stopped his pacing. "I started seeing the doctor, my feelings of loneliness ... he didn't cure them, really, but then I met Adam" — a look came over her face, but he kept going — "and I remember us, together. But no one else does. Adam — or Lexus — he, he says I have him confused for someone else, that he's never been the guy I remember. And none of my friends, sisters, no one I think I introduced him to remembers Adam, or us."

He felt like crying. But didn't. He continued.

"Except for the doctor. He's the only link. He tells me Lexus really *is* Adam, and he's just confused. He tells me to be patient, to keep talking to Lexus ... that one day he'll remember, too, and become Adam again. He tells me … and he was with Lexus … not the Adam or the Lexus I remember, someone else … and then at the hospital …" His voice trailed off. He didn't want to say it. But she waited, quiet for only so long.

"What happened at the hospital?"

"They called me," he said, "I was listed as Adam's contact. I went to see him, and … and he *attacked* me. Said I … I was a rapist, a monster … he just … it was so real, his anger. He was convinced that I … I never did, of course. I remember us, and that wasn't …

"But now, now I wonder … why does no one remember Adam and me? Why did Lexus attack me? *Accuse* me … and then there's the doctor and his *cure* and …"

**

"That's right. You think of Greg when you're reminded of how you two met," Dr. Renesque said. "And when you see Sarah's brown eyes …?"

"Sarah's … brown eyes …"

"Yes, you think of Greg."

"Right."

"Okay, let's go back to the grocery store."

"Okay."

"Can you picture it?"

"Yes."

"Greg's talking to you, right?"

"Yes."

"You remember him talking to you. Can you imagine what he said? You can hear him, now …"

**

Erik sat in his beat-up Oldsmobile, a hulk of faded paint and rust that still ran despite all outward appearances, the kind of big, generic car that most New Yorkers would never really see unless it roared up on the sidewalk to plow into a herd of pedestrians. And even then, half the witnesses would get the make wrong, and the other half the color.

He sat with a newspaper open across the steering wheel, nursing a cup of lukewarm coffee, bundled in a scarf, overcoat, layers of shirts, leather gloves, cocooned for what he figured would be a long surveillance.

The description Sarah gave of the man who broke into her apartment had to be Dr. Renesque — the psychiatrist Lexus used to see every Thursday before he abruptly stopped. Around that time, Erik's contact at LM Industries got even more curious about his day-to-day activities. Erik always assumed the two were related — the drug trials he was supposedly being paid to participate in and his weekly visits to Dr. Renesque — because Lexus had no other regular contact with any kind of doctor or lab or anyone who'd be qualified to monitor the clinical trial.

But when Lexus stopped visiting Dr. Renesque, the trial didn't end — at least not according to LM, who kept paying Erik to watch their outpatient — and so he changed his theory. The two were unrelated, and Lexus must check in with LM some other way.

He took a sip of coffee, eyeing the offices of Dr. Renesque. But there was nothing to see. A silhouette passed behind some drawn drapes on the third floor, pacing back and forth, but he couldn't see if it was the doctor, Lexus, or someone he wasn't interested in.

He was pretty sure Lexus was in there, with the doctor. Just a hunch. It came from Sarah's description of the man who entered her apartment — a description that matched Dr. Renesque. It was just a hunch, but a pretty good one. Enough to start checking it out, anyway. So he went back to the hospital and asked around. Sure enough, a couple of on-duty nurses remembered seeing a man who matched the doctor's description eating lunch in the cafeteria with a patient who could've been Lexus.

So why would the doctor break into the apartment Sarah shared with Lexus? Why would he visit Lexus in the hospital and convince him to leave AMA?

How did he even *know* Lexus was in that hospital? From the news? They didn't mention which hospital the paramedics took Adam to after his scrape with the governor's assassin. Lexus could've called him, sure.

But he had a better idea. One that fit. Dr. Gilbert Renesque worked for LM. He was running this weird show. And he knew where to look for Lexus because Erik called in and reported where Lexus was, down to the room number. Dr. Renesque probably went to the apartment, now, because Erik had just quit — because unlike the past few months, there was no one watching the prized patient. Dr. Gilbert Renesque even sounded like Dale, Erik's contact at LM, when he called from a pay phone a couple of blocks away.

**

Dr. Renesque stopped the tape recorder, swapped tapes, and hit record.

"Well, that should be enough for today," he said, "I want you to come back, to awake gently but firmly, as I count backwards from ten. Waking up. Nine ... slowly ... eight. You can hear the other sounds around us. Seven ... six ... waking ... five, aware of your body, now ... four ... sitting on the couch, relaxed, three ... awake. Two. Awake now, opening your eyes ... one. You're awake."

Lexus sat forward and rubbed his eyes.

"Can you hand this to my assistant on your way out?" He ejected the cassette in the tape recorder and handed it to Lexus. "She'll transcribe it —"

"I remember the drill," he said, blinking quickly. He took the cassette, stood, stretched, and walked out of the office.

"Same time tomorrow," Dr. Renesque said to his back.

**

Sarah filled a tall glass with tap water, hesitated in the kitchen for a quiet moment, and then walked into the living room. She handed the glass to Greg, the strange man who knocked on her door half an hour ago, who arrived desperate and lost and full of ideas and conspiracies and a past with Adam Williams.

He took the glass and smiled. "Thanks."

She nodded and sat down beside him, took a deep breath. Most of what he said hadn't made much sense, and she would've dismissed it all if it weren't for the bit about Dr. Renesque; that resonated with her own feelings — suspicious feelings that told her the doctor wasn't helping Lexus, suspicions strengthened every time he came home dazed, traumatized, the mystery pills — all without any progress, any success.

But.

But it'd been days of stunned worry, anger, unable to think about much without turning back to Lexus and wondering what happened to him and where he was and if he was okay. Days and nights. Days and nights of restless, mental pacing — and then some stranger shows up with a neat and clean answer and a person to blame for all that worry and anger.

Tempting, but not enough; it was too easy an answer, too hard to trust. So she told him what she knew about "Adam" — his fake high school diploma, the phony records the police found tied to the information he'd left at the hospital — because she needed more, and she felt the only way to keep this stranger talking was by taking her turn at it, too. But *he* is real, Greg said. I've seen him. She nodded but didn't know what to say.

"Who I remember and who you remember can't be the same person. They can't both be real," he said, finally, and drank from the glass.

She nodded.

"So we should find out, then," she said, "together. When's the last time you saw him? That time at the hospital?"

He drank the rest of the water. "No, he was at the doctor's place," he said, frowning. He put the glass down on the coffee table. Shifted. "He … he was there. And I … fuck, I'm exactly what he said I am."

**

Lexus stood in the bathroom, confronting his reflection in the water-spotted mirror, staring it down — not his face, but the face of the man he'd become — the man caught between Adam and Lexus, past and future, in a limbo with now. His car accident with Sarah — that event was like the tide, coming and receding, washing the beach clean of the ramparts in the sand he built, the life he tried to form between the ebb and flow of it. So much of what he'd done in the past year was driven by foreknowledge, but it was the cause, and the effect was his life and the lives of the few people he touched. That paradox left him without a future, it seemed. Predestination canceled free will. That canceled his future. His past was part of his future, so then... then it was neither.

Dr. Renesque wasn't getting anywhere with him, day after day, in their sessions because maybe Lexus didn't have amnesia. That was just a symptom. The cause was much harder to articulate, incurable through hypnotic suggestion and recall and pills and therapy and all that talk recorded on the little cassettes that Dr. Renesque handed him at the end of every hour that felt like four.

All of it was a wasted effort — chasing a past through memories that weren't there because the past hadn't occurred yet, the memories unformed — searching for a name and an identity — one that wouldn't fit, now, even if he found it.

**

Sarah sat on the coffee table, facing Greg, who cupped his face in his hands, elbows propped on his knees, and stared at the floor between his feet. She waited. Waited for this man to come around instead of grabbing him by both shoulders and shaking the doctor's address out of him, yelling, "Take me to Lexus!"

You know where he is. You've seen him. You know. You're hiding something, avoiding something, but you know. You *know*.

"Greg, you came here for a reason," she said. "If you weren't looking for Lexus —"

"What if I was?"

"If you were, we should go back to the doctor's office. We should see if Lexus is there and face him together. Like you said, he can't be the same guy —"

"What if he's neither?" His voice cracked. His eyes shot up to meet hers — just a flash of a look. "What if we're both wrong?"

She stumbled. "I'm not sure I understand."

She heard that little voice, the skeptic, the one that never truly believed Lexus and his story of how they met in a past life or *would* meet, get suddenly louder, bigger.

What if?

She watched Greg twist and fidget. His fingers dug trenches through the hair lining his temples, fat, gorged earthworms after a rain, twisting out of blind instinct, not knowing what they sought.

He was convinced of a past with Adam, Adam being Lexus — things she couldn't imagine or understand, that didn't, that couldn't fit with what she knew or remembered, things that sounded made up.

Complete fiction.

But his strength of certainty bought credence — and part of her listened and wondered "what if." The same way Lexus made her consider and wonder about everything he told her about them, their past, their future together.

"I don't understand, either," he said, his words drooling from his mouth to dribble on the floor, "but I want to. And, okay, that's why I'm here. I came looking for Lexus ..."

"Then let's go —"

"But I didn't want to find him. I wanted it to be ... I don't know what or how, but I wanted it to be over. It's like, I don't care what the verdict *is,* not anymore, but can't the jury make up their minds? Can't someone end the trial?

230

"I wanted to come here and see some stranger's name on the buzzer and come to this floor and recognize nothing. I wanted to knock on that door" — one hand of worming fingers stopped their tunneling for a moment to jab one, rigid-straight, at the front door — "and have you, or some other stranger, open it and not know Lexus or Adam and tell me no one by that name has ever lived here ... I wanted to know —"

"It wasn't real."

He gave her another look. But it held.

"Because then you could shrug it off, dismiss it, get on with your normal life," she said, nodding. "That, I understand. That ... paradox. You want it to be true. With me and Lexus, he was this guy who knew me, thought we were together or *will be* together, who ... he just forced his way into my life with his confidence. Even though it's insane, it can't be ..."

"It can't be."

"But then if it isn't? Then you're —"

"Crazy?"

"Crazy," she said, nodding. "Crazy for not trusting your common sense, for getting wrapped up in ..."

"I don't know what."

"Nope."

"But if you were just crazy," Greg said, dropping his hands from his temples, "then you could deal with it. You could be like, okay, that was a weird episode, but whatever. It's over. It wasn't real. Forget it, move on."

Sarah nodded along with him, not trusting herself to speak or think or feel but knowing all the same that her skeptic's voice had become incarnate, personified in this stranger and his stranger claim to Adam — and the things she knew she suspected all along deep down — ever since meeting Lexus — but never admitted, couldn't be ignored any longer.

"Part of me has been waiting for that ever since I met him," she said, finally. "But Lexus, he … he has a way of staying with me, of fitting …"

"Me too," Greg said, a tilt in his voice, "me too … but then I wake up, and it's all been — it's not real, anymore."

"But I'm real. This apartment is real. If you want to forget it and move on, you — we — have to do something."

Greg's fingers worked their way back through his tangled hair. He draped one leg over the other, at the knee, and twisted his body away from her and her idea.

"Can you just walk away?"

Greg sighed. "No," he said, to the ceiling, "it doesn't feel over."

"It doesn't to me either —"

"But what can we do? He's a grown man, if he wants to stay with Dr. Renesque —"

"That's where he is?"

"I think so."

"So let's go," Sarah said, standing. "There are answers at Dr. Renesque's. There have to be."

Chapter Twenty-Four

Lexus heard talking from the rooms below, muffled by the thin floor and the bathroom door. New voices. He glanced at the stranger's face in the mirror for the last time and turned from it. He twisted the old faux ivory door handle, its mechanism rusted and strained, and creaked the door open.

It traced a sweeping arc over the faded bathmat, brushing the grain of the stained and flattened shag; his attention oddly caught by the sight, he stared. The portion combed over by the door was a different color than the rest of the rug — darker, newer looking, a discernible change that'd be undone by the door's passage in reverse. With the door shut, the mat would look the same, as if it had never changed. But it would change back. And forth. And back.

He bent, pulled the mat free of its lose hold on the floor, and tossed it in the bathtub. There. Forever combed, marked — "Lexus was here" written in shag.

One of the new voices said his name.

He left the bathroom and crept closer to the staircase so he could hear.

"… can wait all day to see the doctor …"

I recognize that voice.

"I saw Adam in here …"

And that one.

They both seemed to be arguing with the receptionist through the intercom's speaker — the little chrome one she kept next to her phone, with the big push buttons to talk and unlock the door. It projected their half of the conversation through the empty spaces of the townhouse — while her responses were too quiet, evident only in the pauses from the speaker as they — Sarah *and* Greg — listened.

Sarah *and* Greg.

Not Sarah or Greg, Lexus or Adam.

Lexus, Adam, laughed.

It burst out of him — out of some corner untouched by all of this — and he laughed and laughed until tears came to his eyes and spilled on the exposed floor.

He leapt for the stairs, free of the paradox. The doctor was wrong. He had to be. It wasn't Sarah or Greg. It wasn't Lexus or Adam, past or future. The doctor was wrong.

**

Now this is interesting, Erik thought. He watched Sarah and Greg take turns arguing with someone on the other end of the intercom to Dr. Renesque's office.

**

Lexus galloped down the stairs to the second floor, each groaning and creaking, and reached the secretary's desk, which was in the center of an empty foyer.

Dr. Renesque burst into the lobby, just ahead of Lexus, and rushed over to the intercom.

"Do you know who that is?" Lexus asked, the edge back in his voice.

Dr. Renesque didn't answer. He reached over the secretary's desk — "Sorry, Doctor, but they're…" — and grabbed the little speaker — "… pretty insistent, they say that …" — and yanked it with both hands, ripping cords out of the back. Sarah's voice cut out mid-sentence. Silence replaced the commotion. He slammed the speaker on the desk.

He glared at her.

"Go downstairs. Explain that this is private property. Make them leave. Call the cops if they don't."

The secretary raised an eyebrow, her own little editorial, stood, and smoothed her skirt. She walked around the open stairwell, hand trailing on the banister, heels click-clacking on the floor.

Dr. Renesque faced the desk, half-turned away, head tucked down in thought.

Lexus cleared his throat.

"You know, I went to a doctor, once," he said, "and I complained about headaches and made up some story about repeated concussions because I needed to see. And you know what he found? Healed fractures. Head trauma. Broken ribs, collarbone. I'd taken a beating, the kind of injuries a person might receive in a bad car accident —"

"Not the one you remember."

An admission, then. Finally. In the pause, Lexus waited for a denial, an explaining lie, something. But if Dr. Renesque held anything in his mind other than clinical logic, it didn't escape out of the dark wells of his eyes to find expression.

"So, you have been lying to me?"

Dr. Renesque unwound his ponytail and shook out the strands of graying black hair that clumped together in fat Medusa coils.

"I was trying to help."

"Help me? How can I remember my past if you *lie* about it? Sarah is real. Adam Williams isn't."

"No?"

"No!"

"And Greg? Is Greg fake? Because I just heard his voice on the intercom, and he's here to see Adam."

Conflicting waves surged through him — glimpses, snatches of a past and a future. Greg was real. What he felt for Adam was real.

"Adam *was* real," Lexus said, "or still is. I don't know … but not … not in the sense of the car accident. That person, driving then, that person who was in this body with its healed fractures and scrambled memories … that person is —"

"Gone."

Dr. Renesque reassembled his ponytail.

"This is a dangerous time for you," he said. "Remember what you did at the hospital? You can't have any visitors."

"But I did," Lexus said, frowning, "the other day, with Greg. He and I …"

Dr. Renesque raised his eyebrow. "But Greg was with Adam, remember? If that's not you, why do you remember a visit with Greg?"

"But there *was* a visit," Lexus said. "I was … drugged."

"No, you weren't," Dr. Renesque said. And then he was right in front of Lexus. It seemed that a trick of the eye brought them toe to toe without progression, like a vampire rising up out of the shadows in some black-and-white horror film, he was just there, with one hand on Lexus's shoulder, leading him away from the stairs. "We should talk about all this," he said, the pitch in his voice changed, monotone and low again, "in my office."

Lexus shrugged off his hand, spun, and grabbed the doctor by the lapels of his suit coat. He yanked him close. "I was in that car accident," he said, his voice a snarl, his fists clenching and twisting fabric, "and the governor *was* shot."

236

"Adam, I don't think you …"

"These things *are* real."

"… should put too much faith …"

"That's not me!" he yelled. He pulled Renesque closer, so that their faces were inches apart, their eyes locked. He felt like biting him on the face, the nose, somewhere that'd bleed.

He forced the thought, the image, the taste, from his head and relaxed his grip, pulled away. Relax. You can just walk out of here. You *should* just walk out of here. But Renesque was so sure, so calm — his half-sneer still twisting the corners of his mouth.

"That's not me," Lexus repeated, his voice lowered, "and you know it."

A smile oozed across Dr. Renesque's face like oil over water. It spread quickly, coating his expression in a shimmering myriad, a taint that seemed to cast off rainbows, *seemed* to be real, joyous — the smile of a gift-giver at Christmas, anxious to see your reaction — but that impression belied its toxic nature even as it reached his eyes, coated them in its cascading sheen. This was the man's real smile, then: poison over a mask of flesh that was over a man of nothing, of tape cassette reels spinning, of typewriter keys hammering, mechanical and methodic and cold and false — the smile of a dog's, imitation only, an instinctive muscle reflex, devoid of meaning or intent, like sneezing in sunshine — but on a dog, it was disarming, the emotion genuine even if the animal did not know *why* it tried to smile — on this man of calculations and observations, it looked like mockery.

"Yes," he said, his smile shifting and running, pooling in different corners of his mouth, "I know."

Without the smile, Lexus would dismiss what he heard — or thought he heard — as gibberish, imaginations of paranoia, of his confused state and slipping grip on whatever made the world real.

But that fucking smile. Those weren't rainbows it cast off but snares, the brilliance was the bright reds and yellows ringing a poisonous snake, the shimmering lure of a fisherman's tackle. The oil slick wasn't a spill, some accident that was regrettable and lamented with apologies and promises to do better, chagrined; it was dumping for the insurance money, blatant polluting, intentional and brazen.

That fucking smile.

He was gloating.

"You … know?"

Dr. Renesque just stood there, almost bored, adjusting his suit with a shrug of his shoulders, tugging at the sleeves. He paused to inspect the wrinkles on his lapels.

"You know I'm not Adam Williams?" he repeated, staring, struck by the casual admission. He imagined it felt like being told you'd been adopted, after years and years of denial, like a lover's confession after an affair. Yes, it's true. What you'd feared, suspected, somehow knew. It's true.

So?

Now what?

"You're not — or I should say, you *weren't* — Adam Williams."

"What do you mean I wasn't, I'm *not* Adam Williams?"

"But you will be." His eyes flicked from the piece of lint he rubbed between his thumb and forefinger and up at Lexus. "Maybe you are, already."

Lexus stared at him, his unflinching eyes, searching the gaze for some hint of a wink, a look that let him know it was all just a sick joke. A gag. But he heard what he heard. You will be. It was staggering to know, to think that what he'd chased through phone books, the diploma, the drama he played out with Greg, with the governor, Leila, with everyone, his endless chants — little spells without magic — told to the stranger's face in the mirror — the face shrink-wrapped over his, the one he was mummified with, so only his eyes showed through — was right. He was right. I was right. I was right — confirmed with contempt.

You will be.

"I will be?"

Dr. Renesque nodded.

"You can't just …"

"Yes, I can."

"… tell me a lie, over and over."

"I can cure you, if you'd listen. You were a ghost. No ID, no relatives to respond to the police bulletins, to come to claim you," he said. He then walked out of the lobby, toward his inner office, still talking over his shoulder, gesturing to an unseen audience, "You were a ghost, terrified and alone, when I met you as John Doe in Grossmont's ER. So I gave you a name … Hold on, I have the files."

He stepped through the open doorway to his office and turned left, disappearing behind the wall.

"You *gave* me a name?" Lexus asked, calling out to the doorway. "You can't."

Dr. Renesque returned, holding a manila folder thick with pages stuffed and paper-clipped in it.

"Hell, yes, I can. It's like what Milton wrote, how the mind can make a Heaven of Hell, a Hell of Heaven … all of it, just perception. So I gave you Adam Williams," he said, walking over, offering the thick folder. "Is it your 'real' name? Not if you mean your name at birth. But that's lost to you, along with everything else. So do you have a real name? A real personality?"

Lexus took the folder, cradled it open in his right hand, sifted through its contents with his left. There was a police report from San Bernardino County out in California with a black-and-white photograph of a car wreck, the remains rammed into the concrete pole of an overpass, nearly split in two. The words "suicide attempt?" were circled, as were "remit to psych" on the next sheet — some interoffice form from a hospital called Grossmont.

"Everything you've done and felt, that's you. Whether that you is Lexus or Adam or John Doe, desperate to try anything, sign any waiver ..."

Sure enough, the next clump of pages was dedicated to a contract printed on LM Industries stationery, with the initials "J. D." printed, unmistakably, in his hand on the bottom-right corner of every page.

"... move anywhere, even across the country ..."

There was a copy of a two-year lease on his New York apartment, made out between "a signatory for LM Industries, Dale Riven," and his landlord.

"... but none of that would help to *create* Adam Williams, if you didn't believe — or, failing that, if there wasn't an absence of *disbelief*."

The next pages were more documents from Grossmont. Waivers for a laundry list of therapies.

"What have you done to me?"

"Nothing you didn't ask for, urged for, even. It wasn't the amnesia that drove you to it, I think, it was ... these 'damned echoes,' you called them — afterimages of your old life that were never enough to give you a clear handle on who you were, what you'd done, but just enough to tantalize. Or torture."

Lexus glared up from the folder. "Sarah and the car accident."

Dr. Renesque shrugged. "I didn't pay much attention."

"Jesus Christ, you — you've known all along."

"I've *known* that you were troubled. That you had no name, no family, that you'd driven some mystery car that the police never did manage to trace to an owner or insurance records or anything into a concrete pole at something like eighty miles an hour on a cloudless day on a straight stretch of accident-free road in what had to be a suicide attempt."

Lexus crumpled the folder in both hands and shoved it back at him. "Why don't I remember this?"

"Because you have amnesia."

"No, fuck, this car accident, the concrete pole, *that* caused my amnesia, right?"

"Undoubtedly."

"So I should remember all this shit, right? Signing that waiver, agreeing to move to New York, all of it, my hospital stay, meeting you …"

"No, you shouldn't," Dr. Renesque said, with another dismissive wave. "Like I was saying, Adam Williams couldn't help you unless you believed — or didn't have reason *not* to. Waking up in a hospital in California one day as John Doe, and here, the next, as Adam Williams would work against us."

"You mean *you*. I'm just …"

"I make no apologies for our work," Dr. Renesque said, "and I'm thrilled at the prospect of success, of course. It's a bit more impressive than curing smokers of the habit."

"… an experiment to you. Someone with a clean slate and no past, no family, uncared for, unloved — the perfect test subject, right? No strings attached."

Dr. Renesque slapped him, hard, across the mouth. The sting sent little fireworks of flashing pain across his cheek and lips — and for a moment, he was stunned into silence, into listening.

"The martyr role suits you," Dr. Renesque said, "righteous little punk that you are. But if you were just a 'no strings attached'

241

body, why keep the records? Why tell you now? Because we're doing *well,* here, you and I. Because before, you wanted me to do everything I've done to you — and telling you, explaining it, I think you'll come to the same decision you did before."

"Why would I? Sarah's real; she's just downstairs."

"And so is Greg."

"Greg … he must … he must remember *someone*, sure, but not …"

Dr. Renesque's oil-and-water smile rippled. "Greg was depressed and lonely," he said, "when he came to me, so I gave him Adam Williams too."

"You …"

"Don't you see? We could be on the path to a cure for … for, well, what? Sadness, depression, loneliness, defeat, disappointment. What if you could wake up and be exactly who you *wanted* to be? Wouldn't you be happy, unbelievably happy, that your life turned out exactly how you wanted it to?

"And the power to grant that has been in God's hands since we learned to walk — but what if *anyone* could be that happy, not just the lucky few? And not by some genie-in-a-lamp granting miracles, no, instead of changing you or your world, magically, we'd change your dreams and desires."

The words pummeled Lexus. The snow and ice of a verbal avalanche, tripping, pinning. Suffocating.

"The asthmatic kid who always wanted to be the star athlete, consistently failing, miserable, becomes the kid who he'd wanted to be: the smart, witty writer, or the steady, dependable father, or whoever. It wouldn't matter, to him, if that's what he'd wanted all along. He'd be happy. More than content."

Lexus took one step back, then another.

"Or what about the one with a pregnant wife he didn't really love, suicidal, a heavy drinker to numb it all? For him, we could more than save his life, we'd save his wife the pain of a loveless marriage, or the widow's sadness, survivor's guilt, we'd save his kid a father, we'd make a heaven for him, real and tangible, to live in. And that has to be worth something. It has to be worth a lot."

It was wrong. Wrong. It doesn't matter what John Doe signed. His agreements, his terms, aren't mine.

"But it's not real."

"No? Why did Greg come, here, then?" Dr. Renesque asked, his arms wide, palms up. "Why'd he suffer that assault of yours and not press charges? And agree to see you again? To listen, to think about reconciling?"

Lexus looked at the floor, shook his head.

"Why?"

"He... thinks ..."

"He doesn't *think*."

"I know."

"What's that?"

Lexus looked up. "I said, I know. I know ..."

"And it's no less real, is it?" Dr. Renesque's voice eager, pressing, the smile pulling his lips back like the zipper on a costume, splitting his face. "It isn't! It really isn't, that's ... that's amazing —"

Lexus yelled in a wordless, guttural roar that reverberated up from some pit, tension smashing through his grinding, clenched teeth, a mindless quake of white emotion through the fault lines of his composure.

And he chased the sound across the few feet separating him and the doctor, fists swinging, colliding with something moments before the rest of him did. He shut his eyes against the impact. And opened them on Dr. Renesque, sprawled on the floor, surprise on his face.

"You!" he heard himself shout.

The doctor scrambled across the floor. Blood in his mouth. Lip split. He kicked out. Didn't hurt. He shimmied back, away, away. Not fast enough. Not far enough. Lexus grabbed squirming wrists. Forced them clear. Drove his knee down into his stomach. Soft. It gave. He leaned his weight on it. Dove forward. Something clawed at his back. Tendons tightened between his hands, clenched, tightened and then yielded. He throttled, strangled, mind blinded and struggling to comprehend.

Pain, then.

His left arm bent back, twisted. He fell to one side but then stopped, levitated, hung up by his arm, another strong hand on his right shoulder, lifting, dragging him clear of Dr. Renesque — or what was left of him. His vision cleared, a bit. He saw the doctor in the middle of a pile of sprayed papers, panting, shirt torn loose, buttons ripped off, jacket pulled down around his elbows, hair in his face and matted to his forehead, cheeks slick with blood.

Lexus bled, too. A steady drip of blood pooled on the floor inches from his face. He gained his knees. Someone hauled him up to his feet with pressure on his arm, guiding him, like his arm was a leash.

Voices spoke — the secretary screaming, running, her heels cantering, Dr. Renesque coughing, trying to talk, yell — but not at Lexus, at the man behind him, weak demands that didn't make any sense, while he floated over to the staircase.

"… are you okay, Dr. Renesque …"

"… this … is … private," Dr. Renesque wrenched the words out of his throat. "You can't … just … take him … he's sick …"

"… this is Detective Rose, he just forced his way in …"

Lexus smelled aftershave, felt warm breath on the back of his neck, that reminded him of a gym teacher, not his, he didn't remember gym, just a collage of masculine impressions personified in a mid-forties gym teacher barking out drills and advice, snickering behind his dead-stern eyes at the kids who couldn't climb a rope or pull their chin over some cold metal bar.

"Adam Williams," the gym teacher said, his voice firm in his ear, "you have the right to remain silent ..."

"... needs treatment, here, at this facility ..."

"... anything you say ..."

"... treatment? Doctor, he was trying ..."

"... can and will be used ..."

"... and he represents a significant investment in time ..."

Lexus saw the desk, the intercom speaker on its side, where Dr. Renesque dropped it after ripping its connection out, and remembered their voices, Sarah, Greg, remembered that feeling he had rushing down the stairs only moments ago.

"... against you in a court of law. You have the right to ..."

"... and money by LM Industries, my employers ..."

"... an attorney. If you don't have ..."

"... you can't seriously want him to stay ..."

And he started to laugh. "I'm not Adam Williams," he said. "I'm not."

"I know," the gym teacher whispered into his ear. "Now shut up while I get you out of here."

Chapter Twenty-Five

Erik looked at the face, the eyes staring at him from the rearview mirror of his beat-up Olds and wondered how to answer, what to say, if he even should, and thinking how very fucking likely this stupid little stunt of his would make Elle proud of him and white-hot livid at the same time — a kind of paradox only the right kind of girl could pull off. Part of him tensed for that outburst. But part was eager for it, too, and glad she *was* that kind of girl, the right kind.

He floored it. The Olds sputtered to life with a guttural, hiccupping roar — responding more like a diesel freight train than an automobile.

How much time, he wondered, threading between a car making a left and another making a right. He jammed through the intersection just as the light went from yellow to red. Once clear, he checked the dashboard clock, probably the only thing left that was steady and true among all the readouts. Five minutes. It'd been five minutes. Still no sirens.

They'd be on the phone in a few minutes. The secretary bought his cop act when she caught him jimmying the front door open with a set of "police-issue" lock picks; the badge cowed her, his confidence and angry growl got her moving back up the stairs — and just in time, too. When he finally got inside and up the stairs, it looked like Lexus was about a minute and a half away from throttling Dr. Renesque — private psychiatrist and one of LM Industries's leading researchers, according to what Elle had managed to dig up and relay to him in a matter-of-fact conversation on his cell, just moments ago, while he hurtled through the streets in a car that was barely up to the task of making beer runs but was now tasked with getting the fuck out of the vicinity before the real cops showed up and realized some poser had just made off with a key witness in a murder case who had no real ID, no motive, and no reason on paper to be totally innocent, either — a witness who might be on the mob's list, too, according to the scuttlebutt he'd picked up in the dank dives a guy like Erik could pick shit up at with a few drinks or threats of phone calls. Rumor had it the Pizarro captains behind bars didn't like the idea of some guy spooking the governor's sister enough to get the governor on the warpath against organized crime, briefly, before organized crime got just a little too organized and put a bullet through his skull.

He was wondering how long Renesque would sit on his hands, recovering, coughing, and halting the spin of his head. Not long. That fucker was probably quick, sharp. He'd have to be to pass as a doctor.

Pass as a doctor. Right. That guy was a con artist, faking it, somehow. He wasn't licensed. He couldn't be. Just like Adam Williams wasn't real. But you had to look real close to tell. He doubted he'd have the chance to look at Dr. Renesque or LM Industries, so he just assumed his title was faked. It was better to assume than to think of him as a real doctor. It made more sense. Fit better. Some quack running a mindfuck of an experiment. A fraud. Some smiling devil.

If anything Greg told him, near hysterics, outside Renesque's office — about false memories and brainwashing under hypnosis — was true, then this guy wasn't a doctor — couldn't be. He was like an anti-doctor. And if he was, if he somehow managed to get through whatever screening process they put those guys through, well, then he needed to be shunned and stripped of his license, or whatever the medical profession did to its own when they found out they had a bad apple in the bunch. But that wasn't enough. Negligent doctors lost their licenses. This wasn't negligent. It was intentional — it needed a condemning. Abolish his works — whatever maze he'd constructed for Greg and Lexus and others, maybe — and refute his practices. Burn them as heretics at the stake of modern judgment.

"So, really, what's going on?" the face in his rearview asked, for the third time. "You're not a cop, are you?"

He shook his head.

"Detective Rose — you talked to Sarah."

He tightened his grip on the steering wheel. "Sure I did," he said, and grinned. "She didn't buy it, either."

"So, she's … real."

He glanced up at the rearview. Lexus still watched Erik's reflection — studying it — waiting for an answer.

"Sure she's real," he said. "What kind of question is that?"

The face relaxed a bit, his body of taut wires loosened, slightly, just enough slack to ease back half an inch against the Oldsmobile's plush seats.

"I don't know," Lexus said. "Everything's … I don't know."

Erik nodded out of habit. Lots of times on the force he'd picked people up who talked nonsense. So he let them talk and nodded along. He couldn't imagine what Lexus meant. She's real? She lived with you for months, he thought. She's cried and screamed and fought for you. He eased off the gas a little. They were getting close. Still no sirens.

"Listen, Lexus —"

"I don't need that name anymore."

Erik squinted in the setting sun, looking for his turn. "No, I guess you don't," he said, deciding to be agreeable if nothing else. "But, listen, I haven't figured this all out — your case, I mean. What that doctor was trying to do to you, why ... how ... But there's one thing I do know —"

"My name?"

"No ... just advice. Forget everything that doctor told you. I mean everything — just get it out of your head, purge it, go on a big fucking bender and puke it down the toilet with some undigested seafood and a quart of rum."

**

The car shuddered to a stop, tires complaining with a short screech, and Detective Rose — Lexus didn't know what else to call him — jumped out. He yanked open the back door, curbside, and helped Lexus out. He spun him around so that he faced the car, deftly uncuffed him, and then spun him back so that they faced each other. He clapped him on his shoulders, maybe for the benefit of the curious passersby who slowed to look, to gape, to ask themselves, "Hey, was that guy handcuffed a moment ago?' and to wonder, but only wonder, while they said and did nothing but walk on, pausing when their dog paused or talking into their wireless headsets. Maybe it was just a show for them, but he looked Lexus in the eye and nodded — a slight apology and a best-of-luck-kid-punch-on-the-shoulder kind of sentiment.

But it was over before he could respond, and Detective Rose was back in his car, the tires complaining, the motor gunning, and then the big rusting Oldsmobile lurched down the street in a cloud of thick, greasy fumes. Anonymous in the traffic. Gone.

He stood on the sidewalk, watching it go, cold in the chilled air, free but not feeling it, knuckles, ribs, aching — bloodied from his fight, battered worse in mind than in body.

"Lexus?"

He turned and saw Sarah, leaving the Starbucks that Detective Rose had dropped him off at, her coat and scarf gathered up in her arms. She rushed up to him, smiling but sad, too.

Greg followed, pale, not looking but still watching, moving slowly, silently, a hesitant shadow.

He felt something like vertigo, something like waking in an unfamiliar place and trying to sort out where you are and why, and then getting on with your day, something like seeing through an optical illusion for the first time, something like all of that rolled into one sensation that washed over him and down him and through him even as his feet stumbled across the sidewalk.

They collided in a hug, awkward but warm.

"It's ... good," he said, "good to see you."

He hugged her tight, resisting the urge to squirm, to push her away, to cry — glad but not, somehow. Not at all. Not with Greg here too. Greg. Watching and standing off in the background, threatening to fade away for good.

What do you mean, I wasn't*?* he said in memory. *I'm not Adam Williams.*

But you will be.

You will be.

He looked at Sarah — and saw Greg — her eyes were his eyes, her smile, and she was smiling, now, was his smile, her past — their past — was his past with Greg, his apartment with Greg, his first date — it was and it wasn't. It wasn't. He blinked and looked again. Her eyes — his eyes — were ... nothing alike. He laughed out of surprise at the illusion, like a magician's audience, delighted. He looked again, searching for the wires, the marked card, the stacked deck, the trap door, whatever. Sarah's eyes were emerald green shot through with golden flecks, little sparklers that made the black of her pupils darker in contrast. But his mind just … skipped, his needle hopped, the song — his thoughts — jumped ahead. It was disorienting, jarring, but it just went to Greg, like that, skipping ahead from Sarah's eyes — Greg's eyes — from the physical sight of them, the green, the golden flecks, to Greg, to seeing him in the grocery store, their eyes meeting the first time, that long look — his needle just skipped to that track, only the song didn't just advance, jumping over a scratch on the record to the end of the chorus or the next verse or progression or whatever, it was like the fucking record changed. Now it played a part of a song that wasn't even on the album … a song he couldn't recognize, that shouldn't be here, next to Sarah's song. And it wasn't even that their eyes *looked* similar. Greg's were dark brown and narrower, oblong pools of chocolate compared to Sarah's perfectly round jewels of sparking emerald.

Looking at them side by side was like some trick of the eye; it was like seeing double, mirror images, only one mirror was from a circus funhouse — distorting, changing, twisting — so that he could look at Sarah and see Greg as he was in whatever groove his mind skipped to. But it wasn't Greg whom she reminded him of — not the Greg who stood there, behind her, but some blend of the two, some invented memory of some man with Sarah's eyes and her smile and her laugh and none of that *fit,* not on Greg, not on any man, but he just went there, over and over, and if he looked at Greg he felt the same skip, the same jump in his thoughts, the same reminders from the same cues, the same pointers to the same song that didn't belong here at all.

He didn't know how long his thoughts skipped and the songs changed, but Sarah broke in, interrupting the loop.

"Lexus? Are you okay?"

Lexus.

I'm not Lexus Sam. Not always. I was John Doe at a hospital called Grossmont. He tried to remember it, the hospital room, meeting Dr. Renesque for the first time and listening to his promise of a brand new, happy life. And before that? Before that I, well … You don't know, he thought. You don't.

"No," he said, "but I will be."

He watched her, fought the vertigo. His mind jumped and skipped, the funhouse mirror made Sarah's face shift and dance, so he shut his eyes and gathered her up tighter in his arms.

"I will be."

He looked past her at Greg, who held one arm with the other behind his back, his eyebrows arched, his mouth a thin, set line.

He knew, then.

He turned back to Sarah, burying his face in her hair, smelling of some impossible citrus scent — smelling like *her* hair, her scent, her.

Her.

Here was something, then, untouched, untampered, something the doctor forgot to bulldoze with his insidious suggestions, his constant false reminders, something pure: the smell of her hair. It reminded him only of her.

He shut his eyes and breathed deeply and thought back to A. D. Secondary, to that brick-and-mortar hallway, their first meeting; to the coffee shop; to his apartment, Sarah, with her back to him, pulling up her shirt, raising it inch by inch, like the canvas of some grand sail of an even grander ship, straining against its moorings like a leashed dog on the scent of a fox, that sail the instrument of their upcoming voyage to the horizon and beneath, chasing the setting sun and the falling rainbow and the shooting star and everything else wondrous and beautiful; he smelled her hair and remembered these things, these memories, whole and intact, like individual black boxes on a fleet of downed airliners, memories that survived, inexplicably, that were an accounting when everything else seemed to be destroyed; he smelled her hair and remembered — he *remembered*. In an epiphany. It was here. This is it. My epiphany — a blinding flash of knowing, just like all those accounts of all those recovering amnesiacs, the teary-eyed recounts of remembering one day, of mailing a letter and hearing a bubble-gum pop and remembering the 4th of July and some bandstand and their first kiss and then everything else came flooding back with it. And did it matter, was it diminished, that it brought only Lexus Sam back to him and not the person he was before Lexus, before Adam, before he was even John Doe, that Mr. X who lurked in the shadows of his knowing — did it matter?

"It … doesn't …" he said, close to tears.

Not to me.

Not to her.

Sarah stirred underneath, worried still, probably, but he just held her tighter, buried her face against his chest, and spoke into the top of her head.

"It's good to see you," he said, quietly and tenderly, finding his voice, the one for her only, again.

I'm not Lexus Sam.

But I *will* be.

And I still love you, Sarah.

Book Four

I know the car accident's going to happen, because everything else has. How much of it did I make and how much just was, I don't know. Sarah, the governor, even Greg ...

But I don't care that it's coming. I'm happy. My dream has come true. It doesn't matter if it lasts for another day, week, or decade — it's happened, and it'll end, and a new dream will take up where this one stopped.

And even then, I'll still love her.

Chapter Twenty-Six

Lexus passed his hands under the motion-activated tap of the Newark airport sink and received a piddle of lukewarm water. He wet his hands and triggered the soap dispenser. A white foam squirted out that lathered as he rubbed his hands.

He saw his reflection in the mirror. Hair short and trimmed, fists of salt at the temples, individual hairs sticking straight out from his scalp like flagpoles planted by age advancing into new territory. He stared, studied it in a long gaze of everyday, pedestrian awe; he'd seen it all before — yesterday and its yesterday and its yesterday — and it was still here, now, whenever that was, and if it was there tomorrow, impossibly, he'd note it with the same nonchalant amazement.

I'm getting older, whoever I am.

And I'm still trapped in there, gaze shifting to his eyes, dark and deep, framed with a few spreading wrinkles at the corners, brown — the brown of locked and bolted doors, the kind guarding an old estate, stained and varnished over the years; in there somewhere, behind those eyes, those locked and bolted doors, there was a person, a consciousness — thoughts and hopes and fears and regrets and experiences — that existed in this body before John Doe, before Lexus Sam.

He rinsed the soap off, dried his hands, and left the bathroom.

**

Outside it was cold. A winter sun hung low and bright in the clear sky. Morning rays crashed over the skyline to the east, across the Hudson, and sliced through the gaps in the skyscrapers, bathing the parking lot's slab of asphalt in white light. It etched a razor-sharp silhouette, his shadow distorted and elongated by the angle, on the row of rentals behind him.

Back in New York.

Back, after the intervening years in California, that bungalow on the beach, premonitions or dreams or just illusions, fantasies made real through belief — back.

"This is it," Sarah said, beside him.

He looked in the direction she was pointing — a red Mazda hatch, two-door, with chromed accents and subtle fog lights peering out from either side of the front bumper.

She unlocked the doors and popped the hatch with a touch — it rose on silent hydraulics and revealed a decent space behind the back seats.

Lexus dropped his duffel to the ground and used both hands to lift Sarah's wheeled luggage in first. Then he bent, retrieved his duffel, and tossed it in on top. He shut the hatch while Sarah got into the driver's seat. He followed her in through the passenger side and dropped into a low seat. It was one of those racing-style, molded and formed seats that hugged your hips and lower back. He groped under the seat, pulled a handle, and slid the seat as far back as it would go.

Sarah started the car and turned the heat up. She adjusted her mirrors, buckled up, and put the car in reverse.

She glanced over and asked, "You okay?"

He nodded. Tried to smile.

"It's just ..."

Driving. Being in a moving car. Putting myself in fate's way. It's just that I'm crazy, that I have an irrational fear, irrational foreknowledge, of this accident, of having to follow these footsteps in the snow, of having nothing else left of you to follow but these footsteps.

Sarah had called it a superstition and left it at that.

Others had pried more.

A doctor had asked him once when it started. Lexus had laughed at that. When? Right.

"I know," she said. "It's okay."

"Yeah."

She leaned across from her seat and kissed him. On one cheek, then the other, then his forehead. And smiled.

"Okay," she said, settling back, "let's go visit your new nephew."

"Well, my nephew-in-law."

She punched him, lightly, on the shoulder. "Shut up," she said, putting the car in reverse.

"I don't think his parents want to think of me as his uncle either. His commie uncle."

She laughed. "No, probably not." She shifted into Drive. "I thought everyone knew not to talk politics at the dinner table."

Grinning, he said, "They started it."

"Lex," she said, glaring at him in faux warning.

"Okay, okay. Eyes on the road, please."

**

The rain fell lightly and intermittently on the rain-sensing windshield. Wipers wiped and stopped, wiped, wiped, stopped.

Lay dormant. Wiped again. He tried not to focus on them. On anything. But his eyes stayed fixed on the road ahead. On what might be coming. His hand flexed, tightening on the steering wheel, and relaxed. Flexed. Relaxed. He knew the words to some autogenic training that was meant to calm him down. He repeated them to himself, silently, again and again. Focused on his breathing. Deep breaths. Slow, steady. Perfectly calm. Maybe it helped a bit. He couldn't really tell. Didn't care. Every time he was in a car could be it. He didn't drive anymore. That was the best he could do, the concession he made to this madness, but he still rode as a passenger knowing, sure, he didn't have to be driving to cause the accident like he caused everything else. This time, next time, last time. Sometime.

Ahead, the clouds thinned; the last wisp of torn cotton covering the sun pulled apart. Quanta of light, infinitesimal, refracted in rain drops; scattered, rainbowing light made brighter from the sudden contrast to the curtained gloom of cloudy skies, forcing his eyes shut for a long blink.

He opened them, squinting, and reached for his sunglasses. They were on the dash in front of him. He leaned forward, felt the seatbelt tug against his chest, holding him back. He tugged at the seatbelt with his left hand to give him enough slack to reach forward. Reached with his right. Focused on the tips of his fingers, an inch away from the arm of his black sunglasses, open and unfolded, in the far corner where windshield met the dash. So close, just another —

— his wheels slid off the pavement, dropped into the dirt-and-gravel ditch some six inches below with a crunch that wrenched the steering wheel free from the loose grip he kept on it with his left hand.

The directions, written on a single sheet of newsprint torn from one of those free commuter rags they gave away, that he'd

260

stretched, reached for, slid from the corner of the dash and drifted onto the empty passenger seat.

His attention snapped, and then returned to look at the road curving away and to the left — pulled out of view by a trajectory aiming him toward an onrushing concrete pole — and for a panicked instant, he could not form rational thoughts, could not understand how he was driving, what he was doing here, in the California sun, bombing down some freeway alone — alone and driving when it seemed to him, then, that he hadn't been, that he had been somewhere else. But that couldn't be.

Shit.

His seatbelt, unbuckled, a loose loop around his left shoulder, seemed important now. He grabbed at it with his left hand. Sat back in the seat. Pulled the loop away, slid his hand down its length to the buckle. Slow, automatic movements.

He'd taken his foot off the gas and planted it off to the right and away from the pedals, to provide leverage to stretch his body across the center console. But now he needed it on the brake. Like, now. Disoriented. His foot felt the floor underneath the steering column. Automatic movements that groped blindly for the brake pedal.

Slowly, too slowly, his right hand came away from the dash.

The left tire dropped off the road. Crunched gravel. The car drifted further right. The overpass loomed, blocking out the sun. The back tires dropped off the road. He grabbed the wheel with his right hand. Tried to buckle in with his left. Turned the wheel to the left, hard, away from the ramp's solid wall of concrete. Jabbed the buckle into nothingness. Slammed his foot down on a pedal. The concrete support swung into view, dead center. The engine roared. The car lurched forward, faster and faster and faster. He didn't have time to realize his foot had found the gas pedal. He only pressed down harder and —

— Lexus dropped his sunglasses and leaned to his left, grabbed at the wheel. He didn't have time. To think. To warn. To look. He twisted the wheel to the left. As hard as he could. He heard Sarah yell. The car swerved, dipped. Momentum pulled. But he did have time to see. To remember. To realize there was no overpass, no concrete pole. Not now. Not this when. Now there was just a pickup truck in the lane of oncoming traffic, directly ahead.

So when was the overpass? When? That was nonsense. The kind he'd scribble down in his most recent journal, the collection grown to a hundred-odd notebooks full, now, with questions and irrational haiku and dreams, so many dreams, maybe even memories masked as dreams. He'd have to write this one down. When? And underline it. Because, really, when did that overpass come from? That phantasm of past decades, ghost of nightmares past, made real just long enough to cause the accident happening now in trying to avoid it.

When?

Was it conjured up out of his lost past and set in front of him, again, to close the logic loop, the hiccup in the reality of the waking world — had the time between his first car accident and now been a mistake? Or an illusion — like some afterimage of a shining star long gone, supernovaed in a brilliant and beautiful display of nature, that hadn't existed, been real, since the first human eyes wished on its twinkle or stared up at it, dreaming or hoping for a new life, a new start, a second chance with the trappings of the first.

No, he thought, not a mistake. It was all self-contained and reinforcing. A bubble in which his actions were trapped echoes, reverberating off the rainbow-shimmering membrane walls, coming back to him again and again, decayed signals that didn't transmit the whole message, didn't impart the real wisdom or insight into his situation, but just left fragments, like a shout across a huge canyon: an echoing voice whose words were easily lost, and those that weren't had a maddeningly vague and cryptic air to them; they contained enough to catch your attention, to make you stop and listen and try to figure out the whole message, what those voices were telling you, like hearing "danger … don't … helicopter … tomorrow" from somewhere above on the mountain pass you climbed. It could make you stop and turn around, or hurry up to the summit, or radio for a helicopter, or radio to ensure a helicopter didn't come, or just make camp and sit in your tent and do nothing, fearing you'd trigger the danger, or wait, at least, until tomorrow before going on, going back, making camp — all these actions and permutations of actions based on guesses of meaning behind a perfectly imperfect message. Sarah. Blood. The accident. This accident. Dreams and déjà vu and coincidence, all colluding to make a perfectly symmetrical event, alpha and omega, the beginning the end, the end the beginning, that'd seem like an imperfection in the real world — too many coincidences — if it weren't for the feedback, for the echoes of what's happened making what's to come, like a climber's shout of "Avalanche!" causing other climbers to scamper and hurry and get careless and dislodge more snow and ice and perpetuate the avalanche and shout "Avalanche!" to the next poor bastard lower down the line, all around the entire globe, until the last climber's shout of avalanche becomes, really, the "Avalanche!" the first climber heard, the climber who scampers and slips and shouts — a mountain of climbers trapped in an Escher painting. And so it wasn't really a coincidence, wasn't fated, wasn't premonitions and predictions and clairvoyance; it was cause and effect, where the two were one — it was just that, a bubble, trapping, reflecting everything.

They hit the oncoming pickup truck.

Hard, and —

— sounds and forces hammered all around him, into him, over him. He shattered a wall of glass with his head, shoulders. Dark and weightless, he flew, fell. Somewhere distant a horn blared, stuck in the death wail of a crashed and wrecked car, repeated again in film and TV as the camera panned out and everything went dark, dark, quiet, and —

— he felt a lash of fiery pain like a lightning whip burned into his chest, taut, restricting. Suffocating. He groaned. The harder he tugged, strained against it, the more pain he felt. The hotter the fire. He couldn't breathe. Couldn't. His eyes were shut. He clenched his teeth. Pulled harder. The boa constricted. On its prey. His chest.

Numb fingers, stinging with pins and needles, moved along the belt, searching, moving on their own, seeking blindly. Stars burst across his black, confused vision. He reached the belt buckle, pushed. It clicked open. And he fell forward, released.

Pain.

He slumped forward, face in his hands. That hurt worse. He sat back. Opened his eyes, downcast, and stared. Blood on his hands. Splintered glass. Thousands of spiderwebbed lines. The world was draped in a thin veil of red silk, curtains of blood that parted with his touch. He wiped his eyes clear. More spilled. The curtain kept falling.

He leaned to his right. The door gave way. Opened. He sprawled out. Elbow bracing against empty air where the armrest used to be. He tilted over, out of the car's open door, caught himself on asphalt. Cold. Saw the road below, its black bleached, stained white with salt and forested with boots.

Hands on his arms. Under his armpit. Pulling, supporting, lifting.

There were people all around him. Voices were speaking, but he didn't listen. He swayed.

It was cold.

Snow fell.

From high, high above him.

Streamers thrown for a surprise party he didn't want to attend.

"Sarah?"

Sirens wailed nearby, approaching.

People talked, some shouted.

He thought he heard his name, once, in the discordant choir. But he couldn't be sure. His name was gone. Whatever it was. It was gone.

Shapes focused into faces, set expressions. It's okay. Just take it easy. Soothing sentiments betrayed by the tension in their voices. Too many eyes, watching. They talked too slowly. Everything was not fine.

"Sarah?"

Beyond the faces with scared eyes burning within identical poker faces, and beyond the road, was an empty lot collecting trash. Someone had trampled down the orange, plastic webbing strung up as a makeshift fence around a few lampposts. They had made a path through the middle of the empty lot. He stared. Traced their footprints in the snow, leading away from the road.

He said he needed some air — voice sounding strange, words mumbled and confused — and they let him go. He took a few steps toward the empty lot.

Sarah.

He looked over his shoulder. At the wreck. Mazda and pickup fused. Glass splintered and sprayed. An ambulance, lights flashing red and white, pulled alongside. He turned, saying, "I remember."

Disordered thoughts came to him. Memories of an aftermath of a different car accident, slipping back into that battered body, feeling and pain returning like warmth spreading, radiating.

No.

They were more than just memories surfacing — lying in the shade of the overpass, the road cool on his back, eyes stuck on his big toe in the middle ground of his vision, unable to refocus, everything beyond and in front blurry, staring at his big toe, bare, the nail cracked, twitching on its own — they felt more real — ambulance arriving, flashing lights, hurried movements, pen lights peering into his skull through open eyes — more vivid, more simultaneous than simply remembering — panicked thoughts reaching out for Sarah unexpressed except in the limbo of a waking coma — like the trained associations Dr. Renesque tried to force into him under hypnosis, turning Sarah into Greg, training his mind to skip to Greg when he thought of Sarah, even when he saw her, at the height of its power, it was like that seeing this only stronger —

— I remember, he thought. Green eyes, sparkling, watching, waiting, flecked with gold. Sarah's eyes. Wake up, she whispered with those eyes. She winked one, then the other —

— stronger because it was more than just a coincidence —

— wait, no wait. More thoughts, like a yellow rose tattoo. Her shirt, lifted up over her bare back. Bare. She didn't have a tattoo. She did. Eyes young, old. A man's face, eyes. They didn't make sense to him. A name. Adam Williams. But that's not —

— stronger because it wasn't some cheap imitation, an approximation, like Dr. Renesque's attempts.

Stronger, because this had to happen. It formed something necessary. A metaphysical underpinning to the atemporal Lexus Sam, to the paradox — the hiccup in causality — that allowed Lexus to be informed by memories before they happened for him and allowed memories of events to inspire the actions that caused the events themselves.

Stronger than memories because they weren't.

They were happening.

As he stood at the side of the road watching the crowd part, the backs of paramedics visible now as they lifted a stretcher, he was also in an ambulance. Or part of him was — the part that was going back as Lexus Sam, again. Not back, really — there was no geography or chronology that truly fit. But it was close enough to the realization that part of him was moving from here to then, taking some of these memories, associations, back — the connection between sight and thought so strong it traversed time and space to form a link through the ether like quantum entanglement applied to consciousness instead of particles. A link that he could feel, now, entranced, associating this crash to the other, the beginning to the end, the end to the beginning, timeless, infinite, mirrors held up to mirrors, reflecting further and further, deeper, so that he could feel now what he felt then, what the part going back would feel, like drowning in a vacuum — black, empty space devoid of air and pressure — a vacuum of his mind, being, devoid of thought, devoid of him, knowing the stress and anxiety, the pain and longing, that he'd go through, sympathizing, empathizing, but knowing it was the only way for the paradox to happen, for any of this to happen.

But he'd have help.

A memory. Clear, concise, perfect.

The singular memory he would need to follow, again, back here. The last memory of Lexus Sam and the first. Once he created it.

The blowing snow cut across his path in a downward slant, drawing stinging lines of white over the empty plain. A path of footprints, little craters in the sheet covering the hard ground, trailed away in a gently curving arc over the horizon — each print a signpost pointing the way to his girl with green eyes. But the drifting, falling snow filled them in bit by bit, and unless he caught up soon, it'd cover her tracks forever.

He pulled his scarf up over his mouth against the blowing snow and stepped off the road. He matched her stride step for step, walking in her footprints.

Something caught his eye and —

— he turned to look. Everything was different. The car crash was a minor spectacle, an obstacle to holiday traffic, but nothing more. He looked at the Mazda, its hood crumpled and peeled back, the passenger door open to show deployed airbags, now deflated, inside, and saw nothing else.

For a moment, that seemed strange. Like it lacked a dimension. But then he saw the paramedics wheel a stretcher towards the open bay of the ambulance, oxygen mask in place. It was Sarah. Alive and awake and breathing, clouding the clear mask with the condensation of her warm breath.

Sarah.

Her green eyes met his, for a moment, through the crowds. She winked at him.

END

Iguana Books
iguanabooks.com

If you enjoyed *Lexus Sam*...
Look for other books coming soon from Iguana Books! Subscribe to our blog for updates as they happen.

iguanabooks.com/blog/

You can also learn more about BP Gallucci and his upcoming work on his website:

http://bpgallucci.com/

If you're a writer ...
Iguana Books is always looking for great new writers, in every genre. We produce primarily ebooks but, as you can see, we do the occasional print book as well. Visit us at iguanabooks.com to see what Iguana Books has to offer both emerging and established authors.

iguanabooks.com/publishing-with-iguana/

If you're looking for another good book ...
All Iguana Books books are available on our website. We pride ourselves on making sure that every Iguana book is a great read.

iguanabooks.com/bookstore/

Visit our bookstore today and support your favourite author.

IGUANA

CPSIA information can be obtained at www.ICGtesting.com
Printed in the USA
LVOW11s1414170415

435039LV00004B/26/P